BURNT

BOOK ONE OF
THE BALANCE OF KERR

Kevin Steverson & Tyler Ackerman

New Mythology Press
Virginia Beach, VA

Chris Kennedy/New Mythology Press
2052 Bierce Dr.
Virginia Beach, VA 23454
http://chriskennedypublishing.com/

Publisher's Note: This is a work of fiction. Names, characters, places, and incidents are a product of the author's imagination. Locales and public names are sometimes used for atmospheric purposes. Any resemblance to actual people, living or dead, or to businesses, companies, events, institutions, or locales is completely coincidental.

Cover Design J Caleb Design.

Ordering Information:
Quantity sales. Special discounts are available on quantity purchases by corporations, associations, and others. For details, contact the "Special Sales Department" at the address above.

Burnt/Kevin Steverson & Tyler Ackerman -- 1st ed.
ISBN: 978-1950420988

I would like to dedicate this book to my wife, my six children, my sons and daughter in law, and my ten grandchildren. When we get together it's a houseful. They're my favorite crowd.

Kevin Steverson

* * *

I would like to dedicate this book to my better half, Melissa, and my sons Hudson and Carter. I would also like to include my parents.

Tyler Ackerman

Chapter One

In the beginning, there was nothing. The Creator said, "Let there be." And there was. What was... was one of many, in infinite numbers only the Creator could comprehend.

– first paragraph of The Book Of The One.

Note: *though the discussion of the various interpretations of this paragraph continue among clergy and scholars, the consensus is the Creator, in infinite wisdom, created realities with worlds such as Kerr in numbers unknown to mortals. Of the various sub-theories, several submit there are realities where magic does not exist and prayers to various deities are unanswered, as the Creator did not designate any in that particular reality.*

The huge oak door opened, which was only to be expected in an establishment on the good side of town; many of the locals stopped for a meal or drink in the evenings. The fact it was held open longer than most of the patrons in the tavern felt necessary was the issue. The brisk winds foretelling the oncoming winter blew in and caused the flames to dance on candles stuck on the wagon wheel hung from the center beam high above the room.

The fire in the huge fireplace covering most of one wall leaped and spun, the breeze fueling it. It crackled and popped as ashes and small sparks swirled out to land on the worn wooden floor. Shouts at the culprit were followed by empty mugs sailing through the air. Kryder ducked as droplets of beer and wine flew from the earthen mugs, and metal cups sailed above him.

Tog grinned at Kryder, drained his beer, and hurled the mug with abandon. Unlike most of the others, his shattered when it struck the closing door above the head of the small person struggling to close it. The pieces rained down on the hood and shoulders of a grey cloak.

Her shape gave away that she was a woman, though her face was concealed in the darkness of the deep hood. Like the others partaking in the fun, guilt formed on his face when he realized the culprit couldn't help the situation. With her size, it took all she had to fight the winds and close the door.

"What's wrong with ye?" shouted the owner of the place from behind the bar. His cheeks turned red as he shook a big fist. "She's but a wee thing! Everyone without a mug er cup in front o' them is paying for it, be it broken or not. If ye don't like it, there's the matter of me boys tae answer to, and you'll not cross the doorway of the Hobbled Goat err again!"

Kryder glanced over at the two hulking figures as they moved to pick up the earthenware mugs and tin cups. They weren't as big as his companion, but they were two of the largest men he had seen since leaving his village. A cleaning maid followed with a straw broom and a thin piece of wood to clean up the pieces. She moved slowly, and by the look on her face, she was concentrating on the simple task. It was obvious her mind was burnt, and she was little more than a simpleton. Kryder felt for her.

Looking away from her and back at Tog, it was Kryder's turn to grin. "Don't look to me for a few extra coppers later. When your coins are gone, I'll be sure to let you watch me eat a sticky pie or roasted chicken leg in the next village or town."

"Some friend you are," complained Tog as he poured copper coins out of a small pouch into his huge hand. "And to think we're kin."

With a grimace he dropped three into the waitress' open hand. She closed her fist around them and beckoned with her forefinger for more. A groan escaped Tog as he dropped one more into the now open palm. The hand stayed open; Tog looked up at her raised eyebrow and dropped another. She smiled, closed her hand, and placed a new mug of beer in front of him with the other. At least it was a larger mug than the last.

Kryder glanced around the room. Whoever the small woman was, she was nowhere to be seen. *She must have a room upstairs*, he thought. He reached down to his side and pulled a dagger out of its sheath. The hunk of smoked hog surrounded by taters, onions, and redroot on the wood platter in front of him was uncut. He inhaled deeply, for the smell was amazing. He cut a large slice, stabbed it with the point, and blew softly on it. It was still hot, but he took a small bite anyway.

"This is why you don't waste coin on broken mugs," Kryder said after he chewed and swallowed, indicating the smoking meat remaining on the end of the dagger. "We'll be able to take some of this with us after I talk our barmaid into wrapping it for us. I might get an extra tater or two, as well."

Tog snorted and said, "First you wish me to be coinless, now you want to starve me to death with a small meal. You can imagine there'll be any of this left before we leave this table tonight if you want. It's a wasted thought, though, if you ask me."

Kryder tilted his head slightly, looked at Tog, and nodded. "You're probably right. I have no idea how Aunt Katheen and Uncle Lur were able to feed you enough for you grow as big as you are."

"Hey!" Tog complained. "You were seated at the table, too. I'm not the only one who asked for another helping each night."

Kryder pointed his greasy dagger at Tog. "Another helping maybe, not another whole chicken."

Tog shrugged. "I like chicken," he said as he pulled out his dagger. Standing nearly seven feet tall and weighing nearly three hundred and twenty pounds, a dagger for him was a short sword to most men. He cut a piece off. He didn't bother blowing on it and poked it into his mouth. There was instant regret on his face. He began breathing through his teeth with the piece of meat between them, the sharpness of his incisors giving away that he was half Orc, if his size didn't already reveal it. He grabbed his mug and drained it.

Kryder shook his head, cut another piece for himself, and blew on it. Before he took a bite, he said, "If I had a copper for every time I've seen you do that, I could exchange them for a piece of gold. I'm talking about a whole coin and not a quarter piece."

Tog wiped his mouth with the back of his hand, ignoring the remark, and said, "So when are we going to be contacted? Besides the cost of mugs, this place isn't cheap. It's not like we have coin to spare. We should think about an inn more in line with our coin purses."

"I don't know," Kryder answered. "The old man said someone would contact us here. If we go across town, whoever it is may not find us."

"Well I..." Tog started to say when he was interrupted by a loud voice two tables away.

"Look here, halfbreed," a man dressed similarly to them, in leather armor covered with a travel cloak and a sword on his hip, said loudly. One side of his face had a scar stretching from eyebrow to lips. He was speaking to them. "I don't eat with such as your kind." The three men sitting with him laughed. One wearing a half-helmet with leather flaps hanging on each side added his own loud insult, "Since the rape didn't kill his mother, surely bearing an Orc bastard did the deed." The group laughed even louder.

Kryder reached down to his side and drew another smaller, more ornate dagger with his free hand. He laid them both on the table. He stood, turned around, and looked at the four men. Tog, on his feet nearly as quickly, reached over his shoulder and grabbed the axe strapped to his back with one hand. It was dual-headed and meant for two hands when used by a normal-sized man. He placed it on the table beside his own large dagger. A hand's length of the worn leather-covered handle hung over the edge.

The four men realized the object of their harassment and his companion didn't intend to leave. They meant to fight. They scrambled to their feet, knocking over chairs. Several groups stood and moved away from the center of the room, while others left the tavern completely.

The owner's sons looked toward their father. He shook his head. Fights happened, even in his establishment on the better part of town. Usually he had his boys put a stop to it. This time, the insult thrown at the large patron was more than he could tolerate. He decided to let the man demand his apology, even if it meant he had to beat it out of the four. It was an easy decision.

Kryder stepped toward the group, shifting to the side as he moved. Tog's huge strides had him even with him in no time. Kryder watched as the four men came forward. Two of them crossed each other behind the forward two, moving to the opposite sides. Kryder knew then these men had fought together often, perhaps in a military unit or mercenary company. Out of the corner of his eye he saw Tog's posture change slightly. Tog recognized the same coordinated movement. Kryder also noticed the men didn't disarm before they shifted to fight.

Kryder moved suddenly. He rushed farther to the side as he dove toward the man on the far left. The man, thinking the group had the advantage, and he wouldn't have to fight one-on-one, was clearly surprised when he was tackled.

With a shout Tog kept the attention of the other three, and he swung a hammer blow from above his head that came down across his chest. With the others hemming him in, the lead man was unable to dodge the blow. His helmet went flying, and he saw stars as he was knocked into one of his companions. His body slightly turned, Tog twisted back, putting his torso into the punch from his opposite hand. The man still standing was knocked sideways, unconscious before he hit the floor.

Kryder straddled and rained punches down on the hapless man he'd tackled. The fourth punch connected between the man's arms shielding his face, and his defense dropped. One more blow ensured he was out of the fight. Kryder stood and turned toward Tog and the other three. His eyes widened, and he raised a hand.

Tog grabbed the now-standing victim of his hammer blow by his leather vest. The man offered no resistance in his daze. Tog threw him sliding across the room into a table, his head striking a leg. His back was turned to the last of them, so he never saw the man draw his short sword. He felt the pressure as the tip pressed against his undershirt between his leather top and his breeches as he heard Kryder shout. He tried to arch and tensed, expecting the worst.

The blade went no farther. Tog turned to see the man straining to push his arm forward, a determined grimace on his face. Kryder stood several paces beyond, his hand outstretched and trembling along with his body. Realizing he didn't understand the words Kryder was shouting, Tog knew his cousin had cast a spell.

No longer hesitating, Tog kicked the man, his foot connecting with the shoulder of the hand holding the sword. The hardened leather of his leg and knee armor sent the sword flying away as the man was knocked over a table. The last thing the man saw was the chair coming down on his head as Tog broke it on him.

Once the fight was over, the owner motioned his sons toward the troublemakers. They grabbed one each and dragged them outside. One of the regulars, a Dwarf with a long, flowing beard and dressed well, held the door for them and pulled it closed quickly. They came back in and grabbed the last two, took them out, and tossed them on the others.

Kryder sat down and shook his hand, sore from the punches thrown. The ring on his middle finger was no longer glowing red, though no one else in the establishment had seen it when it was glowing, except the barmaid assigned to clean up. She didn't have the wits to understand what she'd seen or explain it. The ability was long gone, along with part of her mind.

The owner walked over to their table as Tog settled himself on the bench. His lips were held in a tight line as he glanced at the broken chair pieces being picked up by the barmaid. "I'm to be sorry for that, lads, sure as I'm standing here. Don't ye worry none o' the chair, and I'll see that ye have a hot meal brought out. Keep that for traveling as well." He nodded at the wood platter in the center of their table.

"Thank you," Kryder said, raising an eyebrow in question.

"Lucas," the large man said. "Lucas Trant is the name."

"Thank you, Lucas," Kryder said. "Are you sure you won't let us pay for the damages?"

"I should think not," Lucas answered. "They deserved what they got, and then some. I'll not have that kind of hatred in me place. To be honest with ye, if the two of ye hadn't looked the kind to handle yerselves, I'd have had me boys set them straight."

Kryder nodded, his evaluation of the man rising. "My name is Kryder. This is Tog. Thank you again for the offer of a new meal. We'd like to take some with us, should we leave in the morning."

Later, after the crowd cleared out and those staying upstairs had left the tavern area, Lucas came over to their table and pulled up a bench. No one else was in the room but the cleaning maid, wiping tables on the other side.

"How'd ye like the hog?" Lucas asked. "It's me own blend o' spices rubbed agin it before roasting."

Kryder grinned and held his mug up in salute. "It was the best I've had in a long time. Maybe ever."

Tog leaned back and rubbed his stomach. He burped silently and blew it out. "It was the best I've had," he admitted. He looked over and tilted his head slightly. "Not to be rude, but this isn't usually the kind of acceptance I'm used to this far from home. Thank you for that."

Lucas waved it off. "Lad, I don't know yer story, but I'll tell ye a bit o' mine." He looked off into the distance, into a memory from long ago. Finally he spoke, "How d'ye think I'm as big as I am, not to mention those two boys o' mine? Me mother's great grandpappy was half. When I was a wee thing, she told me of him. Said he was a good man. He died long before her grandpappy brought the family south from Minth, fighting those that helped bring him about, if you know what I mean."

"The last time raiding parties came out of Orcanth and made it that far was…over one hundred years ago," Kryder said, understanding fully what Lucas was referring to.

Lucas nodded. "Thereabouts, I suppose. Who's to say how these things happen, but I'm bigger than me brothers were, and me boys are both bigger than me. Runs in the blood and skips a few, I'm to be thinking."

"There have been some rogue tribes that raided since," Tog added, "but they never made it that far. The Baronies West stopped them…with help."

"It happens time to time, so I hear,' Lucas said, "not that much news of the Baronies makes its way this far south, mind you. A few o' the Gnomes trading down this way pass it along. That what does is not always to be believed."

Suddenly the door slammed open, once again allowing the wind to whip through the place. Four of the town guard came in, led by an older man in chainmail armor. The look on his face showed he meant business. He looked around the empty room, noticed Lucas sitting, and stomped over. One of the guards had the sense to close the door.

He looked Kryder and Tog over, stiffening slightly at Tog's size, or his mixture of races, Kryder couldn't tell. "Lucas, ye mind explaining why yer dumped four o' the Razors out on the street like the night's used dishwater?"

"Aye," Lucas said, not bothering to stand. "They started a fight, and those they fought ended it for them. If they say different, they're lying, and I'll stand before the magistrate and swear to it."

"Yeah, well," the sergeant of the guard said, "I've got a mercenary lieutenant screaming like a banshee about it. Filed a complaint on behalf o' his commander, he did."

"Let him scream, Johan," Lucas dismissed. "Are ye to believe me, an upstanding proprietor and a friend of yours for nigh on thirty years, or mercenaries from a unit without the best o' reputations?"

"It's a point ye have," admitted Johan. "If the king is looking to contract the likes o' that company to bolster the forces, all is lost, and we may all end up swearing fealty to King Westell the 3rd of Gar-Noth. We're on the brink of war if the parlay fails."

"King Bainhon is not what his father was. Our kingdom isn't to be having the forces to stop Gar-Nath, not with the lord mage backing him. I'm not to be knowing if contracting all the mercenary companies on Kerr would help," Lucas said. "We may have no choice."

The sergeant pursed his lips and nodded. He said, "I'll not eat their bland food if they do manage to force the king's hand, I'll tell ye. If I wasn't a bit past me prime, I'd be joining the king's own, me-self."

"I'd be beside ye, like old times," agreed Lucas.

The sergeant nodded at them, turned, and led his squad out of the establishment. The three of them watched the flames slowly settle down after the door closed again. The barmaid waved goodbye enthusiastically to Lucas, took off her apron, and tried to fold it. It was a task beyond her comprehension. She ended up placing the wadded ball of cloth on a table and went upstairs.

Kryder noticed the slight smile on Lucas's face as the man watched her. He realized the look of a father watching a very young child attempt to do things on her own. Once again, he felt for the woman. He knew what had caused her to be the way she was.

Lucas walked over to the table, picked up the apron, and folded it. The movements were automatic, as if he'd been doing it for years. He walked around the bar and put it out of sight. He then filled a pitcher of beer, fetched himself a mug, and came back to the table.

He filled all three mugs, took a sip, and said, "Now lads, if ye have the time, I have the ears. What brings a couple of travelers such as yerselves this far south? The accent, the armor ye wear, and the look of ye tells me yer from a little farther than the Baronies West."

He turned to Kryder. "Ye used a bit o' magic to hold that one's hand. What's nobility—or at the very least, someone from incredible wealth—doing traveling in leather and carrying duel daggers like ye know the use o' them? I can be trusted with the tale, to be sure."

The last he said to Tog, "After all, me and ye are some kin, though it may go so far back it's impossible to find."

Kryder thought for a moment. He knew Lucas was referring to the legend that all Orcs came from the same tribe originally, a tale passed from generation to generation along with many others among the tribes in Orcanth.

"Tog's story is his to tell," Kryder said, his mind made up. He'd let Tog go first. If they were to base here for a while, it would do to have a place to come and go from. Besides, it felt right, and he was usually a good judge of men.

Tog grinned, his incisors showing, and said, "You're of the blood. You claim it. I acknowledge it. Though you don't know if you are of the Red Fist Tribe, I say we share blood."

Kryder's eyes widened. It was the first time he'd heard Tog make this proclamation. As little Orc blood as Lucas had running through his veins, he was acknowledged as a distant relative to Tog, and by the words spoken, to all of the Red Fist Tribe.

Lucas, through tales told by his mother and grandpappy, knew something profound had been said. Though he'd never known which tribe had sired his long past ancestor, even if it was under the worst of circumstances, it was a part of him.

He put his beer on the table. He did know what he'd heard was something rarely done, and he appreciated the gesture. What he didn't know was, it wasn't merely words. If he did, it would leave him speechless, because Tog actually had the right to bestow kinship on Lucas.

"Will ye tell me the story, Tog?" Lucas asked again.

"Sure," Tog answered. "We…"

"Allow me," a voice said. It was a beautiful voice, the sound soothing, yet sharp and clear as the chime of a church bell ringing across an open field.

All three heads turned, startled at the intrusion. No one was there, yet they'd all heard her. The top of her head revealed itself as she pushed the hood back, breaking the power of the cloak's enchantment. Before them was a small woman, having both human and what Kryder thought might be elvish traits, and so much more. They stood, Tog's bench flipping on its side behind him.

Kryder stared. He'd seen beautiful women before, and the one time he'd seen a Half-Elf before she'd pulled her cloak's hood over her had astounded him, but this…this was something different. Something…almost holy.

Her hair, a deep auburn color, hung below her shoulders in soft curls. Her eyes had the slight almond shape of the one Half-Elf Kryder had seen, but were a striking green color, unlike the dark brown Elves were rumored to have. He knew, like his blue ones, human eyes came in different shades but never had he seen this color before. Her skin was tanned, a definite contrast with what was known of Elves and even Half-Elves. When she smiled, Kryder found himself lost in it, the weariness of a long day and the high and low of the fight and its aftermath lifted from him like the smoke from the fire up the chimney.

She spoke again, "Tog, forgive me, you could certainly tell your story…but it would be from your perspective. If you'll allow me, I can tell the whole story."

* * * * *

Chapter Two

The three men, though surprised at her sudden appearance, didn't panic; even Lucas was aware of items like the cloak. He'd been around powerful mages in his youth when he was a soldier, and there were several in town and a few working directly with his king. He rarely dealt with them, but he did have more knowledge about them than the average person.

Kryder and Tog knew from experience mages tended to keep the enchanted items they possessed a secret. When an enchanted item was used, anyone with the gift of magic in sight of it would know it for what it was. Not its actual abilities, but they would know it was enchanted.

There were, of course, spells to determine what an item was capable of, if a mage knew them. Spells, like enchanted items, were kept close, too. Most mages had a book of spells they used, often on their person. Some were memorized permanently and didn't need to be referenced. Those only required a few words. Others were more complicated.

The ability to remember spells for long periods, or memorize complicated ones, depended on the power of the mage and their experience at casting. All spells took a toll on the caster. Exhaustion was the price one paid for their use, and how powerful spells were, once successfully cast, depended upon the individual and the strength of the gift they possessed.

The effort a caster put into them was a very real thing. Too much use without resting was dangerous and could cause one to drop from exhaustion into a type of coma. Depending on the situation, this could mean the end of the mage.

Kryder kept his book in an inside pocket of his undershirt, wrapped in a thin waterproof sheepskin. His book wasn't large; it was hand-sized. Most of the spells were written in a flowing script. Others, not as neat, had been added later. He didn't have one that would tell him what the cloak could do, not that its owner would allow him the time to use it if he had it. He doubted he could even cast the spell.

"His whole story?" Kryder asked, the skepticism plain in his tone. "This I have to hear. Maybe afterward you can tell mine."

Kryder looked over at his cousin, tilted his head a little, and glanced toward the woman. They'd run into fortune tellers and even the occasional seer in the past. Even the ones proving they had a little talent were limited to specific events and areas. They had yet to run into one claiming to know the past of someone they'd never met. Well, not their entire past.

This should be good, he thought. *She may be beautiful, and she wears a powerful enchanted item, but what she's claiming is impossible...unless there's a spell or object that can do that.* There were many spells Kryder had no knowledge of, and items, too.

Her lips moved as she whispered. Kryder strained to hear her and see if he recognized any of the words in the spell. His eyes widened when he realized she wasn't casting...she was praying. Before he could say anything, everything around him faded away in a grey mist. The mist faded, and he was somewhere, standing in a town unlike any he had seen.

He looked around and found he wasn't alone. He started to shout in warning when he realized Tog was going to be run over by a horse and cart full of loose hay. Before he could, they passed right through Tog, and did the same to Lucas, walking behind him. Unsure of anything and everything, Kryder stopped and stared at his cousin until he heard the woman calling him. She was up ahead, closer to the blue sea in the distance.

The three approached her. Out of the corner of his eye, Kryder saw Tog still patting his chest and stomach to be sure he was solid. Lucas was pale; the look on his face showed this was more than he'd ever thought he'd experience with magic. *Magic?* thought Kryder. *This isn't magic. This is something else.*

"Son of a fat flying carrion bird," Tog said, looking at Kryder. "Did you see that?"

"Rest assured, Tog," said the woman, amusement in her voice, "you are still whole. We can see and speak to each other. Those we observe cannot. We were not there, after all. Wait, I have misspoken. That is not correct. Some of us were there in some places. You will understand as the story unfolds before us."

"Who are you?" demanded Kryder as he crossed his arms, determined not to move from the spot until he received some answers. "I know you're some type of cleric or priestess. Who do you pray to?"

Once again she smiled. The simple act eased the tension in Kryder's shoulders, but he stood firm, waiting on an answer. She waved a hand, and the scene around them froze in place. Time stopped.

Kryder could see the dust as it hung in the air in the shafts of sunlight streaming between the stable and the building across the street. Smoke from the farrier's fire pit was a motionless column extending up and off to one side in the stilled breeze. Besides the four of them, there was no sound.

"Kryder Narvok, I can see you have many questions," she said. "Ask. I will answer what I may, but know that some things I cannot answer."

Kryder stood his ground. "You're right. I have a lot of questions. Who are you? How do you know our names? Our story...our lives. How did you do this?" He waved his hand around at everything around them. "This is something out of bedside tales told to children by candlelight in the dead of winter. Amusement when they become restless at being shut in by the weather."

"I have many names," she answered. "I am no cleric or priestess. Then again, perhaps I am. To some, I am known as Saint Lanae, Keeper of Memories. To others, Sister Time. The Elves know me as Lanaeth the Timeless, when I am even mentioned at all. Orcs know me as Lan. You may call me that which is most comfortable to you."

Tog's eyes widened, and he was visibly shaken. "Lan...she who brings the season's change," he whispered. "You honor me."

Lucas dropped to a knee and bowed his head. "Saint Lanae, thank you for the gift o' memories. I pray you, may I never forget the smell o' me mother's hair as she hugged me when I was but a wee lad."

"This is a prayer to be commended, asking for it with no ulterior motives other than to be reminded of one lost. It has been and always will be a request I grant to you, Lucas Trant, for you are a good man," she answered solemnly as she placed a hand on his shoulder and gently pulled so he would stand. "And you have thanked me countless times when the smell of flowers in the field reminded you of her."

Somehow, Kryder knew she spoke the truth. Deep inside he knew it couldn't be denied. They were standing in the presence of one with abilities far beyond any race known. He realized now, why he had not detected magic being used when she was concealed in her cloak. It wasn't because of a concealing spell masking it...it wasn't magic. It was an answered prayer. *Wait,* he thought. *A prayer? No...could it be that she...?*

"Yes, Kryder," Lan said, "it is not magic. It is answered prayer. I must pray for my greatest prayer spells to work. Even one such as I pray to the Creator."

"You...I—" Tog said. The look of confusion was plain to see on his face.

"I am but a saint," Lan explained. "To some, a goddess. Yes, there are others like me, worshipped by all the thinking races. Men, Orcs, Dwarves, and Gnomes. Even Goblins, Trolls, Ogres, and Elves have their own deities. All were of our Creator's design. We all know there is one above us. The foulest of demons know they do not reign supreme. Getting one to admit it...is another matter.

"Today is not the day for that discussion. Know the Creator has sent me, and I obey. In time, if it is within our Creator's plans, you will know more. Today...today I am to show you of your past, starting with Tog. Will you allow me to continue?"

"Allow?" Kryder asked, shaking his head in amazement. "You are Lan...I'm pretty sure we can't stop you from doing anything."

"There is where you are wrong," she explained. "All mortals with the ability to think are born with free will. It has always been so, and always will be. Only when the balance of this world shifts has our Creator decided to step in and even things. Hence, I am here."

"Wait," Kryder said, realizing the weight of what she'd said. "Tog and I are supposed to be part of the Creator's plan? What balance needs to be evened? You do know we're only a couple of men from beyond the Baronies West, right? We're traveling, trying to bring a little information and coin back home. Right now we're working for Baron Arnwald. I mean, it's not like anyone in our village has a lot of spare coin. Our families can use all we take back. We're too young to be part of some world-changing prophecy; I mean, neither of us is more'n twenty years old."

"I am aware," Lan said, "and rest assured, our Creator knows. He decided long ago you two are a part of his plan."

"Are you sure?" Tog asked, finally able to speak coherently. "We're not special. I can fight, I can farm, and I can take down a tree as fast as anyone. I not someone to be noticed by the Creator. I know someone who may be, but not me. I mean, I've been to services, but I'm just a Half-Orc from the Western Borderlands."

"The Creator understands," Lan said with a smile, "and watches and knows those who are trying to live a good and just life. Those who are evil and spread evil are also known. Why they are not struck down where they stand is not for me to ask. Our Creator's will is our Creator's will. Perhaps one day it will be revealed to me, should I be so blessed."

"So you're saying this is some kind of prophesy, and we're in the middle of it," Kryder surmised. He shook his head again, looking down. He looked up. "Look, I don't mean to displease you or the Creator, but I think you have the wrong ones. I'm like Tog. I can fight, I can farm, and I can even cast a few spells. This sounds like a story told by my aunt. They were great when we were children, but really?"

He continued, "I'm not a Half-Orc like Tog, and I'm an orphan. Don't get me wrong, I have a family with Orcs in it, which I admit sounds like the beginnings of one, but it's not. My aunt and uncle took me in, but I am no mage, that's for sure. I'm barely more powerful than an Orc shaman."

Kryder paused, then continued, "Not to mention, poor Lucas." He motioned toward the dumbfounded man. "We've done some risky stuff before, trying to make a coin or two, but this time we managed to drag an innkeeper with us to…to who knows where."

Lucas spoke for the first time since they arrived, "Lad, I've no idea where we are, but if Saint Lanae brought us here, it's where we're needed, to be sure."

"Yes, Lucas, you're to play a part in this," Lan said. "Kryder, there are things you must know, but for now, I am to show you Tog's past. Will the three of you come with me?"

"I will," Tog answered. "I want to know why we have to see this, and…I want to know."

Tog turned to his much smaller cousin. "Kryder, this is the town my mother lived in as a child. It matches the descriptions she and grandpapa told me. I can smell the sea. I don't know how I know what it smells like, other than how she described it, but it's the sea, I'm sure of it."

Kryder looked at his cousin and saw the determined look on Tog's face. He glanced over at Lucas, who nodded in affirmation. With a sigh, he turned to Lan.

"Fine. It's obvious we were meant to see this. Show us," he agreed.

"Before I continue," Lan said, "I would ask you to hold all questions. Those around us cannot hear us, but it will be easier if you allow it to happen around you without interruption. This takes a great deal of concentration to maintain, even for one such as I."

She waited until the three of them nodded, and waved her hand. The smoke again rose from the fire, and the sounds of seagulls crying overhead resumed. In the distance, the sound continuous, they could hear the sea as it rolled in wave after wave against the beach.

* * * * *

Chapter Three

Katheen Narvok giggled as she raced the water up the sandy beach, the frothy foam at the edge of the wave lapping at the bottom of her dress. She was barefoot, as she always was. Only in the dead of winter were boots needed on the northern coast of Minth. She had never seen frost, much less snow, in her entire life. Granted, it was only eight years, but not many in the small fishing town of Lornt, the villages, or the surrounding farms had seen it either. Her father spoke of it once occurring when he was a boy.

Without a care in the world, the little girl played all afternoon. She dug great holes with a piece of driftwood, looking for treasure, and chased the small birds scratching along the edge of the water, hoping to find what they dug up for themselves. When she was tired, she took the small collection with her to inspect it.

She was sitting in the sand under the dock counting seashells in her lap when she heard her brother Marnell call to her, "Katheen! Papa is ready to go. Katheen, come on, you've played enough. We have to get back home and do our chores. It's already going to be dark when I try to round up the pigs. Katheen!"

"Coming!" Katheen called out.

She stepped out of the shadows under the dock into the bright sunshine and the glare off the light brown sand, squinted up at her brother standing atop a dune, and waved. She worked her way toward him in the soft sand with a handful of the prettiest finds of the day. When she got home, her mother would help her make a necklace.

Playfully, her brother tugged her hair before he helped her into the wagon. Only three years older than his sister, Marnell had no problem lifting her up into the wagon. He was large for his age, already showing proof he would grow into a man of his father's size, able to handle the work on the farm easily.

Her father smiled at his younger child, the miniature image of her mother, with long dark curls and pretty blue eyes, as she made her way through the supplies in the bed of the wagon toward the front. She didn't come to town often. It didn't hurt to let her spend the afternoon playing on the beach, as long as she didn't go into the water. She wouldn't disobey him; she didn't know how to swim yet.

There would be time for the chores later, even if they had to be done by lantern. This was not a concern, for the next few months, anyway. Included in the supplies he had purchased, after selling two young cows, was a small cask of fish oil used in lanterns. Katheen wrinkled her nose when she realized she was using the cask as a seat so she could see ahead between her brother and father as they made their way through the town toward the countryside. It didn't smell very good when burned, but it provided light.

Katheen waved and smiled as a squad of the local troops marched by, working their rounds, with a tall sergeant barking orders. She was impressed at the sight of a woman wearing britches instead of a dress. The grizzled old swordswoman gave her a wink and a smile, then proceeded to reprimand one of her troops for doing the same thing.

The lone draft horse plodded along as the flatland gave way to gently rolling hills, while the pine forests thinned into farmland. They received friendly waves from everyone, whether it was someone sitting in the shade of a tree shucking corn, shelling beans, or any number of small chores farming families did, or from young boys tending to sheep or cattle in unfenced fields behind the thatch-roofed homes.

Most farms did well enough every year to continue improvements, even after paying the taxes to the local lord.

Very few owned their own lands in Minth; those who did were very wealthy or had been granted a parcel from their local lord as part of the payment to a family for a son or daughter promoted to the lord's own personal troops. Many teenage boys, and some girls, joined the ranks of the forces. Only when their skills and deeds gained recognition did they receive the offers to advance beyond local militia or the lord's foot soldiers and cavalry.

Jynal Narvok was a large man, strong and intelligent. When he was young, he'd spent some time working with the king's own engineers as a laborer until he was moved into an engineer's position.

He'd joined the foot soldiers as a way to earn coin but had been singled out by his captain for his intelligence and common sense. A decision was made to trade him to the king's engineers for three young soldiers who hadn't worked out in the specialty unit. It was there he learned of construction, digging wells, and proper sewage, along with the building of bridges, catapults, and other war machines.

His left hand was injured when he'd struggled with and un-jammed a catapult during a minor siege. His efforts to repair the machine resulted in success, and using it, they'd been able to gain access to the upstart lord's castle. It had cost him two fingers and left a nasty scar on the outside of his forearm.

The bit of land he owned had been granted to him for his service. He'd left the king's army as a corporal, ready to find a wife and settle down on his farm. He was granted tenant status on the land surrounding his. On the extra land he farmed surrounding his property, he had to pay the taxes all tenants did to the local lord, who in turn paid taxes to the king.

In time, the arm strengthened, and he used it as any other man would. Even now, it held the reins as he kept his other hand on the old short sword on the seat beside him. This part of the trip, the road wound through a long stretch of hardwoods frequented by cougars, bears, or worse—men living off the land as brigands, ready to attack the unwary.

He glanced over at his son, satisfied to see the boy holding the bow he'd made for him in one hand and his leather quiver full of arrows in the other. He was thankful Goblins hadn't been seen in over fifty years; they were farther inland in the nearest mountain range.

Several hours later, they came to a crossroad of sorts. Several homes were clustered around it, forming a village. On the far end was a small church, the symbols showing it was an outreach of the kingdom's main religion dedicated to Minokath, Lord of the Seas. This far from the coast, there were very few attendees to its services, yet the young priest was steadfast in his duties and worked hard to become a trusted member in his village, in the villages at other cross-roads, and the surrounding countryside.

Jynal nodded at the priest sweeping the upper level of the steps in front of the small stone building as the wagon went past. He glanced back at his daughter as she waved. Brother Pynon waved back at her, followed by an exaggerated bow, making Katheen giggle in delight.

For at least the tenth time, Jynal vowed to himself to bring his family to attend a service. He knew the priest was having a hard time growing his small flock, or was it called a school? Jynal didn't know. He didn't really follow any particular god.

He knew Brother Pynon's biggest obstacle was the local herbalist two villages away, with her questionable cures, potions, and charms. She had the ability to convince others of nearly anything to make a copper for herself. He felt for the man. The old woman seemed to thrive on rumors, lies, and discontent.

An hour later, they arrived at the farm as the sun was setting. They were greeted by Jynal's wife Nyissa, and his youngest son, Teel. The boy struggled in his mother's arms as he tried to get down. Since he'd started walking, he'd been a handful. The horse and moving wagon was too tempting for anything other than complete restraint of the young child.

After the wagon was unloaded and the horse fed, watered, and brushed, Jynal and Marnell joined the family in the small house for dinner. As they ate stew from wooden bowls, Katheen told her mother all about the shells she'd found and was excited about having her mom help with the necklace once her baby brother was asleep. It would do them no good to attempt it with him still up.

"I know it's dark, but we all have some chores to do," Jynal reminded his two older children.

"Yes, Papa," Katheen said.

She was a little disappointed the egg gathering for the day still awaited her. They'd left before sunup that morning, so all the eggs were uncollected. She didn't look forward to going out into the night, but was glad she didn't have her brother's chore.

"The chores won't do themselves," Marnell said, imitating his father's voice. The whole family laughed.

Before they'd left for the day-long trip, her brother had led three pigs on a rope to the tree line and turned them out. Typically they rooted in the shade of the forest all day and were waiting at its edge to be led back to their pen, where they hoped scraps waited for them. This time of year, they didn't have to worry about piglets. All had been sold on the last trip to town. Three pigs or a small herd, Katheen had no desire to cross the open field to the edge of the forest at night to lead them back like her brother often did.

Her father filled a lantern with fish oil using the last of the old cask, and she walked toward the barn with it held high. She remembered what she'd been told, and didn't look at the burning wick directly, lest it make it hard to see beyond it once she looked away. It wouldn't do for her to trip and fall with a lit lantern in one hand and the egg basket in the other, so she walked carefully. At only eight years old, she was careful enough to be trusted with the lantern.

Katheen walked around the inside of the barn, looking for eggs. She knew all the places the hens liked to hide them. She gathered several in each spot until the basket was half full.

Once she'd checked them all, she held the lantern up high and counted the chickens roosting in the rafters. She counted nineteen dark shapes. She recounted. She knew there should be twenty, eighteen hens and the two roosters.

Her mother hadn't mentioned any of the chickens missing, and she knew her brother had caught the fox killing them last month in a rope snare. Besides, there would've been feathers scattered if it had started happening again. One of them was attempting to sit a nest. Katheen looked around for the likely spot.

Near the front of the barn was a set of shelves built into the wall with various tools on it. A small anvil was on the bottom shelf. On the second, there were shoes and nails for the horses. A file and several hammers occupied the third shelf. None of them had been cheap, but her father was competent enough with them that he saved coin by taking care of the horses himself. Not many farmers had horses with shoes.

Katheen eyed the fourth and fifth shelf. There on the fifth shelf was an old wooden pail lying on its side. She knew it was empty, though she couldn't see into it. Her papa had put it up there because it had a leak.

She suspected the chicken was there, deep in the bucket, covering the eggs. She was a smart girl with farm sense, so even at her age, she knew once a hen laid enough eggs in one place, instinct took over, and the urge to cover them until they hatched would control the chicken. The bird would only leave the nest for short periods to eat and drink.

Katheen looked around and decided to put the lantern on the top of the corner fence post on one side of the pig pen. She couldn't set it on the ground like she did other places. If she did, the bucket would be in shadows. She needed it up high. She set her basket down and started climbing.

She stood on the second shelf but still wasn't high enough to see into the bucket. She placed her right foot carefully on the third shelf and pulled herself up partially. There was no room for her left foot so she could stand fully to see and reach into the bucket. She felt with her foot and realized the file was in the way. It was laying at an angle across a hammer. She scooted it over more, and the file made an eerie screech as it slid over the head of the hammer.

She flinched at the loud noise, and then let go of the shelf she was holding onto as the hen panicked at the sound and flew from the bucket down at her head. Katheen fell back against the fence, striking her head and shoulders against the bottom rail.

She was slightly dazed and looking up when she saw the lantern tilt and fall. Time seemed to slow as she threw an arm up to cover her face. The lantern broke when one end hit the bottom rail and the other struck her elbow, covering her with its contents. The pain was beyond what any mortal man should ever feel. Katheen screamed until she could no longer draw breath as she rolled, covered in burning fish oil.

* * *

Marnell was headed to the barn, leading the boar on a small rope, the two sows following, when he heard his little sister scream. He'd never heard a cry of pain like that. It seemed to last forever as he sprinted for the barn, the inside lit brighter than he'd ever seen at night. Shadows danced crazily on the back wall as he ran through the opening.

Inside was the stuff of nightmares. Flames were everywhere around his sister as she writhed, burning, no longer able to scream. Marnell didn't hesitate as he grabbed his sister, burning dress and all, and ran out of the barn, straight for the water trough. He shouted for his papa as he ran.

He never felt the pain of his own burns as he threw her into the long trough. Twice the flames tried to reignite in what remained of his sister's smoldering hair. He ducked her again and again. Through his tears he could see the fire was out. He fell back as his father picked his sister up out of the trough and ran toward the house.

* * *

His hands blistered. Marnell urged the horse to run faster. He was almost to the village where the church was located. As he got closer, he called out for Brother Pynon. Several villagers heard him calling and came out of their homes to see what it was all about. One of them, slow to follow the rest, stared with a blank expression.

Marnell jumped from the wagon as it slowed to a stop and met the brother as he was coming out the door of the church. The shouting had been loud enough to wake him. It didn't take him long to come out.

Marnell cried out, "Brother, you have to come with me! My sister has been burnt…she's burnt real bad. My papa sent me to fetch you.

The herb woman is at our home, and she says there's no saving Katheen. Mama went to get her; she's been there since midnight."

Marnell sobbed and continued, "Nothing she did worked, and she said sometimes burns heal, but Katheen is burnt inside. She won't stop coughing, and she wheezes. She's burnt bad. Almost all of her." The last came out in a whisper.

Brother Pynon could see the burns on the boy's hands and redness on his arms, his singed hair, and his tear-streaked face. "Wait here, child," he said and ran back into the church, his blue robes pulled up in one hand so he could move quicker. He came out of the church moments later with a wooden flask and two books.

To his credit, the horse ran back to the farm as fast as he'd left it, urged by Marnell as he cried uncontrollably. Brother Pynon spoke quietly to him, alternating between that and prayer. The brother could smell burnt flesh on the boy. It might not have been his flesh, but the smell of it was in his clothes and hair.

* * *

"No!" shouted Jynal. "Get away from her!" He pushed Jalette away from the bed.

"It's for the best," the old woman argued, "there's no hope for her. I can do it. You take your wife and youngest outside. I'll do it. It's not my first time, you know."

"You get out, or I'll kill you," Jynal said, anger evident in his voice. He stepped toward the old woman, intent on following through with his threat.

"Jynal Narvok," the old woman said as she slid the small knife back up her sleeve into its sheath, "you're being selfish. Think of the girl. Even now, she hasn't woken up yet. She's wheezing and coughing in her sleep. When she wakes, and she will, she'll scream until her voice is gone, you mark my words."

Jynal glared at her. "Go," he said through clenched teeth.

The old woman gathered her things. "Well, I won't be here when Brother Pynon gets here, that's a fact. Him trying to start a church out here. He's a fraud, and that sea god he follows is, too."

She pointed he long bony finger at Jynal. "There's only what we do in this world, not some mythical being granting miracles. When the rot starts in, you'll wish you hadn't run me off. You'll see."

Jalette stomped past the children's mother as she sat on another bed, holding her youngest tight. The herb woman ignored her and slammed the door behind her when she left. The sound of Katheen wheezing as she struggled to breathe filled the room.

Nyissa was numb as she stared off in the distance, her eyes unfocused. She had no tears left. Though she was no longer looking at her only daughter, in her mind she could still see the blackened flesh as some of it peeled away with the girl's dress, some coming off with clumps of burnt hair. She knew, once Katheen woke, the pain would be unbearable.

She buried her face in her youngest's hair and held him tightly, the boy crying because his mother had been. He didn't understand what was happening, but like most children, he felt the emotions around him. For once since he started walking, he made no attempt to get out of his mother's arms.

Outside, the old woman threw her bag into the two-wheeled cart, climbed up in the seat, grabbed the reins in one hand, and urged the big goat forward. She reached into the side pocket of her dress and pulled out two metal flasks. She threw them in the back with the bag.

She muttered to herself, "A waste. That's what it is. A waste. I could have the blood of a dying virgin filling both my flasks right now. There's so much I could have done with that, starting with my looks. May Lethrall take him to the depths of hell!"

Though she might deny the sea god, she knew of demons. Jalette denied all the gods. She preferred demons. She rode off into the dark.

* * *

As the scenes unfolded around them, Kryder looked over at Tog and Lucas, their images slightly blurred, as tears were streaming down his face. What they were witnessing was heartbreaking, but he was completely surprised to see his cousin crying with him and the innkeeper. He'd never seen the Half-Orc cry. Orcs didn't do that. Ever.

He glanced over again when they heard the old woman mutter. Lucas' face turned red, and there was a look on Tog's showing his own rage.

* * *

As the wagon slowed to a stop, Brother Pynon leapt off. He hurried to the front door of the home, ignoring the still-smoldering barn. Marnell was close behind him. Without bothering to knock, the brother entered the home. The first thing to hit him was the smell.

He rushed across the room to the bed where Jynal stood. Brother Pynon didn't speak as he went to work. The first thing he did was move his hand down the length of the burned child, above her, his hand and fingers moving up and down mimicking the motions of waves as he prayed and called for his god's mercy. His other hand slid along the length of his necklace of seashells, the fingers seemingly counting on their own.

Brother Pynon felt his god answer like a blow to his very being. It knocked him to his knees. Shaking his head, he stood slowly, knowing now what he must do. He pulled the wood flask from an inner pocket of his robes and both books from another. The edge of the bottom of the cork, where it met the flask, glowed with a soft blue light for a few seconds, and then faded.

The brother turned to Nyissa and said, "Please bring me a metal pot. Have you one?"

She didn't answer. She still stared off, barely registering the man was present. Brother Pynon turned to Jynal.

"Nyissa," Jynal said softly as he touched her. "Please, she needs us here. Now. Fetch a pot."

Shaken from her thoughts, Nyissa scrambled to the fireplace and her small collection of pots and pans. She was back quickly with a small dented pot. She handed it to the brother.

Brother Pynon pulled the cork from the flask, closed his eyes, and poured some of the holy seawater into the pot until he felt the urge to stop. He carefully replaced the stopper and set it aside. He put the pot on the floor beside the bed and opened the smaller of the two books. He read quickly, nodded to himself, and turned to Jynal.

"You must turn her on her side," the brother said, "so her head is hanging over the side of the bed and she faces downward." He walked over to the fireplace and took a pinch of ashes from the edge.

His face showing the pain his daughter must feel from being touched, much less placed on her side, Jynal did as the young clergyman had asked. Through his hands he could feel his daughter's breath coming faster until she was nearly panting. He looked up and saw his oldest son helping, holding Katheen's feet so they wouldn't slip off the bed. Tears flowed from his eyes in helplessness.

Brother Pynon spoke the words of prayer and power he had memorized while he spread the ashes on the bottom of the pot. The pot began glowing, and the seawater started boiling. He held it below the young girl's face as the steam rose. It wasn't close enough to burn her more, but with every breath, she inhaled the vapors.

Brother Pynon held the pot until all the holy seawater was gone, leaving a thin white crust of salt at the bottom of the pan. Once it was gone, the bottom of the pot stopped glowing and was as cool to the touch as the handle had been.

Amazed, Jynal could feel Katheen breathing easier, though she still coughed occasionally in her unconscious state. He nodded at his son, and they gently rolled her onto her back again. They no longer heard her wheezing.

Brother Pynon stood over Katheen, placed a hand on her stomach, one of the few places that was red but not blistered, and prayed again, thanking his god for the gift given to the child and asking for continued guidance. Once again he felt the answer reverberate in his mind as he stumbled backward.

"Sit her up," Brother Pynon said, his voice shaking, knowing what was coming. "We must wake her so she drinks."

He looked at Nyissa. "Listen to me carefully, for this is very important. When she wakes, she will be in pain. Terrible pain. I will take this pain unto me until I can no longer. You must have her drink from the holy flask. She can breathe now, but she must swallow the holy seawater, too."

Nyissa, now much more aware of her surroundings, nodded her head quickly in understanding and took the flask. She pulled the stopper out, put it in a pocket on her dress, and moved to the head of the bed.

Once again Brother Pynon placed his hand on the child. This time it was on her thigh. Truly the only areas not burnt on the girl were below her ribs down to right below her knees. Her upper body, head, face, arms, and hands were blistered and charred, as well as her feet.

The brother nodded at the girl's father. Jynal raised Katheen to a sitting position as her mother held her head steady. Brother Pynon prayed for the power, opened his eyes, and spoke the girl's name.

Instantly Brother Pynon felt pain as he had never felt it before. He sucked in his breath and closed his eyes tight, his entire body shaking. The pain was unbearable. He kept his hand in place as long as he could.

When Nyissa felt Katheen hold her own head up at the sound of her name being spoken, she quickly put the flask to her daughter's ruined lips. Some of the seawater dribbled down, but by instinct, Katheen swallowed a mouthful…once, twice, three times, before she became limp again.

Brother Pynon fell back and dropped to his knees, holding his hand by the wrist with the other. He took deep breaths, and the unbearable pain receded as if it was never there. It might have been gone, but he knew he would always remember it. Always.

He slowly stood, nearly exhausted. "Please hand me the flask," he asked.

Nyissa handed him the flask, then realizing she still had the cork, she handed it to him, too. The brother felt the weight of the holy seawater remaining. He swirled the flask, thinking. He nodded to himself. He knew what to do with the remaining water. Grateful this bit of knowledge hadn't come to him as hard as the others, he went back to work.

He looked at the child, at her ruined face, her burnt eyelids, the lips mostly gone, along with her nose. All of her hair was gone with the scalp on one side. The other had some hair. He poured a little of the remining contents into his hand and wiped it over both eyes. He poured more and did the same for her nose and lips.

Swirling the flask again to determine how much was left, he thought more of this child's future life. His decision made, he poured some on both feet and rubbed it all over, ensuring he covered the toes, the top and bottom of both, and her ankles. He did the same with her wrists, hands, and the inside and outside of both elbows. There was very little left, as most was used on the bones of her hand where there was no more flesh.

He poured the last, and he wiped it over both breasts with the back of his hand, should the girl decide to become a mother one day. The flask was nearly dry. He tapped the bottom of the flask as he held it over one cheek, and the last drops fell. He spread it as much as he could over it.

The next night, as everyone else slept, Jynal jerked awake from a deep sleep. He checked on Katheen and found her sleeping, though she shifted about as if uncomfortable. Without knowing why, he walked over to the fireplace and picked up the small pot Nyissa had set back on the shelf. With a wooden spoon, he scraped the salt from the bottom and poured it in a small piece of leather. He twisted it up, tied off the top, and put it away. Feeling tired again, he laid back down beside his wife.

Brother Pynon stayed with them for four weeks, taking turns sitting with Katheen as she slowly healed. He was able to pray, as he counted shells, and use the spells he knew to ease her pain somewhat. The most important thing his spells did was prevent infection from setting in. Daily he blessed spring water and helped clean the burns. It was not the holy seawater touched by Minokath himself, but it did have healing properties.

During this time, Jynal and Marnell cut trees and made lumber to replace what had burned in the barn. They replaced the thatch roof over it and built a new pig pen, stopping often to check on Katheen. Several neighbors did the same, as did some people they knew from nearby villages.

Their friends didn't say much when they left. They didn't know what to say. It was obvious the girl would live, but the scars she would bear were hideous in their eyes. When Brother Pynon had held the steaming pot under her face, some bone had been showing. The steam had healed the deep burns, and the flesh had grown back, but half of Katheen's face was deeply scarred.

Her hairless scalp bore the same, save for part of one side, where the holy seawater had dripped as Brother Pynon worked. That ear was whole, as well. Her shoulders, upper arms, forearms, back, lower legs, and some of her upper chest was scarred. Her neck was streaked with deep ones, except where it had dripped when she drank.

It wasn't spoken of, but Jynal and Nyissa knew their beautiful little girl, though still beautiful in their eyes, would never grow up to be a woman a man would desire for marriage. She would live, and she would heal, but her life would never be what it could have been.

She was strong, and even though she was in some pain as she healed, she was determined to get out of the bed. She never asked why it had happened to her, she just dealt with it, practicing sitting up and entertaining her baby brother as he sat in bed with her, careful around her, as if he understood.

"I must go," Brother Pynon said one day. "I wish you all well, but I must take the long trip to the city and receive counsel from the head of my church. The miracle must be recorded, and I am to receive more training in the healing arts before I return and continue to build my congregation. I must also replace the flask with a new one, filled from the sea fountain there."

Before Brother Pynon left, Katheen held his hand and said, "Thank you. Thank you for helping me."

"My child, you are most welcome," the brother said, "but it wasn't I. Saint Minokath, in his infinite wisdom, had mercy on you and gifted me the knowledge and power to do what little I could."

"I know," Katheen said as she looked up at Brother Pynon, her pretty blue eyes clear in understanding. "I saw him."

"My child," Brother Pynon whispered. He dropped to his knees to be closer to her. His faith was strong. He believed her. "You saw the Lord of the Seas..." His eyes glistened.

Katheen nodded. "I saw him. It was kind of blurry, like he was underwater. He was a tall man. He had long, green hair, shiny chain armor, and his cloak floated behind him. He dropped to his knees and was praying, then he stood up, looked right at me, and smiled. After that, I think I remember tasting something salty. The next thing I remember is waking up hurting all over with Papa, Mama, and you there with a bucket of spring water to cool me."

His hand trembling, Brother Pynon reached into his robe and pulled out both books. The smaller of the two was the one he had read from the first night there. The other, thicker book was the one he looked at now. It was an ancient book, passed down through his family for many generations. It was a copy of The Book Of The One. All the brothers of his order had one. His happened to be a family heirloom.

"All belong to the Creator. Verily, I say to you, even the saints and gods," he quoted reverently.

* * * * *

Chapter Four

Jynal and his son continued to farm. In the lord's fields, he grew corn. It would provide enough coin once harvested to pay his taxes, with some left over. They were to be higher this year, by edict. The local lord was raising coin for something, though the peasants and farmers didn't know why. It wasn't their lot in life to know what was happening around the kingdom.

Unknown to Jynal and his family, rumors started to spread. It was said the girl should never have lived. How could there be no infection? Witchcraft and demons were involved. "Jynal must have made a deal with a demon. Look at his hand, he's done it before." Several demon names were mentioned, including demon lords. Being a superstitious lot anyway, the rumors spread easily from village to village, and through the farming community.

Once on the way back from town in the village with the church, its doors still shut waiting on the return of Brother Pynon, insults were shouted at Jynal and Marnell. Rocks and old fruit were thrown. Jalette stood in the shadows of one of the huts, smiling as she watched. The goodwill Brother Pynon had built in the area was all but gone. The old woman shoved the simpleton standing near her aside as she turned and walked away. "Move, idiot."

No one came to visit anymore. One evening, the pigs didn't return from the forest. All three of the big pigs and twelve young piglets had vanished. They searched the forest near the farm for two days, to no avail. Two nights later, the chickens lay dead beneath the rafters where they roosted, all of them killed by rocks the size to fit the pocket of a sling. Whoever had done it hadn't bothered to pick up the stones.

The small herd of cows, fenced in a field behind the barn, broke through the cut wood fencing and couldn't be found. It had happened several times before, and one or another of their neighbors always brought them back. Everyone in the area knew his mark. This time no one did. The only one remaining was a young calf with a lame leg from birth. Her mother had never strayed far from the calf, except this once. Jynal penned her in the barn.

They survived the summer on fruit from the apple and plum trees, garden vegetables, and by butchering the young cow and smoking the meat. Marnell collected a half bucket full of berries from the thorny bushes on the forest's edge. The pigs were no longer there to eat them all before they ripened. Nyissa made a spread for the simple flat cake she made on Katheen's ninth Day of Life celebration.

There were no coins left, not that many places in the villages would do business with him anyway. He was turned away at all the neighboring farms when he tried to trade work for things. No one wanted shoes for their horses or work on their buildings and fences, even though he could see they sorely needed it. The last coins earned from selling items from within the home in town had long been spent.

One morning they woke to find the cornfields burning. The dry stalks seemed to invite the flames as they swept across in the breeze. They saved a couple of bushels, but the rest of the crop was burnt. It was mere days before they were to harvest it all and take it to town. A week later, when the time came to pay taxes, Jynal could not.

The tax collector looked down his nose at Jynal. He stood there in his fine clothes, flanked by four of the lord's guard. "The lord will have his taxes, or he will have your home," he sneered, looking around and noticing the quality of the home, the barn, and the fencing. It was skillfully put together, unlike many farms he'd seen.

"He'll not have my home," Jynal said defiantly. "I have a writ from the king's court. It was gifted to me by the king himself. It's not on the lord's property."

This angered the tax collector. He hated being proven wrong in front of his men. "The home and barn may not belong to our lord, but the fields you farm do. You *will* pay for the use of them and the taxes, or you *will* be hauled to debtor's prison, and we'll see if your wife and children can maintain it for you."

"I can make lumber from the trees and sell it," Jynal suggested.

The tax collector climbed onto the wagon, and the guards mounted their horses. Before the driver could urge the horses to move, the collector raised his hand to stop him. He looked over at Jynal and said, "You have one week." They rode off in a cloud of dust.

Three days later, they left in the evening. The belongings they could fit in the back of the wagon with the children were packed tight. Jynal had built a small frame covered with blankets to keep Katheen and her baby brother out of the sun, as her scarred skin was still tender. They sat on a rough wooden box holding their spare clothes and balls of home spun yarn.

Marnell rode up front with his mother, reins in his hands. The two plow horses were tied to the back of the wagon. Jynal had taken the blade off the plow and loaded it on the wagon. The wooden plow frame he could build again.

Jynal rode his older horse. The black horse was eighteen years old now and had been retired to an easy life on the farm. He had been five years old and recovering from a wound on his flank when Jynal had ridden him from the city years ago, happy with the price he'd paid. He was even happier when he'd arrived at his land, ready to build a home.

A year later he married a woman he'd met several crossroads away. She came from a long line of farmers, but she was the only child. Her parents had her late in life, and they were gone now. Life had been good. They were happy.

Today he wasn't happy. As they rode away, the house and barn behind them was nearly demolished. The days had been spent tearing them down and salvaging all the nails and pegs they could, packing them with his tools and saws. They were in the wagon next to the double handfuls of corn he'd been able to save as seed, the sacks of taters, dried fruit, and seeds from garden vegetables.

Before leaving, Jynal had thought of selling his horse to pay the taxes. His wife had relentlessly begged him not to, knowing what the horse meant to him; besides, the remaining wood could be collected by the lord's men and would more than compensate for the unpaid taxes. Many of the one-room homes in the area were made simply of logs. Not many had the skills or tools to create actual lumber.

They rode inland through the night until they were beyond their lord's borders. They stopped mid-morning at a crossroads with no village. His family slept while Jynal took care of the horses, allowing them to drink at a small stream near the road. The land was more open, so he wasn't concerned about brigands, though they were closer to the mountain ranges in the distance and the Goblins known to dwell there. Several travelers going the other way did the same with their horses.

Jynal didn't speak to them, preferring to stay near the wagon and his family. After several hours, he hooked the horses back up to the wagon and woke his son. They turned south toward the city, many days ahead, passing a trade caravan of five large wagons moving much slower than they. They were pulled by oxen with two drivers on each.

One of those men, riding up front with a driver, waved like a child. Jynal waved back. He nodded his head at the guards riding with them, all carrying themselves as soldiers, only older than most. It was a common trade, once a soldier lost a step or two. He found himself wondering if he knew any of them from years before.

Three evenings later, after passing through several villages, they were traveling through a stretch of forest when Jynal heard the howl of a wolf. He knew packs of wolves roamed this far south where it was cooler. It was answered almost immediately from the other side of the narrowed road at a distance. They were being hunted.

"Marnell, your bow!" he called out. "Nyissa, keep moving. Katheen, stay low with your brother."

Jynal slowed the big horse and dropped back behind the plow horses tied to the wagon. Nyissa took the reins from her son, and Marnell readied his bow. In the back of the wagon, Katheen put her brother up against the seat, deep under the blanket framework. She crawled back to the back of the wagon, her small sling in hand.

She was a farm girl; hunting was a part of life. With her sling, she had taken rabbits and large fowl in the fields near her home. She didn't know how much it would hurt a wolf, but she wasn't scared to use it. She knew it would probably hurt her; her shoulders were still somewhat tight from the scar tissue.

Her mother had been helping her with the stiffness of the scars with, of all things, the very cause of the burns. Fish oil. It was something she'd learned from her own mother. Katheen pushed the hood of her cloak down so she could see better. Here, where no one was around, she wasn't afraid of being seen.

The horses started to get jittery as they kept moving forward. They could smell and hear the wolves as they called to each other. His horse, however, seemed to react better than normal to his commands. It was as if Coal knew there was danger, and his old training came back to him. The stud moved like a young horse, shifting back and forth in the road, ears up, turning and listening.

When the wolves struck, it was sudden. One moment they weren't there, the next there were ten of them coming down from the hills on the sides of the road, their snarling growls giving them away. Two on one side went for the single horse pulling the wagon. The rest went for the larger group of horses at the rear of the wagon. The draft horse stopped moving forward and tried to buck free of the harness, shaking the whole wagon.

Marnell pulled back as far as the length of the arrow would allow and lined up his shot, trying to adjust for the shaking wagon. His aim, at the chest of the huge grey wolf coming down from the slight hill to his left, didn't fly true as the wagon shook. It was high and farther back. The arrow imbedded itself into the wolf's spine, after it cut through several vertebrae. The leader of the pack tumbled, crying out repeatedly like a scared pup, its back legs useless.

The smaller wolf running beside it veered away out of instinct, the sound of its alpha in pain triggering ancient flight instincts.

Marnell buried an arrow to its fletching in the beast's soft side below the ribs, and it fell, rolling. Whimpering as it scrambled in the fallen leaves, it tried to regain its footing, but another arrow struck its chest, dropping it. The boy let fly another. Neither shot was well placed, but they served their purpose.

Hearing the high-pitched yelps from their leader, the remaining pack slowed, their attack becoming less of a coordinated effort and more of a feinting attack in ones and twos. Jynal leaned down on one side, hoping to swipe with his short sword, holding tight to the reins. His horse took the strong tugging of the bridal to mean spin. The horse turned quickly, reared up, and stomped the wolf with both front feet, crushing its skull and ribcage. Jynal nearly came out of the saddle.

The lighter-colored wolf running beside it went for one of the tied plow horses. The more skittish of the two was tied to the inside. It panicked, sensing its impending doom. It tried to go forward and away, causing the horse tied beside it to turn with it. The horse kicked out with both feet in its own panic. The wolf went flying from the blow, its skull crushed.

The next wolf was stomped by the warhorse repeatedly as he reared up and fell back to the ground, fighting as he was trained. One more came running in, again straight for the plow horses. A rock hit it on the side of the head hard enough that the stone cut its muzzle, turning it away. An arrow shot from Marnell's bow as he stood on the seat of the wagon, now more stable, sank deep into its ribcage. Seeing it still moving, the black horse sprinted toward it in three long strides, almost upending Jynal again as he was thrown back by the sudden move. That wolf was stomped, as well. The rest scattered and disappeared over the hill under the bare trees.

After a few minutes, when the wolves did not appear again, Jynal sheathed his sword and dismounted, the big horse's muscles quivering as it danced sideways a step or two. He leaned over, both hands on his knees, breathing deeply. Marnell jumped from the wagon and ran around the back to check on his sister. Katheen stood, rolling her shoulder slightly, the sling dangling in her hand.

"Papa," Marnell said, "I didn't know old Coal could do that. You were like a knight fighting him, like the stories you tell us."

Marnell stood, looked at his wife, and started laughing. She grinned with him, still trembling with fear, and said, "Now aren't you glad you heeded your nagging wife?"

She continued to soothe the frightened draft horse. Teel peeked out from under the blankets when he heard his mama speak. The dark-haired little boy seemed to have enjoyed the bouncy ride in the back of the wagon.

Turning to his son, Jynal said, "I wasn't fighting on him. I was only trying to hang on. I had no idea what I was doing. I was a foot soldier and an engineer. I never fought on a horse. That was for the calvary to do."

"We should skin them," suggested Katheen, her hands on her hips, the wind blowing the tufts of hair among her scars and the large patch of good hair on one side as she stood looking down at them. "You can sell them."

"Aye, that we can," agreed Jynal. "They won't be back, with the big one dead. It'll be a while before they have another leader or another pack moves into the area. I knew men from these hills when I fought for the king. They spoke of wolf packs."

* * *

The scene faded to a gray void. Kryder turned to Tog. "I remember the story of the wolves. His bow hung in our home, the wood old and brittle. It was never meant to be more than a lad's first bow."

"I remember," Tog said. The big man placed a hand on his cousin's shoulder.

Lucas looked back and forth between them, wondering what was unspoken.

"Come," Lan said. "We move forward."

The grey faded, and they were somewhere else in another time.

* * *

Jynal dismounted his horse, now much leaner and more muscular than it had been in the fields of the farm. Months of travel had worked the fat off all the horses. His family wasn't lean, though. He'd been able to sell the pelts and find some work in the city after searching out his old commander, now in command of many in the king's forces. His writ of recommendation offered many opportunities to earn and save coin before leaving the kingdom.

Now, after coming through several of the estates of barons in the Baronies West, they were in the last one before the unclaimed land between the Baronies West and the edge of the Orcanth border. His family secured at an inn with stables, he rode to the castle in his best clothes, seeking to speak with Baron Arnwald. He'd been told the baron was one who would entertain visitors, if the reason for the request was intriguing enough.

Looking around the courtyard, he saw a man in chainmail, a yellow and black tunic over it with his hood pushed back, striding over. The man looked to be younger than Jynal. A guard he'd met at dinner had relayed Jynal's request and had summoned him the next day from the inn. He stood by his horse and waited.

The man walked up, looking at the horse as he came. He looked away from the horse, glanced at the sword on Jynal's side, and said, "I am Sir Narthon, cousin of Baron Arnwald, and the leader of his men. You're Jynal Narvok?"

"I am, my lord," Jynal said, remembering his time as a soldier, standing tall.

"The baron will see you," Sir Narthon said. He turned to a squire, hovering nearby. "Call a groom for his horse; see that it is stabled, fed, and watered." She nodded and turned toward the side of the courtyard to do his bidding.

The squire called out, and a man ran from the stables. When he took the reins, he reached up and petted the nose of Jynal's horse lovingly. Instead of shying away from the stranger, as was his normal behavior, Coal leaned his head down into it. It surprised Jynal to see the warhorse act that way with any other than his family. It was if the horse sensed the man meant him no harm. Studying him, Jynal could see by the child-like expression on the groom's face that the man's mind was burnt. A simpleton. He'd seen the like many times.

As the horse was led away, the knight remarked, "'Tis a fine animal. A little long in the tooth for fighting these days, but he appears from good stock. Seventeen hands, if he's one…Minth bred, I would guess?"

"He's purebred Minth," Jynal confirmed.

"Indeed," mused Sir Narthon. "After you've completed your business with the Baron, I would speak to you of stud services. Does this interest you?"

"Certainly, Sir Narthon," Jynal agreed.

They walked through the corridors of the castle into a great dining hall. The baron sat off to the side, the table covered with roasted fowl, vegetables, and fruit. He raised a hand in greeting from across the large room.

"Of course, I'll need to examine the horse closer before I let him mount one of my mares," Sir Narthon said with a slight smile. "Come, I'll introduce you."

The baron was younger than Jynal by a few years. He was of average height and appeared to be in fighting shape, like his cousin. He wasn't wearing armor, but did have a sword strapped to his waist over his black and yellow tunic. The symbol of his barony was on his chest, a spiked metal gauntlet, the fist closed around the stem of a red rose. Jynal had been told it meant the one viewing it could accept the rose…or the fist holding it. The choice was theirs.

Jynal wasn't sure of the protocol when meeting one of the barons of the Baronies West, so he started to kneel. He didn't wish to offend. The baron stopped him with a hand on his shoulder.

"Come, man," he said. "I'll not have that. We're the same, you and me. I happen to have been born a baron. Other than the title, I see no reason we cannot speak as equals. You're my guest. Let us be content with simple politeness."

"Sir, I…" Jynal began.

"Sit, sit," Baron Arnwald said. "Besides, if you're other, I'm quite sure my cousin will set you straight and see you out. He gets that way, you know."

Sir Narthon shrugged. "Since we were lads sneaking into the town, Arn. Though if I remember correctly, it was you setting other lads straight when they spoke ill or harmed other lads, and especially the lasses."

"I've never been able to tolerate it," agreed Baron Arnwald. He tilted his head slightly and shrugged his shoulders as he said it.

Jynal, unused to this type of thinking from royalty, was sure he liked these men already. One thing he'd noticed as he rode through the Baronies West, the commoners weren't as thin and didn't wear rags as many in the neighboring kingdom of Minth. Nor were they afraid to speak of the barons or other royalty. Nearly all spoke well of them.

The three ate and spoke of trivial things. Farming in the area. Of horse breeds and cross breeding to produce the best results. The sea on the far coast of Minth. The trip Jynal and his family had taken to get there was of particular interest to the men as they asked questions of the border with the kingdom of Minth and some of the far baronies.

When they were finished and the remains of the meal taken away, the baron turned to Jynal. "Tell me of your request. I'm not sure my man delivered your message accurately. These things happen, you know. Do you really mean to settle deep in the unclaimed land near the Orcanth border…and build a farm?"

* * * * *

Chapter Five

"I do, my lord," Jynal answered.

"Why?" asked Narthon.

It was one word. A simple word. *Why?* Jynal had asked himself this many times while he lay looking up at the stars at night as they traveled farther and farther west. *Why?*

"Once, many years ago," Jynal began as he looked up recalling a friend, "I was saved by a big man. Bigger than most. Our catapult had been overrun by what remained of a company of enemy foot soldiers. They'd slipped around the lines and were intent on destroying it before we could break down the wall of a castle. They did manage to damage it."

He continued, "The squad assigned to protect us fought to the last man and woman, but there were too many of them. At the end there were four of them advancing on me and the one laborer left alive with me. Layton was a quiet man; he never spoke much to others. He only did his job, most times the work of two men, with his great strength. He often spoke to me, though, for he was my friend. It mattered not to me he was part Orc.

"He fought three men at once with a large wooden mallet, breaking it over the last of them as I struggled and finally slew my own attacker. It was not without cost. He died in my arms. It took a while, yet there was nothing I could do for him, as he bled inside.

"In that time, he told me of the times he'd ventured through the unclaimed lands back to Orcanth, of the tribes accepting him without hesitation because he was of the blood. He came back to Minth to care for his mother until she died. He was to leave for good after the siege with his coins. He told me too many men believe the rumors and old stories. Yes, Orcs have raided humans in the past, but it's nowhere near the countless times humans have brought war unto other men."

The baron and his cousin remained silent as Jynal continued, "I've known others of mixed blood. Always they're treated poorly, attacked, even. Rarely does one ever say anything or strike back. Finding little acceptance, they simply move on.

"From everything I've been able to find out, the tribes don't venture from the borders of Orcanth anymore, content to be at peace with humans. From the stories I've heard, the land between your barony and there is unclaimed. I would move deep into it. I don't wish my family to ever go through what we have again."

He continued, "This barony is the closest to the border of Orcanth. Is this true? Do they stay within their borders?"

"Aye," Sir Narthon said, "that they do. Occasionally they send a messenger when the Goblins stir, threatening to come from their mountain homes, or when a tribe has gone rogue against the wishes of the consensus of the council of tribes. It's usually a Half-Orc bringing the message. One like your friend, who made his way to Orcanth. It hasn't happened in tens of years."

"We...I know the Orcs aren't thought highly of among the kingdoms," the baron said, "but we know, here in the baronies, they aren't the monsters they're made out to be. Are they different? Yes. Are they much larger than men? Yes. They may have fangs protruding like tusks, and can fight like the demons people claim they worship, but that doesn't mean they are less than we."

The baron stood and began pacing as he warmed up in an argument he had been part of many times. "They aren't monsters. They think like you and I, man. They *think*. Yes, some go rogue. Name a race that doesn't have its own bad apples ruining the whole barrel full. Saint Lanae take me now if we Humans haven't been the worst of the lot throughout history."

He sat back down. "They have their own gods, though I suspect some of them are the same as ones we know by another name. They don't worship demons. The Book Of The One all but names them as mortals of the Creator's design. The same as Dwarves, Gnomes, and Humans. Elves too, I suppose."

"The book does not name them specifically," reminded Narthon.

"Bah!" Baron Arnwald said, waving a hand in dismissal. "It doesn't name *any* race specifically. It says 'thinking mortals' in several places. They think, and they have free will!"

"So do Dragons, cousin. So do Dragons," Narthon countered.

"Yeah, well, maybe they're thinking mortals, too," the baron argued, "and the book includes them, as well."

"I'm not saying Orcs aren't," Narthon said, his hands up in resignation. "I was only pointing out the other side's argument. We've had peace all these years, and I want nothing less. I would be content to never use my sword other than in training until I grow too old to lead the forces and simply retire to a life of horses."

"I know, cousin, I know," the baron said, calming. "It's those farthest from the borders of Orcanth who keep the rumors swirling. You'd think those in the kingdom of Gar-Noth would know better. They have more mages than any kingdom, with the Halls of Magic there. Surely they have spells or devices letting them see the truth of things. Remind me to ask your sister."

"Aye," Narthon said, "though she's never mentioned the like. It's not like she uses much magic these days. She never had the ability to do much."

"That's good," interjected Jynal, "I've heard they do their best to convince those with real power to stay and teach. I think it's so they can consolidate the strongest. There are always issues on the border of Minth and Gar-Noth, and should war come, mages will be involved."

"So I've heard," agreed the baron. He looked around. "As usual when my cousin is involved, we've traveled down a rabbit trail and made many turns."

Narthon slowly shook his head and said, "Once again you blame me for things when you are clearly the one at fault." He turned to Jynal, nodded his head sideways, and said, "This one needs a good thumping, hey?"

Arnwald laughed. "Back to the matter at hand. You wish to travel deep into the unclaimed lands. I cannot, nor would I, stop you. What is it you wish of me?"

"Protection," answered Jynal.

"Protection?" asked Baron Arnwald, confusion on his face. "I believe we have established that the Orcs stay within Orcanth. Don't tell me you wish to cross their borders."

"No, my lord," Jynal assured him. "I'm not asking for protection from Orcs. I ask it from Humans. If I establish a farm and I'm successful, I believe other farmers will come looking to do the same. Perhaps a village will be established. These are good things, as long as honest, hardworking people come. I fear word will spread, and other types will come rushing in. There are always those who wish to take what they haven't built or earned. A brigand with enough men under his sway could establish themselves there and claim a small kingdom."

"I see," Baron Arnwald said, rubbing his chin. "'Tis a point you have there. The Baronies are ruled by reasonable people. Five barons and one baroness. It wouldn't come from one of them officially, but I wouldn't put it past the king of Gar-Noth to try to establish something in the unclaimed lands."

"It is a lot of land," agreed his cousin, "even if much of it is unfit to farm. Water is an issue in many places. Still, if you become well established, word will spread. Unclaimed land is a rare thing. What are you thinking, Arn?"

Baron Arnwald grinned. "Summon your sister. Ask her to bring the stone."

After a time, a woman dressed in fine clothes, save the fresh stains on the front of her dress at the knees, came into the hall. She was older than both the baron and Sir Narthon, with a touch of grey showing in her reddish hair. She smiled pleasantly and held up her soiled hands.

"You called me from my flower garden, cousin," she said. "Let us hope you have good reason, lest I need a clean tunic to wipe my hands on."

"Don't even think of it," the baron said, grinning, "this is newly made." He indicated his tunic. "Notice the flower resembles that which you have perfected."

"This is Jynal Narvok," Narthon said. "Jynal, meet Lady Shynae. He intends to farm in the unclaimed lands."

"Really?" asked Shynae. "What will you grow? It's very dry there. Well, part of it is. I don't think fruit trees will do well. Perhaps a hearty wheat strain, or corn, if you have water enough. It rains seasonal there, I think…"

"Sister," Narthon interrupted, "the stone? Did you bring your stone?"

"I did," answered Shynae. She turned to the baron, reaching into a pocket. "Do you wish to question him?"

"Only a few questions," confirmed her cousin. "I know it drains you."

Jynal was unsure of what was happening. He watched the woman hold the stone in her palm with her other hand over it. She said several words he had no hope of understanding. The stone remained the same in her palm. She held it over his head and nodded at Baron Arnwald.

"Jynal Narvok, do you mean harm to the Arnwald Barony?" the baron asked.

"No," Jynal said.

There was no reaction from Shynae. The baron continued, "Do you intend to refrain from entering the borders of Orcanth, build your farm, and swear you are not sent by the kingdom of Minth, Gar-Noth, or any other kingdom or lord to establish and claim the land for them?"

"Of course not, my lord," Jynal said, taken aback.

"Are you a good man?" the Baron said, leaning back in his chair, folding his arms, and studying Jynal.

"I would like to think so, but that's for the gods to determine of any mortal," Jynal said after a moment's thought.

"He lies not, Arn," Shynae said. She closed her hand and sat down, obviously tired.

"I didn't think you were, but I had to be sure," Arnwald said as an apology to Jynal.

"I understand, my lord," Jynal said, not really understanding. "That was the first time magic has been used on me. I didn't see or feel anything happen."

"From what I understand, unless you had the gift, you wouldn't," explained Baron Arnwald. "And enough of the 'my lord' business."

Baron Arnwald stood and walked a few paces from the table. "Come here, Jynal."

Jynal stood, confusion on his face, and walked over to the baron. The baron drew his sword and said, "I mean you no harm. Kneel."

Jynal knelt as the baron's cousins stood, both grinning. They'd seen Arnwald do this before on a whim to members of the baron's forces. It was always amusing.

Baron Arnwald laid his blade on Jynal's shoulder. "I dub thee Sir Jynal Narvok, Lord of the Western Borderlands. Rise, Jynal. I will grant you a small plot of land here in my barony. I will safeguard it for you, and it will continue to be used as pasture for my horses in payment of the taxes owed. As a landowner in my barony, you're no longer a commoner."

"But...why?" Jynal asked, unsure of what had transpired.

"You're a lord in my barony," explained Arnwald. "You wish to travel into the unclaimed lands and establish your own land. I support it. If I hear of your survival, I'll send word to the other baronies of my support. Armed with that knowledge, no force shall travel through any of them to the unclaimed lands. To get there they must traverse unpassable mountains inhabited by hordes of Goblins, or they must come through the great northern desert. That is an undertaking no one will attempt."

He continued, "We may be six separate baronies, but we support each other and our people. There is strength in numbers. Who knows, perhaps one day the Western Borderlands will become another barony. Besides, they'll be as amused as I am when I tell them of the expression on your face."

The baron stood and said, "Now, before you leave, let us have a look at this horse of yours. Seventeen hands, you say?"

* * *

Tog turned to Kryder and said, "That's how he became a lord. I've heard him called so only a few times; he doesn't encourage it."

"When I asked him about it, he laughed and said he's the only lord walking behind a plow." Kryder laughed. "He's probably right, though I think if she was able, Lady Shynae would do it."

"Aye," agreed Lan. "That she would. A good woman, that one."

"What were the business o' that stone?" asked Lucas.

"A truth stone," answered Kryder. "I know of one. I could see its soft red glow, though I suspect it would have brightened if he'd lied."

"Come," Lan said. "We move forward."

Once again the grey swirled and shifted, and they found themselves elsewhere.

* * *

Jynal stood on the edge of the plateau looking down into a desolate ravine. It stretched to the south as far as he could see, toward a range of snow-topped mountains. To the north it grew small with distance and disappeared behind some hills, still within the Arnwald Barony.

A trail barely wide enough for the wagons snaked along the wall below him, to the shallow flowing water at the bottom, among the washed-out dirt and rocks. Some of the stone formations visible in the distance were incredible to look at, both in shape and color. The lines of different colored rock and sediment, mostly in shades of orange and reds, were easily visible.

"This is as far as I can take you, my lord," the squire said. "This is as far as we patrol, anyway. By your leave, we'll ride to the next watchtower with these supplies." She indicated the four pack horses with her calvary platoon.

She pointed toward the south and said, "You can see the top of it there."

"Thank you for the escort, Anise," Jynal said.

"You're welcome, my lord," Anise said. "My lord, you do know it won't be safe through the canyons? None of the towers have sent signal of Goblins moving from yon mountains, but some may have slipped through in small numbers."

"I know," Jynal said. "We'll stick to the trail the miners use."

"Yes, but that trail doesn't go beyond the canyons where they prospect," she said, "the miners always hire guards. You have none. No one has ventured beyond the canyons into the unclaimed land since it was abandoned. No human alive knows what you may find beyond in the ruins of the villages."

* * * * *

Chapter Six

Jynal placed Katheen in the saddle on Coal. Next he handed her younger brother up, sitting him in front of her. Katheen wrapped an arm around her brother, gripping the pommel tight with the other. The warhorse stood still throughout. As he'd reverted to his training when it was time to fight, he also knew when to be the docile animal needed for the children.

It wasn't the first time Jynal had led the two of them around on the horse. Granted, the times before were back on their farm in open pasture, and not before descending down a switch back trail. They began the descent.

Marnell led the plow horses, now pulling double duty, as they were hitched to a large wagon carrying supplies bought in the town before they left the barony. Extra axes, saws, shovels, hammers, and plow blades filled a large box. Other boxes were filled with wheat flour, corn meal, and dried meat. Two cages held chickens, the ten of them constantly clucking, the two roosters as nervous as the rest. In the back third of the wagon, three young goats were now tied, their legs hobbled so they wouldn't stand and try to jump out.

Nyissa walked the draft horse pulling their old wagon. Supplies had been added to it, as well, including three barrels of fresh water, fruit tree saplings, and more seed. There was another bow besides the one on Marnell's back, and several quivers of arrows. This one was well made.

Slowly, carefully, they made their way to the bottom. Following the path, occasionally seeing the indentions of wagon wheels, they made their way through the canyons and gullies. The miners knew of their coming long before they arrived at the camp site.

Several miners and four guards with bows were standing beside their cook fire when they rode up. They could see a mine entrance in the wall of what appeared to be the backside of the canyon. A small stream ran out and down one side of the slight rise leading south. Chickens ran around the camp with untethered goats. One of the men stepped forward.

"We heard you coming a way back," the man in dusty clothes said. "Ol' Red, our rooster, has been answering yours as soon as he heard him. He lets us know when the supplies are coming."

"We did bring some for you," answered Jynal. "The baron asked us to drop it off on our way."

"On your way?" asked the man. "I see you have your family with you. Do you mean to continue on into the unclaimed lands?"

"We do," answered Marnell for his father.

"You don't appear to be part Orc to me," the man said as he scratched his beard. "What are you to do there?"

"Farm," Jynal said, "and live."

"Farm, you say?" the man said sadly. "Well, let us get the supplies unloaded so you can be on your way. I'm sorry, but I don't want to get to know you, as I'll never see you again. Nothing good comes of knowing a dead man, I say."

He continued to talk as he unloaded the supplies Nyissa pointed out. "There's nothing good up that cliff there. We don't go into the unclaimed lands. Nobody does except those passing through to Orcanth, and I haven't seen one for years."

"How long have you been here?" Jynal asked as he steadied his horse when a goat came near.

"Eight years now," answered the man. "I return to the castle a few times a year, when we bring a load to the baron, and when the contract is up with the guards."

"Our contract has been up for two weeks," one of the guards interjected. "It's time for that trip."

"I know, Zane," the man said. "We'll have the cart full by the end of the week. You were paid up front, and you'll get the extra when we return."

One of the other guards, wearing the same dark green and leathers as Zane, walked over and pushed back her hood. "Zane, you know I'm not interested in going back to a town, but I don't want to stay here. I grow bored."

"What are you saying, Penae?" Zane asked.

"Perhaps the farmer is looking to hire a couple of guards for the rest of their trip," she answered. "It would be a chance to stretch the horses, and our legs. Hunt for something other than rabbit and wild fowl."

"Aye, that it would," agreed Zane. "We took this job when coin ran low. Perhaps we can go where coin isn't needed, somewhere more like back home."

Zane turned to Jynal. "Would you have use of guards where you're going, farmer? Forgive me, I know not your name?"

"His name is Lord Jynal Narvok," Marnell said proudly.

"My lord," the old miner said, quickly taking off the dusty leather and wool cap he wore. "I didn't mean to say you were a dead man."

Jynal glanced at his son, looked back, and answered, "No offense taken. You didn't know. Besides, I may happen to be a lord, but I'm no better than you, as I didn't introduce myself, either. My apologies."

"I…thank you, my lord," the old man said as he looked at Jynal in a new light. "It's like the baron you are, a good man in my eyes. My name is Jeffrent."

The old miner put his hat back on, the wool flaps hanging on each side, and said, "Well, if you have need of those two, their contract is up. I can vouch for them. They're good people. Yon cart is full of raw stone. Worth a ransom it is, once polished and worked. Never once did they or any of the guards look to leave with it."

Jynal turned his fidgeting horse back in a circle so he was facing the two guards. "I wouldn't say no, but I have no coin. All was spent on supplies. I don't know what we'll find up there. I intend to travel to the far side, where I've been told the best land is."

"My lord," Zane said after reading the look on Penae's face, "if you'll have us, we can make arrangements for pay at a later date. Perhaps we'll build a cabin there, if it's to our liking and the hunting is good, unless you intend to claim all the land."

"I don't," answered Jynal. "We would welcome the company. Let me introduce you to my family."

Zane grinned and said, "Thank you, my lord. The last thing I wanted to do was take my wife to another town. She's happiest among the forest, and you know what that means."

"I do," assured Jynal. "Nyissa would live on a farm and nowhere else."

* * *

They traveled north away from the mountains, following the cliffs marking the western side of the canyons until they came to a draw leading up toward the west. In the beginning, the heavier wagon bogged down in loose sand. Jynal was able to get it moving by tying several ropes to the first wagon and using the strength of all the draft horses.

Zane rode ahead to ensure the draw didn't narrow too much for the wagons to pass. Once he was sure they'd have no issue topping the cliffs to the land above, he rode back and guided the rest of them up. The sun was starting to set when they came out.

Katheen stood behind her mother in the back of the wagon, her hood pulled over her head as usual. The view was amazing. The sky was a shade of purple and pink she'd never seen, reflected in the bottom of the clouds. As far as the eye could see was a dry grassland. There were the occasional groups of small, stunted trees on some of the gently sloping hillsides.

"Papa," Katheen asked, "is this where we will live?"

Jynal, riding beside the wagon, shook his head and answered, "No. We'll ride for a week before we get to the land my friend told me of long ago. Here there is very little water. The few springs are used by the animals. Some of them hunt near the water. Even here, there are wolves."

"And cats," Penae added. "I've heard there are big cats, much bigger than the lynx from the forests of my home."

Katheen reached into the pocket of her cloak, checking to ensure her sling was there. In her other pocket was a handful of stones. She didn't say anything; she only wanted to be ready.

The open plains slowly gave way to light forest. In some places the trees were scattered; in others they formed small dark forests. On the fourth day they came to a creek running down from some hills. The evidence of a village could be seen. Several crumbling stone walls a half hour from the creek were the first evidence other humans had been there.

Only a few stone walls of a church were still fully standing. Everything else was little more than piles of rotted wood and knocked over stone. They let the horses and goats graze and drink their fill of water, and replenished the water barrels from the flowing creek. Katheen and Marnell, warned to stay within sight, set out to explore the ruins.

They poked and prodded among the old houses, finding nothing worth keeping except some old pots and cups. On the far side, Marnell found what could have only been the blacksmith's shop. Several rusty horseshoes and some tools, their wooden handles rotted, were strewn about. An anvil, its surface rusted, was lying on its side. He and his sister gathered all the horseshoes and pieces of scrap metal in a pile next to it. If nothing else, their father could make more nails.

Marnell moved several pieces of rotted fence, thinking something might be under it, when he saw the bones. He scrambled back, heart pounding. Once he was brave enough, he moved the other pieces to reveal the bones of a man. A rotted leather apron revealed it was the blacksmith himself. Part of a broken arrow shaft was beside his ribs.

Marnell reached down and picked up the small piece with the arrowhead still attached. The shaft was much thicker than the ones he used with his bow, and the arrowhead was much more than the hardened tips of his. He did have two with small arrowheads his father had made from scrap metal, but it was nothing like the barbed one he was looking at. He decided to keep it and show his father later.

"You should cover him back up," suggested Katheen as she stood back, her arms crossed, hugging herself. "It's like his grave."

"Yeah," agreed Marnell.

He started putting the pieces of crumbling wood back. Several broke, so he looked around for more pieces. In the corner near the crumbling back wall were several pieces of wood. It appeared as if a box had fallen in on itself. When he moved the top piece, he saw the end of a small sheath. He pulled it free, shook it off, and slipped the dagger out of it. Its blade had been protected by the lee of the wall from weather, along with the wood and the sheath. It still held an edge. He slid it back into its dried leather sheath and tucked it into his belt.

They walked back to the wagons and told their father about the metal. Marnell showed him the dagger. Jynal looked at it closely. He knew it was far better craftmanship than he could ever hope to achieve. The best he could do was reshape shoes and make simple items. He handed it back to Marnell.

"We'll probably need to make a better sheath for it," Jynal said. "Be careful with it. It's sharp."

"Papa," Katheen asked, "can I go look in the church?"

Jynal looked over at the walls of the church. They appeared to be in better shape than the homes the two had been looking in all morning. It wouldn't hurt to let her look. Since the accident and the miracle of surviving it, she'd been asking questions about things he really couldn't answer.

"Be careful," he warned her. "Marnell, show me where the metal is. We'll see if we can move the anvil."

Katheen walked to the remains of the church at the edge of the village. She was curious about who it was dedicated to. Which saint or god had the villagers followed? She walked through the open arch where the doors no longer hung. One of them was lying flat, the wood crumbling. The other was in pieces where, even at her young age, she knew it had been chopped with axes.

She walked past the rubble. Some of it she climbed over as she made her way to the front, where what remained of the walls were. Near them she saw the stone altar. It was still intact, with only a few blocks missing from one corner.

As she got closer, she could see the image on the front of it made from pieces of stone inlaid into the blocks. It was an image of several fields, the growing crops easily identified, as the rows were even lines. She knew it was dedicated to Saint Gonthon, patron saint of farmers. Her mother spoke of him, and her parents had taken her to occasional services when she was young.

Katheen ran her hands over the lines of the fields. One corner of the mural was of a fruit tree. She counted the apples, touching each one as she did. When she pushed one of the small stones, she heard a loud click on the other side of the altar. Curious, she walked around it.

A door made of thin stone was cracked open. She wedged her finger in it and pulled it open. Inside was something wrapped in thin oiled leather. She opened it and discovered two books. One was a copy of the Book Of The One. She read the cover slowly. Her parents had been teaching her to read, along with her brother.

Most commoners where they were from never learned to read more than a few words. Her father insisted his children learn more than that, so he taught his wife. The other book was unmarked. It was much smaller than the first. Inside, the writing was not as easy for her to read. The larger book's text was written neatly with quill and ink. This one had clearly been written by someone who didn't write all day, every day. Only a few pages were used.

She wrapped them both back in the leather, closed the hidden door, and left the church. She walked back over to the wagons and showed the books to her mother. Nyissa looked at the smaller of the two and read some of it.

"It's a book of prayers," Nyissa told her daughter. "It must have belonged to the cleric. The first one is a prayer for a bountiful harvest. The next one is something about healing a cough, but I can't make out some of the words. Your father reads better than I do. We'll ask him."

Before they left the area, Zane edged his horse close to Jynal on his and said, "We found several remains. This village was attacked; some of the homes were burned long before time destroyed them. We found no sign of Goblins. We did find evidence of Orc arrows. There's no denying the size of them. It may have been a long time ago, but it was Orcs that did this. I thought you should know."

* * *

Three days later, after riding for a day through lightly forested land interspersed with open meadows and rocky hillsides, they came to open plain covered in deep, lush grasses. In the distance, like an imposing black wall, a dense forest could be seen. It stretched north and south with no end in sight in either direction.

"That's the edge of Orcanth," Jynal said, "and it looks as it was described."

"Is that where we're headed?" asked Zane. "Hopefully, there's water near the boundary. The last was half a day's ride behind us."

Scattered around them among the trees were the remains of another village. Deciding not to stop and search it, Jynal rode out into the open plain toward the far side, the farmer in him observing the healthy grass and the soil when there was the occasional break in the grass.

On the other side of the grassland, they stopped under several huge oak trees, their bases nearly as large as the width of a wagon. In the shade of the trees, the ground was completely exposed; the grasses, needing sunlight, didn't grow there.

Jynal dismounted with Zane and Penae. The two guards knocked arrows and moved in opposite directions to ensure the area was safe from large predators. They were also hoping to bag one of the antelope or deer they saw from a distance as they rode closer to the Orcanth border.

The animals, though curious, moved away in a quick gallop as they got closer. Some went into the forest, others over the next gentle hill in the open plains. Zane and Penae decided they'd stalk the ones in the open. They didn't intend to get close to the border, especially with weapons in hand.

Jynal left the shade of the trees, his family busy staking the goats so they could reach both the shade and the grass. Water was still an issue, and Jynal was determined to find the source the huge trees used. Without an abundant supply, it was doubtful they would've reached their towering size. He hoped it wasn't deep underground. It would take weeks to dig a well deep enough for them to use it. He didn't look forward to the half day trip every few days to go back and replenish their barrels.

Jynal looked toward the line of trees. There, south of the forest, he saw a hill rise up, ending in a cliff face. From what he could see, it became another hill in the grasslands. At the base of the cliff, he saw what appeared to be a dry creek bed. It was full of rocks and boulders. It split about two hundred feet from the base of the cliff. He might not have noticed it if he weren't standing in what was once a small stream bed. He could see where it branched off from the larger bed. It led his eyes to the cliff in the distance.

One side of the dry bed forked and angled off into the forest, into Orcanth, disappearing underneath the low overhanging branches of several trees. If he were closer, Jynal thought he might have been able to see into the forest for several feet. He didn't let curiosity get the best of him. He had no intention of stepping foot onto Orc tribal lands.

He made his way to the cliff on horseback. As he got closer, he realized the trees of the forest were much larger than the trees he was used to seeing. They weren't as large around the base as the three towering oaks the wagons were parked under, but they were taller.

Jynal looked at the cliff and the obvious empty basin where once, long ago, water had pooled before flowing down the creek bed. About four feet up the cliff, he could see small openings where the now dry spring had once been the headwaters of the creek and whatever river it connected to somewhere. It might have ended in a marshy swamp or a lake, but he had no way of knowing.

* * *

Nar drew his arm back, his huge bow creaking. He hesitated to release. If the human crossed the empty creek bed, he would die. Nar could do no other. As the oldest son of the tribal chief of the Red Fist, it was his duty to lead the warriors to protect this section of the border of Orcanth.

Earlier, one of his warriors had run the two hours through the trails to reach him in their village. Wagons had been seen, with several riders, coming across the fields. They'd been watched for an hour as they slowly moved closer to the border, when the decision was made to fetch him. Nar was at the edge of the border with the other members of the patrol in less than the two hours it had taken to get to him. The warrior sent to retrieve him caught up later.

Nar watched as the man stepped halfway across, examining the wall. The human didn't cross to the near side. He waited, as did the eight others with him. They didn't knock arrows, but were prepared to, should he give the command. Easing the tension on his bow, he watched the man mount his horse and ride back to the trees. Motioning to his warriors, Nar indicated they would continue to wait and watch.

* * * * *

Chapter Seven

Jynal rode back to the campsite, dismounted, and let Coal drink his fill. As the horse drank, it reminded him water was an issue. He would have no choice but to go back a half day's ride and refill.

"Papa, what were you doing over there?" Katheen asked.

"I went to the head of the dry creek to see if there was any trace of water," he answered. "At one time, it ran freely. For some reason it's gone dry, or now runs underground."

"Can we dig it up?" Marnell asked.

"No," Jynal said, "it once flowed from the rocks themselves. We don't have the tools for that. Besides, the openings are still there, only no water."

"We could pray for water," suggested Katheen. She held up the small prayer book.

Jynal smiled at his youngest after a glance at his wife. "I'm afraid that kind of prayer would take a powerful cleric. Probably one of the leaders of Saint Gonthon's church, or whichever saint may reign over things like that."

"I could do it," declared Katheen. "I'll pray to Saint Minokath, Lord of the Seas."

"It doesn't work like that." Marnell laughed. "Everyone know it takes years of service and the blessing of the saint to rise to that level. A ten-year-old girl isn't going to get a miracle."

"I'm alive," stated Katheen with a determined stance, hands on her hips. The light breeze blew a few strands of her hair away from the opening of her hood. "Say it again."

"Well," Marnell stammered. He knew she had a point. "He answered Brother Pynon, not you. He's a cleric."

"Papa," Katheen said, "I could write a prayer in my book and ask. He'll answer; he knows me. I saw him look at me and smile."

Jynal looked over at his wife. They both knew their daughter had received a miracle. They couldn't deny it, but her claim to have actually *seen* the lord of the seas was something they weren't quite ready to believe. Jynal felt it had been the fever making her hallucinate.

His wife gave him the look that meant he'd better let their child have her way. He knew the look. It usually meant a horse ride at the end of a day when he was already exhausted.

Jynal turned back to Katheen. "Are you sure you want to write it first? You could just say it. I mean, your prayer book is for prayers to Gonthon."

"I think I have to write it and prepare," answered Katheen. "The prayers already in the book have instructions with them. There aren't very many, but some of them need things. It doesn't matter if the prayers in it are to another god. He won't mind. All the gods belong to the Creator."

"I won't argue that," Jynal said. "What do you think you'll need?"

If he was going to appease his youngest, he might as well go full out. Nyissa smiled at him. Marnell shook his head and grinned.

"Well, I have this," Katheen said as she pulled her seashell necklace from her shirt through the opening of the cloak, letting it hang on the outside. "I need some water, too. I wish I had seawater. It would help."

"There ain't no seawater around here," observed Marnell, looking around as if it was there, he would spot it. "It's months and months away."

Jynal thought for a moment and said, "Wait. There may be a way to make some." He dug around in one of his bags in the wagon until he found the small leather bundle. He handed it to Katheen.

"Is this sea salt?" Katheen asked as she unwrapped the leather string and opened it in her palm.

"I scraped it from the pot Brother Pynon used," answered her father.

"Alright," Katheen said. She thought for a moment and said, "Can I have a few of the corn kernels?"

"What are you doing?" Marnell asked. "Making some kind of crazy potion? Will there be a dance?" He danced in a circle, waving his arms, his younger brother laughed at him and danced, too. "This I have to see."

Katheen looked around. Zane and Penae were nowhere near them. She pulled her hood back so her brother could see her face, crossed her eyes, and stuck her tongue at him. She pulled her hood back over her head and was serious again. As serious as a ten-year-old could be, anyway.

"I'm going to ask both Saint Minokath and Saint Gonthon to heal the spring," Katheen announced, as if it was a normal thing for a young girl to say. "Mama, will you hold Teel so he doesn't knock anything over?"

Katheen picked up her younger brother, handed him to their mother, and took a wooden flask from their supplies. She dipped it into one of the barrels, filling it, and sat down with it against one of the tree trunks. She opened the leather-wrapped salt and spread it open in her lap. She held the three kernels of corn in one hand, shifting them in her palm. Her other hand moved across her necklace, rotating it by the small shells through her fingers, as she looked at the words she'd written in her prayer book.

The instructions, written with the burnt end of a sharpened stick, took up two pages, because she wrote large. Her father had helped her spell some of the more difficult words, and a few of the letters were backward, but she didn't mind. She didn't think the gods would, either. She read the prayer she'd written after the instructions and decided it was good, but it would be better to really talk to them.

She closed her eyes and prayed as only a child can. *Saint Minokath, it's me, Katheen. You know me, I saw you one time. Thank you for saving me. You have pretty green hair. Will you bless this water, please? I'm going to put salt in it. Saint Gonthon, hello. We haven't met. I saw one of your churches, but it was burnt. I'm sorry that happened. I was burnt one time, too. I took the books I found. I hope that's alright. Will you bless these kernels of corn? If you'll bless this corn, I'll put them into the holes where a spring used to flow, then I'll pour blessed seawater over them. The spring will come back, because I believe it will. I know I'm not really a cleric. I'm only a little girl, but the Book Of The One says believe, so I do. Thank you both very much, your friend, Katheen Narvok.*

* * *

Across the continent in a castle deep in the sea, Minokath looked up, his hair flowing behind him in the current. Seated on his throne in conversation with a creature no man had ever seen, he held up a hand to stop his guest in mid-sentence.

Like all the saints and gods, in the back of his mind he heard prayers daily. A part of him took note, and he acted when he thought it necessary. This prayer was different…this prayer was from a little girl. One he knew.

Minokath bid his guest wait and disappeared. Moments later, the Lord of the Seas walked out of the surf on a deserted coast. He stood ankle deep in the edges of the rolling waves and waited, the wind blowing his hair and his cloak behind him, drying them.

A minute later, Gonthon walked between several palm trees down onto the sand. The scrubby bushes behind him turned a thick, lush green. As the patron saint of farmers passed close to one of the trees, he reached out and touched the trunk, letting his hand slide across. Several coconuts appeared on the barren tree and grew to a ripened size.

"Brother," Gonthon called out. He was dressed in simple, dusty clothes, the clothes of a farmer. His hands were dirty, as always. "It has been too long. You should come from the water more often."

Minokath grinned and reached out to clasp the hand held out to him. "It is good to see you, as well, even if you are in need of a bath. Perhaps you should come into the water more often."

They both laughed as he wiped his hand on his cloak. Gonthon wiped his own hand across his shirt to dry it. It was a joke they'd shared since the beginning of time.

"I take it you heard the prayers of the child?" Gonthon asked. "In all these centuries, has anyone ever come to us together such as this?"

"I don't believe so," Minokath answered. "Some have asked me for rain for their crops, but that is not my domain."

"She said she knew you. I looked inside her. She does, indeed," Gonthon remarked. He pursed his lips and said, "I like this child. She bears the scars of unspeakable pain, yet has never asked why it happened to her. She has knowledge of the growing of plants and how they break through the surface of the soil. Her faith is astounding at such a young age. Then again, she has seen the face of a saint."

"Indeed," Minokath agreed. "Well, brother, what shall we do about this prayer?"

Gonthon took off his hat and wiped his forehead with a sleeve. "It is an unusual request. Not unusual as far as dry wells or springs, though. Many times I have answered those, as I'm sure you have. This time, she has written it as a cleric would upon receiving enlightenment."

He paused a moment before continuing, "At ten years old. Ten."

Minokath laughed. "If we work together and grant her this, she will have created a new technique and prayer spell…with an unusual combination of components. When was the last time a new one was granted?"

"Too long ago, my brother," Gonthon answered. "Too long."

Minokath reached out a hand. "We are in agreement, then. Until I see you next, brother; may it not be so long."

* * *

Jynal watched Katheen take a pinch of the salt and sprinkle it into the flask of water. She put the wood stopper back on it, swirled it around, wrapped the remainder of the salt up, and stood. She put it in the pocket of her cloak with the three kernels of corn. They loaded the wagon and rode to the hillside.

Marnell helped his sister out of the wagon. She straightened her cloak and followed her father up to the base of the cliff. Zane looked over at Penae to see if she had seen what he had. The look of shock was followed by sadness in his wife's eyes. She'd caught the glimpse of the girl's scars, too. They both dismounted, tied their horses to the wagon, and stood near it.

Marnell climbed back onto the wagon's seat with his mother as she held Teel, the small child half asleep. He didn't think they'd need the barrels in the back of the wagon, two of them now empty, but he was ready to help. If his parents were indulging his sister, so would he.

Jynal helped Katheen over the loose gravel and a few of the boulders to the cliff face. He showed her the cracks where water once flowed. She ran her hands over the cracks. When she found space, she pushed a kernel into the hole. Once all three kernels were in place, Katheen closed her eyes and prayed. It was one word. *Please.*

Jynal watched her pull the stopper from the wooden flask and pour the water on the rock wall above the cracks where she'd pushed the corn kernels inside. As it flowed down, some of the water found its way to the corn. Once she was done, he heard her whisper, "Thank you."

To his astonishment, a blue glow came from within the cracks. It was bright enough to see in the daylight. After a moment or two, it faded. Without hesitating, Jynal grabbed his daughter and ran. He had no idea what would happen, but he wanted her safe.

Once they were near the wagon, Jynal put her down, and they turned and watched the cliff. For several seconds nothing happened. They had no idea the kernels had sprouted, the plants rapidly growing into the cracks and crevasses.

Many years before, a huge slab of stone had broken loose and slid down, covering the only path for the spring to flow. Once the three plants reached the solid rock deep inside, they paused their growth as if waiting for one gigantic push. The ears of corn forming on the stalks provided the push.

There was the muffled sound of a crack as the stone split deep inside the hill. A small amount of dust blew out of the fissures, followed by a steady trickle of water. It grew to become a small waterfall, about eight feet wide. It would take time, but it would fill the pool at the base of the cliff, and begin flowing through the old bed once again.

"She did it!" exclaimed Marnell.

"Not me," Katheen said, looking up at her brother; "the saints did it. I just asked."

"By Nalkon," Penae whispered. She reached up and grabbed the claw on her lone dangling earring in awe.

Zane stared at the waterfall. He'd seen small things he couldn't explain back home in Tarlok when hunter clerics were granted gifts from Nalkon the Hunter. Never had he seen it from a child. He started to comment, when out of the corner of his eye he saw movement in the forest three hundred feet away.

Zane thumped his finger against the wood of his bow twice. Immediately Penae started scanning the woods without turning her head. Her body stiffened when she made out what Zane had seen.

Zane stepped over to Jynal and turned his back to the trees. "We must move away now," he whispered. "We're being watched."

Jynal nodded, put Katheen in the back of the wagon, and mounted his horse. They rode back to the campsite. He would check the progress of the water later. Now he wanted to move his family away from the danger and ask the woodsman what he'd seen.

* * *

Sar watched as one of the wagons approached. Near the head of the silent falls, the human he'd observed earlier got off his great horse. Two others dressed as if they knew their way among the trees did the same. These two humans had bows in hand. He signaled four of his warriors to watch those two closely.

He continued watching as one of them climbed off the wagon, walked around, and lifted a small one from the back. He couldn't tell if it was another human, or something else. The figure was cloaked and didn't lower the hood. Nar stepped forward a pace to move past a low hanging limb partially blocking his view.

The man led the small one to the rock face, helping it occasionally. *Could it be a child?* thought Sar. The little one ran a hand over the face of the rock. Sar couldn't tell what was happening at this distance. He watched as the smaller one reached up and poured something on the rocks. The color of them changed, and, even at this distance, he could tell they were wet. He saw the blue glow come from the cracks, and the sight shocked him. He stepped forward another pace, his bow forgotten.

After a brief moment, it was gone. The man picked up the small one and ran. Even at this distance, Nar heard the muffled sound as rock cracked. Seconds later the falls were flowing freely. He knew in his life and his father's life the rocks had never given way to the spring buried deep in the hill. He didn't know if they had in his father's father's life, either.

The little one must be a shaman. A powerful shaman, he thought. He took another step forward for a better look. He remained within the shadows of the trees, but didn't realize a shaft of light had landed on his shoulder and part of his side, glinting off his axe. His attention was on the falling water.

He called his warriors to him. "Go, finish your patrol. I will stay and watch them. I do not think they will come within an arrow's flight of the trees." Unknown to many outside of Orcanth, the boundary of the Orc nation didn't start with the forest. It started one easy bowshot from the trees. "They are not of the blood; they will not enter Orcanth without permission."

* * *

The next morning, shortly after sunrise, Zane and Penae rode off to hunt fresh meat. His family sleeping, Jynal walked over to the small streambed near the three trees.

It barely had a trickle of water flowing. He'd been sure by now there'd be more of a flow. He walked along the streambed toward the larger creek bed. In some places the stream he was in was only an arm's width across.

When he got close to the creek, he could hear and see water moving among the rocks. There was plenty flowing, and in several places the water was more than knee deep. He saw what the problem was. Several rocks were blocking the opening to the stream. Jynal eased into the cold water and began moving stones and larger rocks. The sudden appearance of water again had shifted them. After an hour or so, water was flowing toward their campsite.

Jynal looked up toward the waterfall, still amazed by its sight. He noticed another dry stream bed. It led away toward the dark forest on the border of Orcanth, where there was a large bend taking it much closer to the trees. He walked upstream and then waded across the creek, not realizing a bow was drawn in the shadows, the arrowhead aimed at his chest.

He stopped at the opening of the stream and began removing stones and small boulders. These he piled behind him, making a small island of sorts in the center of the creek, with several flat rocks topping it. Freeing the opening to this stream took more than an hour. Once water was flowing down the bed into the trees, he started to turn away. A movement caught his eye as something stepped out of the trees.

Jynal found himself looking at an Orc. The Orc was dressed in shades of green and light brown with a dark brown leather vest and arm guards. It was hardened as a type of armor. On the front of it was the image of a large closed fist, as if a hand had been dipped in red dye and pressed against it.

The Orc was larger than his friend from so many years ago. His tusks were, too. His hair hung to his shoulders and moved slightly in the breeze. He held a large bow in one hand, and Jynal could see the glint of an axe at his side.

Not a word was spoken. After a tense moment, Jynal raised a hand in greeting, his palm open. The Orc nodded once, turned, and indicated the stream at his feet with a long sweep of the hand holding the bow. He looked sideways at Jynal, slightly raised his free hand, mimicking Jynal's wave, and quickly slipped into the darkness of the tree line, following the newly flowing stream. Jynal finally exhaled, having realized he'd been holding his breath.

* * * * *

Chapter Eight

That afternoon, Jynal was discussing with Zane how they'd go about gathering logs to build cabins. They agreed it would be best to take a wagon back to the last grove of trees and cut some down. It would take many trips, but there was no other choice. Katheen insisted they not cut one of the towering oaks down. She could be persistent from within the darkness of her hood.

Suddenly the sound of a roar echoed from the direction of the forest. Startled, the three of them looked toward the sound. Whatever had made it was big, and angry. Jynal grabbed his new bow and ran toward the creek. Both hunters did the same. Marnell brought up the rear with his own, as the adults moved faster than he.

There in the open, near the stream running under the canopy of trees, was the largest bear Jynal had ever seen, and the Orc. The bear rose up, its head more than twelve feet above the ground. The Orc ducked a mighty sweep of its claw and shot another arrow into its chest. As Jynal waded into the creek, he could see several shafts protruding from the beast. He shot an arrow into its side, the shaft much smaller than the ones already there.

The bear swiped again at the Orc as he backed away, nocking another arrow. The Orc ducked and rolled, spilling several shafts from the quiver on his back. He loosed again as the bear advanced on him. The next time the Orc reached for an arrow, there were none.

The Orc tossed his bow aside and drew his axe, both hands on the handle, resigned to fight the monster close up, ignoring all else around him. The bear rose up once more and roared in defiance, spittle flying. It shuffled on its back legs, ready to fall down on the Orc to grab him, crush him, and attack with its jaws.

Four arrows flew in, the two from the hunters striking the beast in his neck and burying deep. They let fly two more before Jynal or Marnell could loose another. Once again, four more flew in. The bear turned toward the new threat and charged toward the creek, its roar deafening.

Four more arrows flew. Jynal missed, the arrow sailing right over the charging beast. The hunters' arrows sank deep in its chest. Marnell, the last to shoot, aimed for the chest, but shot high when he slipped on a stone while backing up to move away, even though he was across the water from the beast.

The arrow he'd selected was tipped with the Orc barb. It was too heavy for the shaft and was incapable of great distance. In this instance it wasn't needed. The arrow flew straight into the bear's eye and embedded into its brain. It took another great stride, and then the bear's front legs folded, it dropped, and slid to a stop on the far edge of the creek, only 10 feet away from his father.

Breathing heavily, the Orc walked over to ensure the bear was dead. He looked over at Jynal and the others. Jynal could see the bear's claws had managed to cut the Orc. He bled from one shoulder. It was not bleeding bad, but it was cut.

"Why?" the Orc asked in a deep voice. "Why help?"

Jynal was shocked to hear the Orc speak the human language. "It was the right thing to do. We're neighbors."

The Orc narrowed his eyes. "What mean…neighbor?"

"We…live close," Jynal answered. "We live next to Orcanth."

No one else spoke. Zane and Penae kept their hands away from their quivers and the long hunting blades at their sides. Marnell stood still, looking back and forth at the Orc and his father.

"You not live," the Orc said. "You no, you no… " he spoke a word in Orcish none of them had a chance of understanding. Finally, remembering the word, he said, "you no home." He indicated the campsite under the trees. "Only wagons."

"We need wood to build homes," Jynal said. "We were planning a trip to go get some with the wagons."

The Orc stared at Jynal. Then he looked over toward the campsite. He could see Nyissa standing with the two younger children. His mind made up, he turned back to Jynal. "You stay that side of water. Build home, be neighbor."

The Orc continued, "I Sar, son of Pon. Red Fist tribe."

Jynal introduced the four of them and indicated the others near the wagons, telling the Orc their names, too. He explained who was his family, and the two hunters were friends.

Sar pointed at Katheen. "That one…daughter? Not shaman?"

"No," Jynal answered. "She's no shaman. You saw that? She prayed for the spring to open again. The saints granted it. She may become a cleric one day. She may be already; I don't know how it works, but she's no shaman. She doesn't have the gift of magic like shamans."

Sar nodded. "Some shaman have magic. Some shaman pray, do things, but have no magic. Sar not question shaman."

"A wise choice," agreed Zane.

Sar nodded toward the bear and looked at Marnell. "You want? Meat not good. This one old. We hunt long time. Not find. Water make leave cave I not find. Orc killer. Is good dead. You want fur?"

"I," Marnell stammered. He looked at his father, who shook his head slightly. "No, you can keep it."

Sar nodded. "Make good blanket. Tribe use."

He stepped over and started pulling arrows from the beast, the arrowheads pulling loose easily with his great strength. He lay them in piles, separating his from the rest. The last arrow he pulled was the one that killed the beast. He hesitated and looked at the tip closely.

"Where get?" he asked Marnell while pointing at the barbed tip.

"I found it days ago," Marnell answered.

Sar grunted to himself and put the arrow in the pile. "Running Boar Tribe. Always make trouble. Not have tribal lands on border. Council move them long time ago. Before Sar."

With a mighty tug on a front paw, Sar flipped the beast over, preparing to skin it. Zane asked him if he could help. Sar looked at him for a long moment.

Finally Sar said, "Cross border, help Sar."

It was then Jynal realized the border of Orcanth didn't begin with the trees. He was glad they hadn't crossed it before this point. He was sure it wouldn't have ended well.

The next day was spent emptying the large wagon and preparing to make the trip to gather the logs. Jynal was yet undecided if he would leave his family or have them follow in the other wagon. The incident with the bear had him worried.

"Papa!" shouted Katheen. "He's back, with more."

She was running toward him from the stream, an empty bucket in hand. She'd let him know earlier she was going to water the fruit trees planted away from the shadows of the oaks. On her third trip, she'd seen the Orcs.

Jynal walked to the edge of the creek. On the other side stood Sar, with three more Orcs. One was decidedly older, with streaks of gray in his shoulder-length hair. He was dressed similar to Sar except for the red leather bracers on both of his arms. On his back, visible over both shoulders, were the tips of a dual-bladed battle axe.

Standing with them was a younger Orc, in his teens, and another small Orc with long hair, dressed in furs, holding a six-foot twisted staff. The three of them were slightly behind the Orc with the bracers, indicating he was their leader.

The leader stepped into the creek and waded to the island of rocks. Unsure of what was happening, Jynal did the same. The Orc reached over his shoulder and pulled the great axe free from the loops holding the handle. He place it on the flat rocks. Still wary, Jynal slid his short sword from its scabbard and laid it beside the axe.

With a satisfied nod, the Orc spoke, "I am Pon, son of Dol. I am Red Fist chief."

Jynal said, "I am Jynal Narvok."

Pon looked back at the shaman when her heard her huff. The shaman looked into her palm, reached up, rubbed her chin, and shrugged at Pon.

Pon looked back at Jynal, tilted his head slightly and asked. "More?"

Jynal sighed and said, "I am Jynal Narvok, Lord of the Western Borderlands."

This time when Pon looked back at the shaman, he received a nod. Jynal realized, whatever the shaman was holding, he'd better remain truthful, not that it would be an issue.

"You not want be lord?" Pon asked. He heard the sigh and reluctance in Jynal's voice.

"Whether I wanted it or not doesn't matter," Jynal answered. "It's my title and my duty now. My responsibilities will grow every day."

"Yes. Duty to people. A leader must lead. This I know," Pon said. He paused a moment while they both thought of what had been said. "You and your people save Sar from great bear." He looked over at Marnell. "Your son save my son. Perfect shot."

Marnell spoke up, "Sir, it wasn't a perfect shot. I got lucky. I…I need to practice more."

Pon looked at Jynal. "What mean 'sir?'"

"He shows his respect for you, for your position as chief," Jynal explained, proud of his son.

Sar grinned, showing more of his large incisors. "Your son honors me. Honors you by this. Says need use bow more. Good. Brought bow."

Sar turned to the youngest Orc and nudged him. He stepped into the creek while taking a bow off his shoulder. It was nearly identical to the one on his other shoulder. He crossed the creek, and, still standing in the water, he handed the bow and a quiver of arrows up to Marnell with a nod. He walked back over and climbed the bank into Orcanth.

"Thank you," Marnell said as he ran his hand over the stout wood. It was very well built, and more powerful than his father's bow. It wasn't the size of the bow Sar used, but it was better than any bow Jynal had seen. Zane and Penae both admired it.

"You build homes. Be neighbor?" Pon asked. "Sar teach this word, neighbor, to me."

"Yes," Jynal said. "We want to start with two cabins. I would farm the fields. Later, more will come."

The shaman said a few words in Orcish. Pon looked back and asked one word they couldn't understand. The shaman confirmed it.

"More like you, or them?" Pon asked, indicating the hunters.

"Well, more humans like us," Jynal said. "Maybe others. Do you mean Dwarves, or Gnomes?"

"No, like you," Pon said. This time he grinned showing many teeth. "You not know?"

"Know what?" Jynal asked. Confusion showing on his face.

"You big human," Pon said.

"Well, yes," Jynal said, "my father was also a large man. He was a little shorter than I am. I think my youngest son will be bigger than both me and his brother. He's only two, and stands almost as tall as a four-year-old."

"Never slows down, that one," added Penae.

On cue, they all looked toward the camp site. Nyissa was chasing Teel as he ran completely naked toward the stream, holding a chicken. The poor bird was flapping its wings rapidly in an attempt to escape the upcoming bath.

"At least not jump from tree holding bird," Sar commented. "Try fly. Tro do that once. My mate pull hair out with that one." He nodded his head sideways, indicating the boy standing beside him. "Other son much easier."

All of them laughed except Tro. He shrugged and grinned at Marnell. Boys will be boys, no matter their race.

Jynal asked, "How do you know our language?"

"Ones like you," Pon answered. "Some come back and teach long ago. Shaman teach. Tribal council say all border tribes must learn speak human."

"What do you mean ones like…" Jynal trailed off, realizing what Pon meant and what he'd meant by Jynal's size. At six foot three, Jynal knew he was larger than most men but hadn't thought anything about it. "You mean…?"

"You are of the blood," Pon said. "It is from long ago, but I acknowledge it. Big word, 'acknowledge.' It mean I accept. Your young ones are of the blood. You not claim it because not know before. Not know tribe. I say we share blood. You and young ones are of the Red Fist Tribe."

The shaman spoke up, her words much plainer, in a voice a higher pitched than male Orcs, "It has been spoken by the chief. It is so. Only a tribal chief, his sons, or his son's sons may say this. I will inform the tribal council of new members in Red Fist."

Pon nodded and added, "Your mate is Red Fist by your choice. These two," he indicated Zane and Penae, "I say are ally by deed. You can enter Orcanth. Must receive mark. No problem other tribes."

Pon reached out with his hand. Jynal reached across the rocks, and the two clasped forearms. Marnell stepped into the creek. He walk past them up the other bank; he wanted to talk to Tro about the bow. Jynal and Pon placed their weapons back in their holders.

"Wait," Jynal said. "When I'm in Orcanth, you're my chief?"

"Am always chief," Pon said. He pursed his lips, thinking. "This new to me. Tribal lands mine. You lord of that side." He indicated toward the open fields.

"Come," Jynal said attempting to hide his smile. "Enter the Western Border, my lands."

Pon looked at him, trying to figure out what his intentions were. He stepped up on the bank with Jynal. The hunters stepped aside and made room.

Pon stomped a foot, looked around, and said, "Feels same. Not many trees here. Orcanth have grasslands, too. Grow food and granx...human call cows. Long way from village. This first time in human lands."

Jynal drew his sword. Pon's hand reached back for his axe. The hunters backed several paces away. On the other side of the creek, Sar had an arrow knocked in the blink of an eye, as the shaman raised her staff.

Jynal raised his hand. "Easy...easy. I mean my chief no harm."

The shaman looked down into her palm and spoke a word in Orcish. Everyone relaxed, and Sar replaced his arrow in his quiver. Pon's hand lowered. Both boys stared at everyone with their mouths open, unsure of what had almost transpired, as they were caught up in examining and talking about their bows.

"Please kneel," Jynal said. Seeing Pon hesitate, he asked again, "Please kneel."

Pon tilted his head slightly. Trusting the assurance the shaman gave him, the huge Orc slowly knelt on one knee, his eyes never leaving Jynal's. He was ready to dive away in an instant, something Jynal could see by his tense posture.

Slowly Jynal lowered his blade, placing the flat side on Pon's shoulder and then the other. "I dub thee Sir Pon, Lord of the Axe. Rise, Sir Pon."

Pon rose, his eyes narrowed. "What mean?"

Jynal grinned. "It means you're now a minor lord in my lands. I'll send word to Baron Arnwald, an ally. He'll inform the other baronies. You and I can broker trade with them if you desire."

Pon stared as Jynal continued, "I'll grant you a plot of land here. There will be no taxes required. You're a lord in the Western Border, and the second to own some of my land. Zane and Penae have chosen a piece of land on the other side of the grasses in the forest there."

"You honor me," Pon said, realizing he now owned some of the human lands. He paused and said, "Wait, that mean I am your chief always, and you are my lord always." He threw his head back, laughing. Jynal grinned right along with him.

Later, after Jynal introduced Nyissa and his youngest son Teel to Pon and those with him, Pon looked over to the farthest tree at Katheen. She sat against it, watching everything, but didn't come close.

"Your daughter," Pon said, "she bring water back. Why not come meet chief?"

"I would speak to her," the shaman added. Jynal still didn't know her name.

"She was in an accident and chooses to stay covered," Nyissa said quickly. She was ever protective of her daughter.

Katheen heard them. She stood, straightened her cloak and hood, and slowly walked over to stand beside her parents. Jynal placed a hand on her shoulder and introduced her.

The shaman knelt in front of Katheen, looking into the darkness of her hood, and said, "Katheen Narvok, I would tell you my name." She leaned forward and whispered her name to Katheen.

At this, Pon and Sar inhaled sharply. Once an Orc became an accepted shaman, their name was never spoken by the others in the tribes. They were always referred to as 'Shaman.' It didn't matter if they were a shaman of magic, or one of faith. Occasionally a shaman was of both, but this was very rare. The shaman of Red Fist was one of these. Katheen had been given an honor unheard of. What they heard their shaman call Katheen next nearly floored them.

"Sister of faith, why do you hide away?" she asked.

"What?" Katheen asked, surprised a stranger had called her 'sister,' especially an Orc she'd never met.

"Others cannot, but I see the symbol's glow around your neck, sister," the shaman explained patiently. "Tell me, what do you see when you look at my staff?"

Katheen look up at the tip of the staff and said excitedly, "I see it! There's a glowing stone stuck in it. It is so pretty. It has a symbol in it. An hourglass."

"I would tell you of Lan, Bringer of Seasons. Will you tell me of your god, able to bring forth water?"

"Yes!" Katheen said excited. "There are two I follow. Two saints, they both did it together. I mean, I know there are more. It says so in the Book Of The One."

"Yes, sister, there are many," agreed the shaman. "I would hear of those I know little of, but first, I would know your face."

Katheen froze. "I...I don't want anyone to see me," she said, her voice barely above a whisper.

"Sister," the shaman asked, "what does our Creator say about faith in the gods?"

Katheen hesitated. She had read it yesterday. Her reading was improving every day. Her writing was not as good, but she could read with little help from her brother or parents.

"'Hide not your faith in the deities I have given you. In this, you show faith in your Creator,'" Katheen said, her voice growing stronger with each word.

"Hide not, sister," the shaman said. "Hide not."

Slowly Katheen reached up and pushed back her hood. She unclasped it at her neck and let it drop to her feet. For the first time since the accident, she showed herself to others than her family.

Still on her knees, the shaman smiled, reached out, and pushed a tuft of hair growing from a small patch on the side of her head where the scars were the greatest. She tucked it behind the stump of what was once an ear. She ran her fingers through the hair on the other side.

Half of Katheen's face was nearly normal, with a slight discoloration. Her eyes, nose, and lips were normal. The other side of her head, face, neck, and what could be seen of her shoulders were deeply scarred with dark pink and white tissue. Her forearms and upper arms had the same thick scars. Only her elbows, her wrists, and below were normal, if slightly red.

With the long cloak out of the way, the scars could be seen above her ankles, disappearing under her dress. Katheen stared at the ground. Slowly she looked up into the shaman's eyes. The shaman nodded her encouragement. She looked around at everyone gathered. What she saw surprised her.

At ten years old, she was old enough to know the difference in someone looking and someone staring at her. What she saw wasn't pity. She saw those fearless enough to fight giant bears, and who knows what else, looking at her with respect...for she had conquered her own fear.

* * * *

Chapter Nine

Kryder looked over at Tog. "I never knew she hid herself. To me they're a part of her. I mean, they just *are*."

"She never told me that, either," Tog agreed. "Still, to reveal herself that way. I wonder if I could do it?"

"I've seen you wade into a group of Goblins intent on taking your ears!" Kryder laughed. "I doubt you would've been afraid."

"That's different," Tog dismissed with a wave of his large hand. "They were only trying to kill me. It's not like I was hiding what she went through."

Lan looked over at them and shook her head. She glanced at Lucas. The big innkeeper had a thoughtful look on his face as he watched the scene unfold. She smiled to herself.

* * *

Pon asked, "What need make homes? Trees like our homes?"

"Yes," Jynal said. "We need trees. Logs for homes, and to build fences. Some of the crops must be protected from animals, including our goats."

"You not many," Pon observed. "Take long time. How lift logs?"

"Leverage," Jynal said. "I'll build frames and use the rope we brought; we will hoist them."

"Sound like take long time," Pon said. "If build home, when farm?"

"Well," Jynal answered, "we work on our homes and live off our supplies. We may have to wait until next growing season. We would have to plant right away to get crops in before it gets too cold."

Pon turned to Sar and said something in Orcish. Sar answered. They went back and forth for a few minutes until they agreed.

Sar turned toward the forest, placed two fingers against his lips between his tusks, and blew. The sound was like nothing Jynal had ever heard before. It was three shrill whistles in harmony, each a slightly different tone.

From the line of trees, an Orc stepped out. He was followed by several more. The first crossed the creek and came running over. Sar spoke to him for a few minutes. The warrior nodded and ran back. He and the rest of those with him disappeared.

Pon turned to Jynal. "Where you want trees? Warriors bring. Show where you want. Show me my land. Will build home, too. Have two homes, one here, one in village."

"Wait," Jynal said, "what do you mean, you'll bring trees?"

"One in…" Pon started to say. He turned to the shaman with a look asking for help.

"One in twenty," the shaman said. "He does not know your words for numbers. They will go into the forest and cut one out of every twenty trees. If there are not enough saplings growing in the area, they will move some to it. That area will not be cut for a year; if it is cut, then it will be one in twenty again."

"I know why," Katheen said. "It replaces everything cut every year. Twenty years from now, it will be the same. New trees replacing the old."

"Yes, sister," the shaman said, impressed one so young understood. "One cannot only take. It must be replaced."

"How big want trees?" Sar asked.

The next morning, log after log was brought out of the woods, carried by six Orcs at a time. They were followed by several bringing the largest branches. That continued until there were two sizable piles. The Orcs stayed for a week to help trim the logs and lift them into place.

Jynal decided on a section touching the creek for the portion he gave Pon. It bordered the land he intended to hold for himself to farm. In his mind he could envision other sections to give to anyone who decided to move there. That would be in the future, next year at the earliest, when he made a trip back to the Arnwald Barony.

* * *

The next several years went by as the farm grew. Zane and Penae built their home on the other side of the open plain. They made a trip back to their homeland and came back with four more couples, others from Tarlok looking for new forest to hunt. They visited regularly.

Twice a year Jynal and Marnell made the trip back to the barony. On the first, Jynal was shown the young horses sired by Coal, and was paid by several others for stud fees. He sold the beautiful hardwood boards he brought with him, and bought supplies, several more draft horses to breed, and a few goats. The wood was unusual in its color and pattern, and easy to sell. The carpenter assured him he would buy all Jynal brought on his next trip as well.

On the next trip, Baron Arnwald introduced Jynal to a man and his young family. He'd been a tenant farmer when the landowner passed. The landowner's heirs wished to sell the property. After some discussion, the baron provided a wagon for them, and there was another farm in the Western Borderlands.

Orcs came and went, some came to observe and practice the language, and others brought items to trade. One day, Pon came with another chief. He introduced Bay, Chief of the Fang Tribe. He had to translate, as the Fang tribe wasn't a border tribe.

"Bay want make trade," Pon said.

"Trade?" Jynal asked. "What does he want to trade?"

"Bird," Pon said. "Bay want trade you birds."

Katheen stepped over to them. Now at the age of thirteen, she was considered by all of the Red Fist tribe as the shaman of Three Oaks. Pon told Bay of her bringing the water back. The chief looked at her with respect.

Katheen, having spent considerable time with the Orcs who came and stayed for periods of time in Pon's cabin, spoke in Orcish, "What do you wish to trade, Chief of Fang Tribe?"

Surprised at hearing a human speak Orcish, he answered, "In my lands, we have this same kind of bird. It is a different color. All are black and white spotted. Now some die young. The shaman says we need new blood. I do not wish to trade with the Running Boar Tribe, deeper in Orcanth. Red Fist borders this side. Pon told me of your birds…and I wanted to see the human lands."

Katheen turned to her father. "They've inbred their chickens. Ours are only a year or two from the same thing. Marnell said so."

Jynal laughed. "He's right. Make a trade. See what else they have. Maybe we can trade a goat or two for something."

By the time Katheen was seventeen, several families lived nearby on their own land. Their own farm had grown. They had a small herd of cattle; the first three were gained from trade. The Orcanth cows were long-horned and larger than the ones her family had owned so many years ago, but they were fairly docile and easy to work with.

* * *

One day Sar came to their farm with Tro and two other Orcs. The four of them moved slowly, and as they came closer, Katheen realized one was much smaller and walked with a limp. Tro took his time and helped him. Sar introduced his mate Rab, and their youngest son, Lur.

They went inside the cabin and settled around the huge table on benches. Teel used it as an excuse to stop doing chores and headed to the creek to swim, with several other kids and an Orc whose father had come to trade with a family whose turkeys were desired by many Orcs.

"My son not warrior," Sar explained. "Born early. Born small. Leg is problem. Can't run like warrior."

"Heart of warrior," stated Tro in defense of his younger brother.

"Yes," Sar agreed, "but not body. Lur want try farm."

Jynal looked over at Lur. The young Orc was only six feet tall; the size of a man. He clearly wasn't part human, though. He favored one leg, the other obviously malformed from birth. Lur had a determined look.

"Do you want to live here in Three Oaks and farm?" Jynal asked. "It's hard work. I know. I've been a warrior and a farmer. Both serve a purpose, and neither are easy."

"Yes, my lord," Lur said. It was obviously rehearsed. "Can't fight for tribe. Help tribe another way."

Katheen giggled at hearing her father called a lord and received a glance from Lur. He saw the beautiful blue color of her eyes, and he couldn't look away. Katheen realized he was looking at her, and the one side of her face turned pink. She didn't know what to think. Rab was across the room, standing with Nyissa as she showed her some of her sewing. Rab was dressed in leather and thin furs, as was typical for a female Orc. The cloth seemed delicate to her as she held it between her fingers. She glanced up and saw the look between the two. She nudged Katheen's mother.

"Oh, no," Jynal said, "there'll be none of that 'my lord' business. You may call me Jynal. I'll be glad to teach to you to farm like a human. Your father taught Marnell how to cut trees and hunt the forest with Tro; we can return the favor."

"Good," Sar said. "Chief say Lur farm his land. Make trade with bird and goat. Grow crop, make beer. Not have to trade for beer with other tribe. Good plan."

"Ah," Jynal said, "now I understand. It *is* a good plan. If you know how to make beer, I'm all for it. I make wine with fruit now. To be honest, it's not very good."

"Bad drink better than no drink," Sar said with a grin. "Had your wine before. Is bad drink." He shrugged. "Still drink."

Katheen looked at Lur's leg. As she often did, she said a silent prayer. Suddenly she stumbled toward the table, grabbing it to steady herself. She shook her head as her mind cleared. She knew what she had to do.

Over the last few years, she'd been holding services. She taught of both the Lord of the Sea and the Saint of Farmers, of Lan, Bringer of Seasons, as well as other topics from the Book Of The One. Sometimes she felt small nudges when she prepared what to say to the handful of attendees from the farms and the occasional Orc. This nudge was like no other she had felt.

Marnell stepped over, concerned. "What's wrong? Are you alright?"

"Yes," she assured him. "I'm alright. Will you bring me the pan full of water?" She turned to her father and Sar. "Will you help Lur onto the table, remove his boot, and cut the leg of his britches? I've been compelled."

Sar had been watching from the trees when she released the spring. He had been there when she loosed the tourniquet, stopped the bleeding, and closed the cut on one of his warriors, a deep cut caused by a great cat. When their patrol had startled the feeding cat, they were much closer to Three Oaks than they were to their own village. They'd bound the wound and rotated pulling the drag litter to the border.

She was a shaman as far as he was concerned. One didn't question shamans. Only a chief could do so. He made Lur lie down.

Marnell knew which pot she spoke of. It was the one used by Brother Pynon so many years ago. Katheen pulled her prayer book from her pocket, sat down, and began writing in it. Over the years she'd written several more prayer spells. Two she'd learned from other shamans; one of them from a brother in faith from the Fang Tribe involved closing cuts. A gift from Lan, it caused a cut to heal as if time had passed instantly. In the past, she'd used it several times among the farmers, and once on an Orc warrior.

She quickly wrote as it came to her. When she was finished, she read the instructions to the prayer spell. It seemed simple enough, but it would be painful. She looked at Lur, now lying on the table and looking back at her.

"This will hurt," Katheen said in Orcish as they locked eyes. She found she didn't want to look away.

She shook herself and looked at her brother. "Your dagger please?"

Marnell reached to his side and drew the dagger he'd found years ago on their journey to the border. It remained as sharp as the day he'd found it. No matter how often he used it, it never lost its edge. It was his most prized possession.

Katheen sprinkled a pinch of salt in the water and prayed for Minokath to bless it. It glowed softly. She looked at Lur and nodded. He gritted his teeth and nodded back.

Katheen sliced his knee open down the inside of his leg. Lur stiffened but didn't cry out. She had no way of knowing, but the ligaments of the knee had never developed properly. She slowly poured the holy seawater into the bleeding cut while praying for healing. There was a flash of bright blue, causing Lur's mother to gasp out loud.

Next she closed the cut, using a pinch of sand she carried in a leather pouch in another pocket. It was needed for the spell gifted by Lan. The last thing she did was pour the rest of the seawater over the knee and table, and the blood disappeared. Everything was dry, as if the leg and table had never been stained with bright red blood. The knee was left with a long finger-width scar.

Katheen sat down on the bench, exhausted. She watched as Jynal and Sar helped Lur from the table. He stood hesitantly and slowly put weight on the leg. A puzzled look came over his face as he put his full weight on it. It was something he'd never done before. He took a few steps…and walked normally.

"Your leg!" Tro said in Orcish. "You can learn to run. You can become a great warrior."

"No," Lur said as he looked at Katheen, "I will farm."

* * *

The scene faded into the grey mists. Suddenly they were back in the tavern. The fire had burned down a little. Kryder looked around and realized, while it seemed years had passed, only an hour had gone by. Lan was the deity of time; of course it flowed as she willed.

Kryder looked at Tog and said, "They were giving each other the look, aaaand about nine months later, you were born."

"What?" Tog said. He wrinkled his nose. "Ew, don't even say that. I can't even. Don't put that vision in my head. Those are my parents. What's wrong with you anyway?"

"Hey, we all have to come from somewhere," Kryder teased, raising his mug in salute.

Lan, a deity created at the beginning of time, laughed out loud. Sometimes she found mortals to be so amusing.

Lucas looked at Tog. "Lad, ye parents. They… "

"Yes," Tog said, interrupting him, "my parents are living happily ever after on the farm. It's always the same old thing. People think every Half-Orc came from some kind of plunder, pillage, and rape story. Those same stories would have one believe we're evil monsters. That's why I get so angry and lose my mind when someone insinuates how I may have been conceived."

"And that's why I don't even try to talk him out of fighting about it," Kryder said. "Nobody dishonors our family."

"Aye, lad," Lucas said. "I don't blame the two o' ye."

* * * * *

Chapter Ten

L ucas looked at Lan. "Saint Lanae, the night is far from over. Will there be more o' the story of these two?"

"Yes," she said. "There are things which must be made known. I have not completed that which our Creator bid me do this day."

Tog picked up his mug and drained it. He wiped his mouth with his sleeve and said, "I'm ready. Where are we going?"

"And when?" Kryder asked.

Once again they found themselves elsewhere.

Kryder looked around. They were in the main hall of a small castle, though it seemed to be more of a fortress, with narrow windows clearly made for archers to fire through. He looked over at Tog and Lucas. Tog shrugged. He had no idea where they were, either. Lan nodded toward three people standing near the entryway.

* * *

"M y lord," an obvious serving woman said, "her fever has lessened. It lasted for more than two hours this time."

"How high was it?" demanded the man. He was dressed in fine clothes, though he wore a thin sword at his side.

"It wasn't bad, my lord," she answered, "but it did come one week from the last."

"Go," demanded the other woman, dressed as the man was in finery. "Stay with her through the night."

"Yes, my lady," the woman said and ducked her head. She quickly left the room.

"It's the gift," the woman said.

"You don't know that, Thayness," he said.

"I do know it," she snapped. "I've seen it. My sister did the very same. We'll have to send her to the Halls of Magic."

"Do we?" asked the man. He looked sideways at her. "Do we?"

"You are Count Bealnoth, Lord of Marent," she answered coldly. "Of course we do. We can't have others speaking of how our daughter was burnt because we couldn't afford to send her to the Halls. What will the others think? Think of our alliances. My brother will surely use it to drive a wedge between us and the king."

"She could have an accident," he mused as he twirled one end of his long mustache. "She should have had one when she was but a child. The last thing we needed was a daughter. We have our sons, and both of their marriages have put us in good alliances in the kingdom."

"We couldn't and you know it," dismissed his wife. "You know full well the king's mistress doted on her. Even now, she asks about her from time to time and says she was the most beautiful baby, with her long curly black hair and a perfectly proportioned face. It makes me sick."

"It was your indiscretion," he countered. "You should have been more careful with your servant. I had to have him disposed of so no one could compare the child's looks to him later."

"It was only a few times with that one," she said, waving it off as if it was irrelevant.

"Indeed," mused the count. "I'm ever diligent with my mistresses. Still, she grows to become even more burdensome. The yearly fee is substantial, you know."

"As a noble, it won't cost what a commoner would pay, even if they were successful in business. Raise the taxes," she suggested. "We'll gain the costs back."

"I suppose, though I was already considering raising them," Count Marent said. "We'll also have to ensure it's known she comes from a family with some means. I'll send a substantial coin purse with her."

His wife sighed and agreed. "Fine, I'll send her with some jewelry on her person. The swan pendant representing the family crest will do."

The count nodded and said, "Perhaps she'll be more powerful than your sister is, and we can gain something from this. There may be an earl or count with a young son, and no mage to speak of in his employ. The only way to survive is to grow our alliances."

"One can hope," Lady Thayness said. She turned to go upstairs to her bedchambers on the opposite side of the castle from his.

The next week, the teenage girl tossed and turned in her sleep as she broke out in a sweat. She sat up in bed, her dark hair matted, in a room dimly lit by candles. The serving woman beside her reached over with a wet cloth and wiped her face and forehead.

"Shhh, Zalana," she whispered. "I'm here. It will pass shortly."

"What's wrong with me, Trenlis?" asked Zalana, her voice coarse as she reached for the cup of water next to the bed. She drained the cup.

"You have the gift, child," answered Trenlis.

"Me?" Zalana asked, her voice more normal. "How can I have the gift? I'm only fourteen. What will happen to me? Will I become burnt?" The last came out in a whisper as a tear fell.

"Don't cry, child," Trenlis said as she wiped the tears. "That won't happen to you. The count is already planning to send you to the Halls of Magic. This is the age when it shows. My sister's son had the gift."

"Had?" Zalana asked. "What happened? Is he burnt? Why didn't he go to the Halls?"

Trenlis was quiet for a few minutes as she continued to wipe Zalana's face with the wet cloth. She dipped it in a bucket to rinse it. She took her time wringing the excess water out.

Finally, she spoke, "Everyone can't go to the Halls of Magic when the gift shows itself, child. If you aren't nobility, or your father isn't the richest commoner around, you won't be accepted, and there's nothing that can be done for you. The fevers start earlier and last longer and longer. They start coming daily. Not high enough to effect you, mind you, but when it lasts longer than a half day…"

"What?" asked Zalana. "What happens?"

This time the tear rolled down Trenlis' cheek. Zalana reached up and wiped it with the sleeve of her gown. Trenlis had been the mother she'd never had, even with her own mother living within the same walls of the castle.

"At midnight, like all the others, my nephew's temperature climbed until it was burning hot," Trenlis answered. "He stayed that way until the crack of dawn. We tried everything. We kept cold rags on his head, we put him a tub of water. Nothing would cool him. When he woke the next night, he…he was burnt."

She wiped her eyes and sniffed. "The mind can't take that. It does something to you."

She wiped her eyes again and whispered, "He was gone. He was there, but the boy we knew was gone, child. He was gone."

"Where is he now?" asked Zalana gently as she reached out to hold her hand.

"In my home village. He lives with his mother still. He earns a few coins, and she helps him with them. She has to; he wouldn't know how. He'd spend it all on sticky pies and eat them right there in the marketplace."

She smiled at the thought and sniffed. "He pulls the billow handles for the blacksmith all day. It's not too bad. The man is kind to him and makes sure he doesn't burn himself. I mean, he's already burnt in his mind, the saints know he doesn't need to get burned, too. It's the best we could hope for."

Zalana thought about what Trenlis had told her. She was scared. What if that happened to her?

"If there was nothing you could do, what will they do in the Halls of Magic?" Zalana asked. "How will they keep it from happening to me?"

"I don't know," Trenlis answered. "They do something. Maybe it is magic. A spell or some magic item that does it. I don't know any with the gift, so I never asked."

"If there's a way to stop it from happening, why don't they help everyone?" Zalana asked. "Why is it only nobles? That's not right."

"No," agreed Trenlis as she dipped the cloth again. "It's not. You know, they say it wasn't always that way. A long time ago, there weren't very many burnt ones in the world. There were more mages then, too. Now, there are only a few outside of the Halls."

She continued, "Well, a few powerful mages. There are quite a few only able to do small things. It seems the ones with a strong gift stay there and study, or whatever it is they do in that place."

"What about Dwarves or Gnomes?" Zalana asked. "Do they go to the Halls of Magic, too?"

"No, child," answered Trenlis. "Dwarves don't have the gift, nor Gnomes. As for Elves, rarely do the Elves leave Zar. Who knows what they do, or if the gift does that to them? I don't even know if any have the gift. Legends say there were great Elven mages once, but I think those are stories."

"I loved those stories," Zalana said. She laid her head back down. She looked up at the woman she loved more than her own mother. "Even if you did make up most of them as you told them to me."

"Me?" Trenlis asked. "I wouldn't make up a story about Elves being good and just. Those were passed down to me as a child." She winked at Zalana. "Now close your eyes and go to sleep. We have to start packing your things tomorrow."

"Tomorrow?" Zalan asked, sitting up quickly. "I don't want to leave so soon. I'll miss you." She started crying again.

"Shh, child," whispered Trenlis. "I have to pack, too. When you leave, my time has ended here. I'll go home to my family. Besides, I'll miss you, too, but I'd rather miss you and know where you are than lose you forever, lost in your own mind."

* * *

Kryder looked over at Lucas. The innkeeper's eyes glistened. Kryder reached out and placed his hand on the man's shoulders.

"I'm sorry," Kryder said.

"Aye, lad, me too," Lucas said. "Me daughter was a talkative one. Always asking questions about this or that. I'm to be thinking when she…when she changed, that's what drove her mother to an early grave. Lost 'em both, I did."

"She waits on you," Lan said quietly. "She picks flowers with your mother as they both wait for you to join them."

"It eases me heart to know that," Lucas said, "sure and it does, but I won't be joining them anytime soon if I'm to have anything to say about it. Me daughter and me boys need their father. Besides, something tells me there's too much to do before the time comes."

* * *

Two days later, Zalana sat in a carriage. She was being escorted by four of her father's knights, while a squire drove the carriage. Several trunks of clothes and other belongings were tied on top. Beside the squire was a small chest of coins. The escort wasn't for her safety. They were there to protect the small fortune.

The trip took several days as they crossed several estates and a duchy. In each, a knight rode ahead to inform of their passing as a courtesy. They stayed in the best of inns. All of it was for show; pure politics.

Her father was letting his allies and rivals both know he had a daughter soon to be enrolled within the Halls of Magic, putting them on notice. It didn't take long for word to spread among the whole kingdom of Gar-Noth.

On the last day of travel, as they neared the mountain range, the Halls of Magic came into view. As the road turned on a wide sweeping bend, Zalana was able to see the stone towers and high stone wall surrounding the buildings. The Halls of Magic was castle and fortress combined. It was much larger than her family's castle, almost like an enclosed town.

The carriage was driven through the archway of the outer wall, its doors open during the day. The carriage stopped in a courtyard. Zalana stepped down from the door to the carriage and waited patiently while an administrator unrolled and verified the parchment with her name, her family's names, and their proof of nobility.

Next, the small chest was handed down. The administrator opened it, looked at the coins, and nodded. He turned to the leader of her father's knights and said, "She is accepted, sir. On this day, one year from now, the next year's fees are due. Failure to pay will result in expulsion, regardless of her training."

"I will relay to this to the count, Lord of Marent," the knight captain said. "We'll move her belongings to her room and be on our way, if that's acceptable."

"It is," answered the administrator. "She's the last in the new class this month. Her training begins tomorrow."

* * *

The next morning, she was woken early by a knock on her door. A voice called out, "To breakfast! All to breakfast."

A few minutes later Zalana hurried downstairs. At the base of the stairwell stood a stern-looking young woman in grey robes. Three young teenagers were waiting with her nervously. Several more arrived minutes later.

Once Zalana joined them, the woman spoke, "I am Caliese, a third-year apprentice. I'll be your guide for the next two years. I'm not one of the instructors. Only a mage can teach. What I'll do is ensure you're where you're supposed to be until you're familiar with the Halls of Magic."

Caliese looked the group over. "Some of you are from here in Gar-Noth; one or two may be from Minth or Yaylok. Is there anyone in this group from the Baronies West or Tarlok? No? Good." She continued, "Everyone, go back to your rooms. There will be robes waiting for you. All first-year apprentices wear tan-colored robes. If your skills are sufficient to progress, next year you'll receive brown robes. If anyone is still attending in their third year, they'll receive the grey robes I wear. Fourth year will wear the black."

The students were quiet, unsure of what to do next. Zalana turned to go back upstairs, when she heard Caliese say, "Now! Be quick about it. You have to eat breakfast before I take you to the waiting hall. I have classes to attend this morning. Go!"

Once they were back downstairs, the guide led them from the living areas through a maze of hallways, past other students moving in groups or alone, through several courtyards open to the sky, to a set of double doors. She chastised several of the others while they walked.

"Some of you need to figure out how to dress yourselves. You took too long," Caliese said. "Your handmaiden, or whatever else you call your nursemaid, isn't here to dress you. At least there's only one choice of wardrobe for you now, or who knows when you'd leave your room and wander down those stairs. And speaking of your rooms. You're never to have anyone in your rooms, and you know what I mean by that. To do so will see you expelled."

Zalana, walking behind everyone, saw several of the other students look at each other as if to say, "Who does she think she is? My father is so and so." Zalana shook her head.

Her parents may have tried to raise her to have their aristocratic views on others below their stature, but Trenlis had truly raised her. That type of thought made her angry. It inferred the ridiculous notion one's position in life was more important than the person themselves.

Trenlis was a commoner who happened to have been selected to take care of her when she was born. To Zalana, Trenlis was the most important person in her life, regardless of her status. Spending her days with her, Zalana grew to know better than to think like her parents. Even though she worked in the count's castle, Trenlis treated those in the town as friends she hadn't met yet. As equals.

It didn't matter whether they owned a stall in the marketplace, or begged from the opening of an alley, Trenlis had a kind word or a roll to give them from the basket she carried on their outings. As Zalana grew older, she ensured the basket had plenty in it, going to the kitchens herself to get them. The kitchen staff knew what the count's young daughter was about and managed to always cook a few more than was needed for the household. Her parents, often absent, had no idea it was happening.

Zalana was wondering if it was going to be four years of political maneuvering while she was attending, with her only relief being the breaks during holidays to go home. Some events were too important for heirs not to attend. Zalana didn't care for that type of thing, but she could play the part should the need arise. For her, it was an act. Besides, her older brothers were the heirs; she was an afterthought. Still, it might come in handy in the Halls.

"For those of you trying to decide who I am, who my parents are, and whether I should dare speak to you this way," Caliese said, "know this. Here in the Halls of Magic, the only thing that matters are the robes you wear. You wear the tan robes. Even if you continue to progress here, you will never equal me. I'll be a mage and an instructor long before you wear these." She indicated her gray robes. "And...I *am* a commoner."

Caliese opened the doors and led them inside. The room contained rows of desks, with a small stack of books on each. Several desks near the front were occupied. Their occupants' heads were down as they studied.

"Sit down," Caliese said. "The top book is written in mage-speak. The language is as old as time. You don't know it. For the next three weeks, possibly less, you'll practice memorizing letters and simple words. The second book is a translation, word for word, with each pronunciation plainly spelled out."

Zalana glanced down at the books as Caliese continued, "The bottom book will be yours to keep. Your first spellbook. The words you learn here won't be in any combination holding power. They're simply to start your learning process, so don't bother copying any of it into your book. You'll be provided parchment for you to practice writing on."

Zalana raised her hand. Caliese noticed her and said, "Yes?"

"Why for three weeks or less?" Zalana asked. "Shouldn't we spend the time necessary mastering the language?"

"I see at least one of you uses your head for more than holding a tiara or crown," Caliese said. "Yes. It does take much longer than three weeks to learn the language. Here in this room is where you'll be for three weeks. It will continue elsewhere."

She continued, "You'll be here every day until midnight. Your midday and evening meals will be brought to you. As your fevers continue and finally worsen, you'll be taken through those doors." She indicated two doors at the front of the room. "If you aren't here when it happens…well, let's say you'll have no need of the robes ever again."

Several of the others glanced at each other, her insults to them forgotten. They all knew the consequences of not receiving whatever aid was forthcoming. Zalana vowed to memorize the route to this hall tomorrow.

Caliese pointed out several other doors on a side wall, letting them know one was the privy, the other a small storage room stocked with water, rolls, and occasionally cheeses. They were not to eat at their desk and risk a spilled cup.

The days went by slowly. The first few were the hardest to bear for Zalana and the other students. They were left alone all day with each other and their books. They saw servants several times a day, but the servants went about their work without speaking to them.

She learned the other students' names and where they were from, of course. Several couldn't help but attempt to make their home politics the topic of conversation, as they felt they were in positions above the rest. All of them but one were people Zalana had no interest in befriending. She was polite, but made no attempt to initiate conversation with them.

Pelna was from the kingdom of Minth, north of Gar-Noth. She was of noble birth, a minor house whose land was tucked away in the north corner of a duchy. Her father owned a sizable estate, but fell below the duke in hierarchy. He was wealthy from mining in several small mountains on his land. Of course, much of the wealth went to the duke, and ultimately the king, but what he didn't have to pay in taxes still provided enough to make his family one of the wealthiest in the kingdom.

Zalana liked her. From talking to her, she knew Pelna was like her—not impressed with politics. Zalana did ask her how her father had kept his estate from being taken by the duke and his family when the mines were discovered.

"My father treats those residing on our lands with respect," Pelna answered. "He ensures they're clothed and fed properly, spending his own coin to do it. Their homes are properly heated in the few months the weather chills. His father treated the commoners this way before him, and his father before that."

One of the boys sitting in front of them turned and said with a sneer, "If that estate was in my father's duchy, he would take it. No minor noble on our lands is going to be wealthier than our family. No one allows that here in Gar-Noth. That's ridiculous."

Pelna brushed her blond hair out of her eyes and smiled sweetly. "If your father tried, he'd better have an army at his disposal the size of the king's own, or he'd lose his duchy to a minor lord. On our lands, we have towns, not villages. The farms are large, with many working them. People petition to live there."

She continued, her tone matter of fact and without condescending, "Those who cannot find a place live in large villages on the edge of other lords' estates. Those lords are grateful for the jobs and coin provided to their people. Not only does my father have the mines, he breeds the finest warhorses in the kingdom, probably on all of Kerr. My father's calvary troops outnumber several lords' entire armies alone. His foot soldiers double as security for the mine and in the towns. The archers are rivaled only by the legends of Orc archers."

"Other lords could form an alliance and take it," countered the boy.

"They could try," agreed Pelna. "Did I mention the mines are not only precious stone or metals? My family also mines the ore used to make the strongest of steel. There are many blacksmith shops in each town, creating armor and weapons. Some of them Dwarven owned. It's sold all over our kingdom and to others. Several clans of Gnomes earn their living in the trade of it."

"So?" the boy asked. "So they make armor and weapons. Others make them, too."

"So," Pelna said, bored of the conversation, "not only do the commoners own bows, each male above the age of fifteen is allowed a shield and a sword, a spear, or a battle axe. Many weapons have been passed down in the families. If a young woman wishes to own one, she may."

"What?' another of the boys asked, clearly surprised. "You allow the peasants weapons of war?"

"Of course," Pelna said. "They're the militia. They receive some training in the basics of fighting. Many grow to be recruited into the lord's troops. That's why my father's army is one of the most disciplined in the kingdom."

She continued, "And, if our lands were ever threatened, within a day word would spread, and the assembled army would be more than enough to stop any other than the king's own. And even he would hesitate."

Zalana grinned. "A sword in hand is an equalizer, is it not?"

Pelna smiled back at her. "Yes, it is. And so are arrows tipped with steel heads instead of hardened wood. I love my bow."

"I still don't understand why your duke allowed a minor to become so powerful," the first boy said.

Pelna shrugged. "Our duke is a good man. My family is sworn to his and honors it. In return, his family honors us. The king of Minth, and his father before him, have always known that corner of the kingdom could break away if they weren't treated properly, and the war would be enough to tear his kingdom apart. My father says the best defense is a known, strong offense. One you don't have to use because the results are feared."

"Still." The first boy sniffed. "Allowing commoners to think they approach the level of nobility is foolish."

Pelna looked over at Zalana and rolled her eyes. She looked back at the boy and said, "My beloved is a commoner. His family fishes one of the lakes on our estate. His cousins fish in the sea off the coast bordering one side of our estate."

At this revelation, even Zalana's eye's widened. The boy was speechless. Pelna laughed at him.

"My mother was a commoner, her mother a baker," Zalana said. "I'm free to choose my associates. I will not be forced into a marriage of convenience."

The first boy, having gotten over the shock of this absurdity decided now was a time to put this minor noble in her place. He said, "Yeah, well, your beloved is probably in the loft of a barn with some other peasant right now, and will likely have her with child while you're here in the Halls of Magic." He laughed, and his new friend laughed beside him.

Zalana started to say something when Pelna stopped her with a wave of her hand and said, "I don't see how that'll happen, since he's here and wears brown robes. My father pays the admission fee for those with the gift in our lands. There are four here in the Halls now, including me." She grinned at Zalana. "My father has four mages in his employ. There are several others in the towns, but they never advanced beyond the tan or brown robes."

Zalana was impressed. Typically every mage was offered a position within the Halls of Magic. Those who declined usually resided within the castle of their country's king. It was rumored the king of Yaylok had three mages. Of course, the highest known concentration of mages on the entire world of Kerr was within the walls of the Halls of Magic.

Still. *A beloved?* The thought made her blush. There were some things Trenlis had never taught her. Zalana was only fourteen; the woman had felt there was time later for that type of discussion.

* * * * *

Chapter Eleven

In the evenings, several servants came into the room and sat quietly against the wall. Occasionally one would get up to check on those siting up front. Sometimes they would take someone through the doors. Twice they brought one back before midnight, their fever diminished. The next two nights one was taken from the room. Afterward the students weren't seen again. At the end of the week, their group was asked to sit in the front desks.

The two boys from Gar-Noth were the first to go through the doors, both sweating profusely. They weren't seen again in the waiting hall. As the second week progressed, Zalana found herself alone all day. With no distractions, she studied the language diligently, figuring out the word structure and practicing writing the letters and simple words.

In the evenings she felt the fevers come on. One night she was walked through the doors into a room with several beds. She lay down and was taken care of much the way Trenlis had.

The third night in a row with fevers, she was taken beyond the room, through another door on the opposite wall. She walked where she was led, paying little attention to her surroundings.

The room was sparse. There was a stone bed in the center of the room, and a fireplace large enough to cover a side wall completely. It was a deep fireplace, the back wall in shadows. She glanced at it before she laid on the cool stone, wondering why there was no wood in it or stacked nearby. The servant left her alone.

A mage walked in from a door on the opposite side of the fireplace. She had a bored look on her face, as if she would rather be in her chambers in bed as opposed to this room with a first-year apprentice. She spoke a few words Zalana couldn't understand, but seemed familiar.

Zalana's eyes suddenly felt heavy. The mage reached into a pocket and pulled out a fist-sized stone. She tried to focus her vision on the stone. She could see what she now knew were letters written in mage-speak on it, but she couldn't actually read the words. She closed her eyes as she felt sleep coming on. The mage placed her empty hand on Zalana's forehead, held the other out with the stone aimed at the fireplace, and spoke words of power.

The stone glowed red, and light emanated from it. Flames emerged, growing stronger and stronger until they completely covered the stone. In the blink of an eye, the flames roared away from the stone, struck the inside of the fireplace, and spread against the back wall, which was now fully visible. The room warmed considerably.

The mage stood in place for a quarter of an hourglass. Slowly the flames lessened and pulled back, until the only light coming from the mage's hand was from the glow of the stone itself. She moved her hand from Zalana's head, and the stone's glow winked out.

The mage slid the stone into her pocket, turned her head from side to side, and rolled her shoulders, stretching. She yawned, clearly tired. Finally she reached down and gently shook Zalana awake.

When she woke, Zalana blinked several times as she tried to remember where she was. It came to her as the mage helped her sit up. She reached up and wiped her face with her sleeve.

"What do you feel?" asked the mage.

"I feel fine," Zalana answered after a moment.

"No, apprentice," the mage said. "Not *how* do you feel. *What* do you feel?"

"I," Zalana paused. Inside she felt something she couldn't describe. It was a pressure inside, like her pounding heart felt when she ran after the swans, chasing them back and forth, trying to catch one before it could escape to the moat. Only it didn't beat, it stayed steady.

"I feel something inside me," she said. "Like it's a part of me that asks for release."

The mage nodded. "It's the gift. It can only be released when the proper words of power are spoken. You'll learn to release it. You'll learn to channel it through enchanted items. I can't tell you how powerful the release will be, for it's too soon to tell. Even if all you ever grow to do is create sparks to light a candle, there will be release for you. Tomorrow you begin your training. You may go to your chambers."

* * *

The room faded into the familiar grey mists.

Tog reached over and put his hand on his cousin's shoulder, his big hand covering it. Kryder was quiet, lost in thought.

Kryder looked at Lan. She gave him a tight-lipped smile. The power she held within her was something no mortal could ever hope to feel, but she knew Kryder felt something inside him in a different way.

Tog asked quietly, "Is that what you feel?"

"Yeah," Kryder answered. "It's like a pressure in my chest. My head. My whole body. It doesn't bother me anymore. Not like it did in the beginning. It's there waiting for me when I reach for it, but it doesn't push at me anymore. Maybe I am used to it now."

"What were the business o' that rock?" Lucas asked. "Was it a big truth stone? One moment the woman is holding it out with noth-

ing to be happening. The next, flames are shooting out like the pit
ere the black smith's shop with his boy pulling on the billows for all
he's worth."

"It made me jump," Tog admitted. "What in the wild boar droppings was…oh, um, sorry Lan. I'm just saying, I might need a change
of britches."

"I don't know what it was," Kryder said, "but I felt it's power. It
was much more than a truth stone. I've never felt anything like it. Its
glow was enough to light the entire room. I forget you can't see it. I
suppose I could have warned you something was going to happen."

The mist swirled, and they were elsewhere.

* * *

It was a small room. Zalana, in brown robes, sat up front
beside Pelna. There were only two others in her group now.
An older mage was perched on a stool up front explaining a
technique, his hands moving everywhere as he spoke. He was always
smiling and happy.

"So, you use a binding spell to lock the enchantment into the object," he explained. "This way the staff, necklace, or ring, whatever,
isn't a one spell item. That's what scrolls are for."

Zalana raised her hand. The mage looked at her and raised an
eyebrow. "Yes, Zalana?"

"When will we learn the binding spell?" she asked.

"Yes, when?" asked Pelna.

The old man reached up and scratched his chin. "Well, you two
will start next week, after you don the grey robes. It's difficult, you
know. Oh, both of your scroll creation techniques have passed the
test."

"We will? They did?" Zalana asked. "I was wondering what happened to them."

"They were tested," the mage said. "Of course, they were tested in different rooms. Your scroll, once read, plunged the room into darkness quite nicely. I was informed it lasted several minutes. It was longer than I expected for an apprentice in brown robes."

He continued, "Pelna, your scroll was quite nice. Three separate spheres of light occurred. They remained in the same area near the ceiling until they faded, which is not ideal. You could have written it so they slowly separated, in case the area needing light is large, but I was surprised to see three of them."

The two boys in the back continued to write. Their last scrolls hadn't met the satisfaction of their latest instructor. One hadn't worked at all. Due to terrible skills with a quill and ink, one of the words had been mispronounced, because the mage assigned to test it was obligated to say the words of power as they were written.

Of course the mage knew the proper words for the simple spell, but that was irrelevant. The spell should have lifted the caster from the floor, allowing her to float to the balcony above her.

The other created a duplicate arrow beside the one it was supposed to replicate, but the arrow was weak and brittle. Arrows like those would do little good in adding to the lord's stores to defend or siege a castle. The problem wasn't the writing. It was the power the boy was able to imbue the original spell with that was at issue.

When the mage didn't mention the two boys moving from brown robes to grey, Zalana knew they might never do so. They would be given several opportunities. If it continued to be a task beyond them, they would leave the Halls of Magic as magic users, but not mages.

Zalana would be sad to see them go. They'd all become friends once the two instigators had been sent home, having never achieved the brown robes. Like her and Pelna, the boys could cast the five simple spells they'd chosen, but unlike the two young women, they couldn't create scrolls for them.

The ability to have scrolls on hand was important, for it saved a spellcaster's strength for other spells. They were a spell multiplier. Enchanted items were more powerful, but they pulled from the user due to their nature. The spells enchanted in them were usually designed to last a while.

The old man rubbed his chin again and said, "You know, there's a spell that'll allow the spheres of light to follow you for quite some time, but that part of the library won't be accessible until you become a mage and elect to stay here in the Halls to continue your studies and teach."

"Will we learn new spells before we learn the binding spell?" Pelna asked.

"Well, yes, there will be a choice of spells available," the mage said with a pleasant smile. "There's a wonderful spell I devised myself after years of research. It throws a lightning bolt out several feet. I'm quite proud of it."

"Lightning?" Pelna asked. Her father's estates bordered the sea, so she was well aware of lightning storms during heavy rains. "I thought that spell was already known. I understand it takes great power to call in the clouds and rain lightning down, but I've read several mages are suspected of knowing that particular spell."

"Well," the mage admitted, "it's not actual lightning. You see, I got the idea one night as I was adjusting the wool blanket on my bed. I was using my feet to shift it, and in the dark, I saw the sparks. Now these weren't the same as the actual flame sparks form the fire-starting spell. It was like little streaks of lightning. I'm sure you're familiar with it."

"Yes," Pelna said. "There was a game we played when I was young. My brother always delighted in sneaking up on me and touching me with a spark."

The mage continued, comfortable in the telling and retelling of this story, "It occurred to me, everyone knows of this, yet no one's tried to harness it. So, after much trial and error, I've perfected the words of power for the spell. It sends a rather large spark several feet."

Zalana said, "I see. It's a way to have lightning available without waiting on the weather conditions to develop. If you don't mind me asking, Mage Jonthia, what is the purpose of the spell? What does it do?"

"Oh, not at all, young lady," Mage Jonthia said, "I don't mind you asking at all. After all, we're here to learn, aren't we?" He smiled, his eyes twinkling. With the same smile on his face, his eyes changed without changing. They became sinister.

"It's a personal defense spell," he said, "or offense, if one wishes. It will stun a man so you can kill him. It works really well with someone wearing armor. You stun him, and then while he's unable to control his limbs, you can use any number of techniques to kill him. You could slice his throat and let him bleed out, for example."

Zalana and Pelna looked at each other in horror. Mage Jonthia continued without noticing. His voice pleasant again, he said, "Now, where was I? Oh yes, for the binding spell to hold, what's important is a well-written scroll that…"

* * *

Tog looked at Kryder. "There are spells like that?"

"Oh, yeah," Kryder said. "There are many spells that'll kill someone, too. It's been said the library in the

Halls of Magic has different areas only the lord mage has access to. Remember the stories the old man in the barony told us?"

"I didn't believe him," Tog said. "I thought he was drunk."

"He was sober enough to write out the spell for silence," Kryder countered, "not that I can think of a use for it. Still, it's in my book now."

"Ye would be surprised what one can learn from the town drunk," Lucas said. "Many times have I been amazed by one o' them. Though I will say, it's never a good idea to let a mage get drunk in yer place o' business."

* * *

Zalana checked her scroll one last time. It was perfect. She wiped her face with the sleeve of her grey robe. This time of year was warm in Gar-Noth. It wouldn't do for sweat to drip onto the still-drying ink. Casting the bind spell while writing the last sentence at the same time had been difficult and exhausting. Her hands shook as she placed it back on the table.

She looked over at Pelna and could see the concentration on her friend's face as she finished her last word. Pelna let her head fall back and her arms dangle to her side, the quill still in one hand. She looked worse than Zalana felt.

The instructor stepped around them and looked over their shoulders at the scrolls. She nodded, reached between them, and retrieved the spell book taken from the archives. The spell was too complicated for them to memorize, and once their scrolls were spoken aloud, the words would fade from them.

Successfully enchanting an item was their final test as wearers of the grey robes. Their final year would be in black. They both stood, stretching.

Caliese—their old first-year advisor, now instructor—turned toward them before leaving the room and said, "You've done well. I see no reason the scrolls wouldn't work as they should. Tomorrow at noon, you'll enchant your rings. Think hard of the spell you'll make permanent within them. The lord mage will be in attendance to decide *personally* if you two shall wear the black robes. Who knows, perhaps one day you'll earn the red robes of an instructor."

After she left them alone, Pelna turned to Zalana. "The lord mage? Have you met him?"

"No," Zalana said. "I saw a glimpse of him once when I was sent to retrieve a book from the library. He passed by without glancing in my direction as I waited for the librarian to bring the requested tome."

"My beloved met him," Pelna said. She brushed her long blond hair from her face, as was her habit. "That was when he enchanted his staff. The lord mage congratulated him, and then took the staff. My beloved was given a ring instead. The ring was already enchanted with levitation."

"He took it?" asked Zalana. "Why?"

Pelna shrugged. "I don't know. Naylon said he enchanted it with the wind spell. He hoped it would blow strong enough to sway trees. He created it to push the ships when the wind fails to blow. When it was tested in front of the lord mage, the gusts were strong enough to shift flights of arrows."

Zalana said, "I wondered why everyone in grey has been given rings to enchant instead of choosing an item like last year. Perhaps that is why. The other items were too powerful to leave the Halls."

"What spell will you choose?" Pelna asked her as they walked the halls toward their chambers. "I'll use the weaving spell. It will help repair my beloved's family nets quickly. Sometimes when they bring them up, they have been shredded."

"I think I'll use the spell of slowing," Zalana said after a moment's thought.

"Slowing?" Pelna asked. "Why that spell? It's a first-year spell. It doesn't really serve a purpose, except for teaching the casting of spells. It's easily broken by strength of force. We used it on each other the first half year."

Zalana grinned. "I would catch a swan."

* * * * *

Chapter Twelve

The next day, Zalana and Pelna waited with several of the instructors in an open courtyard near the center of the castle. As per their request, servants hung a torn blanket on the limbs of one of several trees. One of them held a goose, borrowed from the pens on the far side of the Halls.

Outside the walls, between the mountains and the Halls of Magic, several farms flourished. Everything produced was purchased by the head cook in the kitchens. It was there where Pelna taught Zalana to ride a horse. At first, Zalana had been embarrassed to wear britches like a man. She soon learned it was necessary in a saddle.

Lord Mage Chauncy Ashdale stepped into the courtyard. He was flanked by several senior instructors and a man in a dark cloak, its front unfastened, showing a hint of leather armor. Zalana stared, trying not to appear obvious. The lord mage was not a large man. In fact, he was slightly shorter than her father. His face was hidden within the hood of his robes, which were a deep red with several black stripes on his sleeves.

As the group walked toward them, the lord mage seemed to be angry as he spoke, his hand up, emphasizing a point to the man in the hooded cloak. Zalana caught the glint of sunlight off several rings on his hand. The stone in one was a deep ruby red. She glanced down at the plain gold band on her finger. It was similar to the steel band Pelna had opted for herself.

The lord mage quit speaking before they reached the waiting students. He reached up, pushed his hood back, and let it drop to his shoulders. "So these are the candidates for the black robes?"

His voice dripped with disdain. Zalana looked at him directly, angry at his tone. The man was her father's age, which surprised her. She'd thought he'd be older. His dark hair was neatly trimmed, and he smelled of citrus and light spices. He hadn't shaven that day, and a shadow of a beard showed.

He was very attractive, and carried himself as if he knew it, which made him unattractive to her. Not that she had experience with that sort of thing, or with boys at all. She only knew the person in front of her was the opposite of what Pelna said of her beloved fisherman.

The lord mage looked back at her, his dark brown eyes unblinking, aware he had insulted her. "Your name?"

"Zalana Bealnoth," Zalana said. "Lord Mage," she added after a slight hesitation.

"That one," dismissed Chauncy. "That count is forever wiggling his way into the upper tiers of the kingdom." He stepped closer to her. "I wonder how his pretty little daughter wiggles?" The last was spoken low and for her ears only.

Abruptly, he turned away. "You. I suppose there's a reason a blanket hangs on my cherry tree? And a torn one at that?"

"Yes, Lord Mage," Pelna said quickly.

The lord mage waved his hand in a circle as if to say, 'get on with it.' Pelna took the ring off her finger, held it in her palm, and cast the weaving spell into it instead of at the blanket. It glowed softly. She took the scroll from the servant holding it and read the binding spell. The ring flared bright red for a moment then faded.

"Well at least the binding was successful," the lord mage said. "Let's see if it'll weave the blanket."

Pelna put the ring on her finger, held her hand toward the blanket, and spoke the word of power etched on the inside of the ring. Several threads hanging from the torn part of the blanket started moving. In a few moments, the blanket was whole.

The lord mage turned to her and said, "Congratulations. You've earned the black robes. You may keep the ring. It was quick, and it took little effort by you. It's enchanted well."

"Thank you, Lord Mage," Pelna said, pleased with the compliment, seemingly unable to hear the tone of his voice.

Still shocked by what had been whispered to her, Zalana didn't hear him speak to her again. Chauncy had to clear his throat to let her know he was waiting in an answer. "Well?" he asked again.

Zalana took her own ring off and cast the slowing spell at it. She went through the same steps Pelna had, and her ring flared as well when she spoke the last word from the scroll.

The lord mage shook his head and sighed. It was a simple spell, one used for teaching more than anything else, after all. Many of the simple spells he knew from memory. "You wasted a binding scroll on this? Very well. Show me."

Zalana slipped the ring on her finger and nodded at the servant. The servant threw the goose up into the air with a flourish. The goose, one wing clipped, flapped its wings hard by instinct as it flew up and then back down, moving away.

Zalana raised her hand and spoke the word of power. Time seemed to slow for the goose. Its wings flapped slowly but mightily as it slowly settled toward the ground. Once it landed, it tried to run, its feet moving slowly. After about fifteen seconds it was able to move normally as the servants chased it. Zalana turned to the lord mage in triumph, his implication forgotten in her elation.

"I don't see why you want this spell in an item," Chauncy said, "but it works well. The goose moved slowly longer than I thought it might. Congratulations. You will be given the black robes."

He turned to the instructor closest to her. "Have her join me for dinner this evening. Perhaps she can explain why she chose that spell."

He walked off, raising his hood as he moved. He assistants and the one she'd never seen before followed closely behind. "You may keep the ring," he called out, throwing a hand up, multiple rings glinting again.

The assigned mage gave Zalana a knowing look and smiled. "When the evening dinner is served, be in the lord mage's personal dining hall. Don't tarry. Don't make him wait."

That evening, as she'd been directed, Zalana stood in the lord mage's personal dining hall. The table was set in finery, with a white tablecloth and flowers. The room wasn't lit by candles. Spheres of light floated at random close to the ceiling, occasionally bumping into a wall and softly bouncing away.

Zalana was mesmerized by the display, having an idea of the level of study and strength it took to cast the spell and have it last a substantial amount of time. It was possible the lights were permanent, but it was from a spell she'd never heard of, much less read. She suspected it was in a tome kept away from others, deep in the library.

She was looking up and didn't notice the lord mage come into the room from a door on the far side. He cleared his throat and said, "The grey robes fit you well."

Embarrassed at being caught in her thoughts, Zalana said, "Thank you, Lord Mage."

He smiled and said, "Please, call me Chauncy."

Zalana wasn't sure what to say. The smile was honest and in no way condescending, as it had appeared earlier in the day. His voice had none of the tones she'd detected earlier, either. Perhaps she'd been wrong in her initial assessment.

Like a gentleman, he pulled her seat out for her, allowing her to sit. He smoothly eased around the other side of the table and seated himself. As soon as he was seated, servants brought in their meal.

It smelled delicious. Zalana was surprised at her sudden hunger, but then again, the last few days of preparation for her enchantment examination had been nonstop. She'd only eaten at odd times and in small portions. She glanced up and saw him watching her. He seemed delighted that she was excited at the prospect of a fine meal.

He was amused when she closed her eyes for a moment, thanking Saint Gonthon for the food as Trenlis had taught her since she was a toddler. She didn't see the change in his smile as she did so, with her eyes closed. If she had, it might have made her think more about why there were no symbols or even mention of the saints and gods in the Halls of Magic. That was something she pondered from time to time.

The evening was spent in polite conversation. The lord mage seemed delighted to hear her stories of growing up and chasing swans in the gardens of her home. He showed the proper remorse at learning she'd grown up without siblings near her in age, and of her parents' strict rule of not allowing her to spend time with commoners' children. Other than her private teachers and her personal servant, she'd seen few others. The trips to the market were the highlight of her days.

She was beginning to understand that she truly had misjudged him when he explained with a wave of his hand that he was expected to act the way he had earlier. Surely she understood the way one behaved in public wasn't necessarily the way one truly was.

They paused their conversation politely as the servants cleared the table, leaving only the small bunch of flowers. As soon as they left the room, he picked up where they left off.

"As the daughter of a count," he said smoothly, "you understand the politics...of politics."

Zalana laughed, finally feeling relaxed in the presence of the most powerful mage in the entire world. There was no other on Kerr with his abilities. "I've never heard it put quite that way, but yes, I do understand it."

Sensing the change in her demeanor, the lord mage turned one of his rings on his hand with his thumb. The lights dimmed. He reached behind him and took out a bottle of wine from a cupboard.

"I've enjoyed the evening but, alas, I have work to do tonight," he said as he opened the bottle. "I have something very important awaiting my attentions. It can wait no longer.

"Let us have one drink together, and then you can make your way to the living halls and your chambers," the lord mage suggested. "I'm sorry I cannot escort you, but you understand. I don't believe you need the other apprentices thinking unsavory thoughts of you."

"Certainly, Lord Mage...I mean Chauncy," Zalana said. *He's charming, and his age isn't truly important,* she thought. *Perhaps there will be other meals.*

He leaned over her as he poured a half glass of wine for her. She inhaled his scent, once again catching the smell of spices and of some of the citrus fruit she was fond of from her own kingdom. Close to her, he glanced into her eyes and smiled slightly without speaking.

He sat down with the bottle, holding it as he looked up at the moving lights. "Do you like them?" he asked. "It is of my own creation from long ago. I combined elements of several spells as I designed it."

Zalana looked up. She watched two move toward one another and nearly bump as they passed closely. She felt she could watch them for hours.

"It's a wonderful spell," Zalana admitted when she finally looked back at him.

The lord mage sat relaxed, leaning back in his chair. His own wine glass was half full now, the bottle put away. "It's one I could teach you one day. Perhaps you can find a way to add color to some of them. I haven't found time to work on it."

"I'd like that," Zalana said.

The lord mage raised his glass. "Here's to each of us getting that which we desire."

Zalana smiled at his toast and sipped from her glass. The lord mage did the same, then he looked at her, his head tilted sideways a little, and grinned like a boy. He shrugged and tipped his glass, draining it. Zalana did the same with hers.

The glass fell from her hand as she slumped over. It bounced on the soft carpet and rolled to a stop against the leg of her chair. The lord mage pointed a hand at her and spoke words of power. Another of his rings glowed.

Zalana's unconscious body lifted from the chair and hovered, waist high, her hands and legs dangling below her. The lord mage pushed off the table and stood. The look of disdain was back on his face.

He smirked with a half-smile and said to the empty room, "I didn't even need to cast a charm spell on this one. Pathetic."

He waved his hand toward the door to his chambers. Zalana floated slowly through the open door. Chauncy Ashdale, lord mage of the Halls of Magic, followed behind her, loosening the belt on his robe. He slammed the door shut behind him.

* * *

Kryder lunged toward the closed door, disbelief on his face. "I'll kill him!" he shouted, over and over. Try as he might, he couldn't get to them. He pounded on the door. It made no sound. Though he'd passed through many walls and other objects this night in their travels, this was one barrier Lan wouldn't permit passing.

"I am sorry, Kryder," the deity said sadly. "I truly am. But I must show you that which our Creator has bid me. I can do no other."

Tog whirled on her, forgetting that he spoke to a god. "There'd better be a good reason for this night." He stared down at her, his incisors showing in a snarl.

"The Creator has reasons for everything. The balance must be restored," Lan said softly.

Lucas looked at her, the expression on his face deadly serious. "I'm not one to be questioning the Creator, truly I'm not. But tonight? Tonight I do."

She wasn't angry at the outburst. She understood, but they had no way of understanding she felt the anger they were feeling. As the goddess of time, the pain and anguish of mortals was a part of her. She could ease a mortal's pain by the passing of time. She could erase memories if she deemed it necessary.

She couldn't forget her own. She remembered everything that had ever happened in the world of Kerr, good or bad. There were more memories she must share. This night wasn't over.

* * * * *

Chapter Thirteen

Zalana woke the next morning in her own bed. She had no idea how she got there. The last thing she remembered was sipping from her glass of wine. As she rolled over to get out of bed, her entire body felt sore. She vowed to never drink wine again.

Pelna met her at the doorway to their scheduled class with a questioning look on her face. "Well," she asked, "how was your dinner? What did you eat? Tell me everything."

Zalana told her of the evening and the floating light spell. How it remained floating around the entire meal. She told her the lord mage was different away from others and of the last glass of wine.

"That's it?" Pelna asked. "You don't remember anything else?"

"No," Zalana admitted. "I woke up in my chambers still in my robes. I'm never drinking wine again."

Pelna reached out and took her hand. She looked up and down the wide hallway. Seeing no one, she whispered urgently, "One glass of wine doesn't do that. Even if you've never had wine before. You're lucky he had someone take you to your chambers."

"It was a half glass," Zalana said, confused, "not a whole glass."

Before Pelna could say anything, the mage instructing the morning's classes rounded the corner, headed toward them. It was the older mage. He was whistling happily.

"Good morning," he said. "Are you ready to learn some protection spells?"

"Protection?" Zalana asked.

"Why, yes," the older mage said. "So far you've mastered basic spells, a few of the more difficult ones, and you successfully cast a binding spell. You don't get to write it in your personal books, though. All those are fun, but what if you have to face someone trying to harm you, or another mage? There's the shielding spell, various kinds, of course, and the spell of rejection. Rejection is my favorite of the bunch."

"What does it do?" Pelna asked.

The old man paused in the doorway to the small room. He scratched his chin and said, "It's kind of a combination of a shield and a gust of wind, I suppose. If another mage casts a spell toward you, you can push back at it with rejection. If you're fast enough and strong enough, you can dissipate their spell."

"What happens if it's two equally powerful mages?" Zalana asked.

"Well," the old mage said, "no two mages are ever going to be exactly equal. Eventually the weaker of the two can no longer call on his gift."

Pelna looked at Zalana and winked. Then she looked at the old man and said, "And then you kill him, right?"

"Yes!" the old man said, his face lighting up in delight. "Precisely." He practically skipped into the room.

Pelna looked at Zalana and wrinkled her nose as if she smelled something bad. They both laughed and entered the room behind him. This class would be interesting.

* * *

Three weeks later, Zalana went to see the herbalist. She hadn't been feeling well. At Pelna's suggestion, she went to see the woman for something to ease her sour stomach. Located in a small outbuilding, it was the first time Zalana had been inside the shop.

The old woman recognized Zalana from previous meetings in the dining hall. "Come in, come in," she said. "Close the door, please. We can't have too much sunlight on the night blooms. They prefer dim light, you know. I just watered them, so of course they opened up."

Zalana pulled the door closed and made her way past pots of growing plants, cut plants hung drying on lines, and boxes of dirt with many small plants in different stages of growth. There was both a dry dusty smell, and one of moisture in the air at the same time. The herbalist everyone called Grandmother was seated at a table lit by several lanterns.

The woman pointed to a stool. "Sit down, Zalana. Tell me, what seems to ail you? Is it a tooth? An earache? Hate those; I just hate them." She reached up and held her ear in memory.

"No, Grandmother," Zalana said, sitting down. "It's my stomach. I've been sick three days in a row."

"I see," the old woman said.

She reached over, picked up a lantern, and held it high so she could see Zalana better. The herbalist got off her stool and stepped closer. She prodded Zalana's cheek with a finger. She then did the same under both eyes. When she poked a breast, Zalana flinched.

"Sore, eh? Both of them?" the herbalist asked. "Tell me, how far along might you be?"

"Far along?" Zalana asked. "What do you mean?"

The woman smiled. "It's plain as the nose on your face. You're with child. Now, I'm not one to go around telling my patrons' business, mind you, but you know that type of thing is discouraged. No guests in the chambers and all that nonsense."

Zalana was shocked. The woman must be wrong. She didn't know much about having a child and everything it took for it to happen, but she knew enough to know it was impossible. *Unless*, she thought...

Horrified, she covered her mouth and stood quickly, causing the woman to reach out and say, "Here now. Don't get sick *here*. There's an empty pot in the corner."

"I have to go," Zalana said. "I have to go right now." She turned to leave as she felt the woman grab her robes.

"There's nothing to be scared about," the woman said. "It's a natural thing. Perhaps you can finish your training and gain the red robes before it's time to deliver. I've never delivered one by an apprentice or a mage here. Plenty of servants through the years, though. I believe it's all the same."

She continued talking as she reached up on a shelf. "Here now, let me give you something for the sour stomach."

The woman gave her a packet of ground herbs to mix with water. Zalana offered to pay for it and was waved away. The woman's needs were taken care of in the Halls of Magic, and she had no need for coins.

Zalana rushed away from the building and went looking for Pelna. She had no idea what her future would hold, but she knew it couldn't be there. She'd wondered why she hadn't been asked back to dinner with the lord mage. Now she knew. She wondered how many times it had happened to others.

As she crossed an open court, she dumped the contents of the package out, crumpled the folded parchment, and threw it down. The herbalist had said she'd never delivered a child to a student in all the years she'd been there.

As she rushed to find Pelna, the old woman slowly put her things away, blew out the lanterns, and left her shop. The lord mage had instructed her to let him know when this type of thing occurred. Several times a year she did so.

Zalana found Pelna in the wide hallway near their chambers. She grabbed her arm and pulled her into hers. Not sure what was happening, Pelna allowed herself to be pulled in.

"What's wrong with you?" Pelna asked.

Zalana started crying quietly. "I'm with child," she whispered. "With child."

"What?" Pelna exclaimed. "How can you be? You have to...oh." Her hand flew to her mouth. "That *despicable* man."

"Yes," Zalana whispered. "It must be his."

"What will you do?" Pelna asked, realizing things were very bad. "He hasn't even spoken to you since that night. This is not good. You know he always has his lackey with him. Last week I heard when a nobleman refused to pay for the second year for his son, not only was the boy expelled, that man and several others went to the lord's manor and took more than the fees. There were rumors of *murder.*" The last she whispered like Zalana had been doing.

"One of them was the apprentice," Zalana said. "My father knows the family. The lord only sent his son to keep him from becoming burnt. They had no intention of him continuing. I received a message demanding I continue to pass and graduate. It happened."

"No one told the king, or one of his dukes?" Pelna asked. "How can murder go unpunished like that? If it was a commoner in this wretched kingdom, I could understand, but that was a nobleman's family."

"King Westell has the Hall of Magic in his kingdom, only miles from his palace," Zalana said as she dried her eyes. "He won't risk their alliance. Besides, from what I know of him, he's no better."

"What will you do?" Pelna asked.

"Leave," Zalana said as she searched for her riding britches. "Leave the Halls, leave the kingdom. Go...somewhere."

"I'll go with you," Pelna said as she helped her pack a small cloth sack with clothes. "We can go to my home. My father will protect you."

"Against the lord mage and his sell-sword?" Zalana said. "No, I can't ask it. You have to stay here and act as if you don't know where I went. And you won't, because I am not telling you my final destination."

"What if they come after you right away?" Pelna asked. "How can I warn you?"

"You can't," Zalana said as she pulled her boots on. "You have to act as if you know *nothing*. For your own safety."

Pelna reached out and pulled her friend close. "One day you'll send word you're alright?" she asked, crying herself now.

"Yes," Zalana said. Her tears stopped. There was no time for it. She needed to leave, and leave soon. "Promise me you'll gain the black robes soon and leave. Go back to your family and your beloved waiting for you."

"I will," Pelna promised. She then told Zalana of the fastest way to put some distance between the Halls of Magic and herself. The way she had arrived three years ago.

Zalana cracked the door, looked up and down the halls, and, seeing no one, left her chambers for the last time. She made her way through the castle and the attached buildings using back stairways and rarely used halls. The guards at the small rear gate thought nothing of her going to the riding stables. They'd seen her do so many times through the years. They went back to their conversation.

Zalana saddled her favorite horse, one Pelna said was part Minth. The horse was nowhere near the size of a Minth warhorse, but she was taller than the others in the stable. As soon as her bag was tied, she slipped the small bag of coins and jewelry into a pouch on the saddle and started to mount the horse. She stopped when she heard a voice she didn't recognize calling her name.

She turned to see the young man in his leather armor, sword on his hip, and his cloak hanging loose on his shoulders, leaning against the jam of the open doorway. He had a dagger out, picking from beneath a fingernail.

Smiling, Zalana said, "Yes?" She walked toward him as if she hadn't a care in the world.

"Going for a ride this morning?" he asked. He glanced down at his hand and then back at her. The dagger tip now balanced on the finger.

"Yes," Zalana said. "I plan on stopping for lunch, as well. I took some herbs this morning, and my appetite has come back. I have plenty of food. Will you be riding today?"

"I'm sorry, I don't know your name. I've seen you in the halls, though." She continued to walk toward him, smiling.

The man visibly relaxed when she said she'd taken some herbs. He let the weapon fall, catching the handle. He sheathed his dagger. With his guard down, Zalana threw up her hand and spoke the words inscribed on the inside of her ring. The man's reactions slowed. His mind slowed as well, and he offered no resistance to the sleep spell Zalana cast next. It took a few phrases to complete, but the man was in no position to interrupt her.

He dropped, unconscious. Zalana felt a drain on herself, as if it were the end of a long day. She'd put as much energy as she could into the simple spell. The man would be out for hours, if not most of the day. Deciding not to use a levitation spell, she dragged him into an empty stall, covered him in straw, and closed the door.

At a steady pace she rode north toward Minth. She kept her hood up on her riding cloak and spoke to no one. At a major crossroad she turned east toward the coast. It would take her two hours to reach it. Had she gone north, she would've been in her father's lands in several days.

When she came to the port town, she rode to the docks. She tied her horse up and searched for a ship leaving soon to Yaylok. She made sure to ask several people. Some had nothing to do with the ships themselves. After ensuring she'd be remembered, she went to the nearest tavern.

She stood at the bar, sipping a cup of water and eating a roll as she listened. When she heard someone speaking with the same accent Pelna had, she listened closely, then approached the table. Surprised, the older of the two men slid over on the bench as she sat beside him.

"I'm sorry," she said, "I overheard you say you're leaving for Minth on the tide. Would it be possible to book passage?"

The older man rubbed his beard. "That would depend, my lady. For how many?"

"Only myself and my horse," Zalana answered.

"Well, now," the man answered. "A horse means I need to have hay on hand, and extra water. I've the room, but it's the trouble you'll put me through, you understand."

Zalana reached into a pocket, put her hand on the table, and opened it. On the table were three whole gold coins. "Will this suffice?"

The captain quickly scooped them up before any others in the bar could see them. "Aye, my lady, that'll do."

His first mate stood and said, "I'll get the hay, Cap'n, and an extra barrel for fresh water."

The old man said, "My name is Barl Jonrig. You can call me Cap'n. Everybody else does. Let's see to that horse of yours. I may need to rig a pen if he's the ornery type."

Without introducing herself, Zalana followed him out of the tavern, untied her horse, and followed the man toward the docks. From what she understood, the trip would take more than a week as they hugged the coast, taking advantage of the winds.

* * *

Garvant couldn't breathe. He couldn't move. He was pinned to the wall with his head tilted sideways as it pressed against the ceiling of the lord mage's study. His eyes wide in fear, he looked down at the man trembling with anger with his hand held up toward him.

"You let her leave," snarled the lord mage. "Tell me why I shouldn't kill you here and now?"

The lord mage let his hand drop to his side. Garvant fell to the floor, stunned. He crawled from the wall and struggled to stand, breathing deeply. The lord mage walked around his huge desk and sat down.

"I tried to reach for my sword, my Lord," Garvant mumbled. "My hand moved slowly, and then the next thing I knew, I woke up covered in hay."

"I know you're young, but I didn't know you were stupid," the lord mage said. "When I hired you, it was with the highest recommendations. An exceptional sell-sword, I was told. Was I lied to?"

"No, my Lord," Garvant said, breathing easier now. "He took me in when I was six. I'm the best with a blade in all of Gar-Noth. I was surprised by her. She didn't look the type to attack me."

"She wears the grey robes, you idiot," the lord mage said. "Of course she has the ability to attack you. What do you think we teach here? Sparkling wands and party tricks?"

He stood and paced as he spoke, "For the last century, these halls have only accepted nobility and the wealthy in an attempt to weed out lesser mages. Very few mages with a strong gift leave here. She had promise."

"She said she took the herbs, my Lord," said Garvant, hoping to appease him.

"Maybe," the lord mage said. "Maybe, but I cannot risk it. A child from my bloodline and hers could rival my own gift. It wouldn't be well received. I won't have it."

He sat with his fingers pressed together in front of his mouth as he thought. Finally, his mind made up, he said, "I cannot send a mage. I need them here. Plans are progressing. These things take time."

He continued, "You'll hire the ones who helped you take care of that little problem last month. Find her, and kill her."

The lord mage moved his hands away from his mouth, looked at the sell-sword, and said, "I don't care how long it takes. Weeks, months, years, it doesn't matter. You *will* find her. If she has a child by the time you catch up with her, you know what to do."

"Bring it to you?" Garvant asked.

"No." His eyes narrowed slightly. "Kill it, too."

* * * * *

Chapter Fourteen

The week on the ship passed quickly for Zalana, despite spending considerable time each morning being sick. The captain and his crew attributed it to seasickness. Most of the occasional passengers experienced this, and it was expected. They ensured she had pieces of the dry flat bread and drank plenty of water. The crunchy bread was lightly salted and helped when she was feeling nauseated.

Within a half hour's glass of docking, she was riding west, away from the port town. The captain told her of a shop dealing in blankets and a variety of other items on the edge of town. She bought a couple of good wool blankets, a small metal pot, and a leather bag to hold water. She looked at the bows hanging on the wall but knew it would be senseless to buy one. She'd never been taught to shoot one. She settled on a small hunting knife. She had no idea what she truly needed, but what she had was a start.

She rode until nearly dark. She had no idea if anyone was looking for her, or if the lord mage would simply let her go to be rid of her. She took a room in a modest inn in what appeared to be the largest town near a small castle. Before she left the town, she purchased clothes suitable for traveling.

Despite many conversations with Pelna about the kingdom of Minth, she had no idea which duchy or estate she was in. The innkeeper didn't ask her for her name, and she didn't volunteer it. He accepted the copper coins without comment. Their value was in the metal content, not the kingdom from which they came, though he did take note of the stamp of Gar-Noth on them.

The next month was spent much the same way. The days after she was able to sleep in an inn, she left early in the morning after a full breakfast. Around noon she would stop in a village or near water and eat the small loaf of bread and a boiled egg or piece of meat she'd bought before leaving the inn.

Several nights she slept in barns, the owners happy for the copper piece she offered. In several of the villages it was all there was available. She was grateful for it and the offer of a meal. At some crossroads she was able to buy fruits and vegetables, others the small loaves of bread popular in the area. As she traveled, she was able to see for herself how commoners and peasants survived. She hoped her coins helped them.

She passed others on the roads and trails as she headed west. Sometimes it was someone walking; others were on horseback or in a wagon. She kept her hood up and didn't speak to them, keeping to herself. Only in the evenings did she have contact with anyone. If asked, she gave a different name every time.

One evening, after a long day, she was walking her horse and startled a rabbit. She threw her hand up and spoke the words. The rabbit slowed, allowing her time to drop the reins and catch it. She felt sadness for it, but she did what she had to do.

That evening she roasted it over her fire and ate it with a handful of dried beans she soaked and cooked. Cooking was something she'd never done for herself. It was a new experience for her, and she ate her scorched beans despite the taste. Food was something she couldn't waste, because her coins wouldn't last forever.

Another evening as she was sitting by her fire, watching the sunset, and debating whether she should cook a pot of beans, or eat two of the half-dozen boiled eggs she'd bought from a farm earlier in the morning, two men rode up.

She stood, unsure of their intentions. It was the first time she'd been truly afraid while traveling by herself. If the two men were some of the local brigands the farmer's wife had talked about that morning, she knew she was in danger.

"What have we here, Tolban?" one of them asked his friend. "A woman out by herself, away from a village, a farm, and nobody around."

"Not very wise, if you ask me," Tolban said.

Zalana could tell by the way he spoke he wasn't from a farm or small village. They were from a town or city somewhere. Troublemakers, or worse, on the run.

The first man dismounted. As he walked closer, Zalana stepped away from the fire and said, "That's close enough, sir. I don't know you. Perhaps you and your friend should ride on and find your own place to stop for the evening."

Tolban laughed, his horse spinning in a circle, startled by his outburst. He managed to control it and turned back, facing the fire. "She called you sir! Jayton, you're many things, but a 'sir' isn't one of them."

"Quit your laughing, Tolban," Jayton said. The tone in his voice showed his embarrassment. He looked at Zalana. "That's alright. I'll introduce myself to you."

"If you insist," Zalana said as she tried to hide the fear in her voice, "but I'm afraid I can't see you very well in the dying light. Let me remedy that, good sir."

Zalana spoke several words in a language the two had never heard, much less had a chance to learn. Three small spheres of bright light appeared above her and hovered. It was enough to light the area of her campsite and allowed her to see the men clearly. They were thin, dirty, and armed with short swords.

Tolban's horse bucked and shied away from the sudden brightness. He struggled to control it, cursing at it the entire time. Jayton stopped in midstride and started backing away, a look of fear on his face.

Zalana raised a hand, took a step toward them, and asked menacingly, "Where are you going? I haven't decided what I want to do to you yet."

At hearing this, Tolban kicked his horse's flanks and rode off. He was quickly followed by Jayton after he mounted his own horse. Neither of the brigands looked back. Moments later, the lights slowly faded. Zalana sat down near her fire, relieved but smiling. She reached for her pot and the rest of her dried beans.

* * *

The firelight faded into swirling grey mists.

Tog turned to Kryder and said, "By herself. Through a and rife with brigands, mercenary companies moving from one contract to another, wolves, hunting cats, and everything else in the night, yet she traveled alone, with no one to take turns through the night watching."

"I know," Kryder said, "and she was younger when she did it than we are."

Lucas looked over and said, "I'm to be thinking this one can take care of herself, lads. Did ye see those two riding away like a banshee was chasing them?"

Lan said, "In those days, there were not so many mercenary companies moving around. Come. It is time we go elsewhere."

The mist swirled once again, and they were in another town. This one familiar.

* * *

Zalana eased herself down from her horse, carefully removing her foot from the stirrup. She was five months pregnant and well aware of the changes in her body and her balance. She didn't think others could tell, as her choice of clothes hid it, but she felt it.

She went into the specialty shop. It appeared to be the only one in town. She could understand why. This deep into the baronies, except for the nobles, a craftsman creating and selling jewelry didn't do much business. Most commoners couldn't afford it.

She took the time to admire several pieces, gave a nod to the guard standing near a window, and walked toward the back, to the worktable lit brightly by several lanterns. A Dwarf was leaning over a rounded piece of glass. Underneath was a ring held tightly between two small wood plates pushed together by wood screws. In one hand he held a steel rod, its tip glowing; the other held a thinner gold rod.

Not wanting to disturb his work, Zalana watched him work the melting gold into a small rose centered on the band of the ring. Occasionally he would place the steel rod back on a brazier, its tip in a bed of glowing coals, and grab another, never looking up.

Once he was satisfied, the dwarf placed the rod in the brazier and put the remainder of the gold in a small stone bowl. He reached up to what appeared to be a short beard and started tugging. Eight more inches of beard was pulled from underneath the leather apron he wore. He fluffed it a little, then turned to Zalana.

"Welcome to my shop," he said. "Did you find anything you'd like to see closer? Perhaps try on?"

"Several were to my liking," admitted Zalana, "but today I'm looking to sell."

The proprietor looked her up and down closely. "Hmm, you're clearly not wealthy. You've the leathers and cloak of a traveler, but not the sword. You don't strike me as the type to go poking around old ruins. If you gain your pieces in the night through windows, I want none of it." He folded his arms and stared. "Well?"

Zavalla smiled. "I can assure you, master craftsman, I am no sneak thief. I'm a traveler, but I feel my traveling has ended. I spent the last of my coin replacing the shoes on my horse. I've a necklace and a pendant to sell to you today. At one time both pieces were my mother's."

"I see," the shop owner said. "My apologies, my lady. Now that I've heard more of your accent, I realize you've traveled quite a ways. Gar-Noth, if I'm not mistaken."

"You'd be correct," admitted Zalana. She placed the necklace and the small pendant on the counter.

He picked up the pendent first, turned it, and held it under the curved glass. He turned it over, checking it from all angles. Next he picked up the necklace and ran the finely woven links through his fingers as he inspected it.

"Very nice," the master craftsman said. "The swan is finely detailed, though of an older style of art. The necklace looks as if it was made for that exact pendant. The style of links is very distinct. I traveled for many years buying, selling, and creating fine work myself.

"I spent a year or so in Gar-Noth," he continued. "Didn't care for the politics of the kingdom. I'd say the work came from somewhere near the coast there. Looks to be Gnomish work."

"If that's your assessment, master craftsman, I'm inclined to believe you," Zalana said, smiling. "My mother owned it long before I was born."

The Dwarf placed both pieces of jewelry on the tray of his scales. He added weight to the other side until it balanced. He crossed an arm over his beard and held the elbow of the hand cupping his chin. He thought for a moment, calculating in his head.

He turned back to her and said, "I'll pay you thirty gold coins for both."

Zalana was shocked. She'd expected to get a gold piece for each of them. Six would allow her the opportunity to buy a small home in town. Thirty would get a small place to build a one-room home and have a garden. It might even be enough to purchase a small field for her horse to graze in.

"I see the look of disbelief on your face, my lady," he said. "It's not the weight in gold that makes them so valuable. It's the age and the fine detail, and the knowledge that particular clan of Gnomes is no more. These pieces are highly prized. I'll hold onto them, and one day I'll more than triple my investment. Let it never be said Moovy Stonepolisher isn't an honest Dwarf."

"Thank you, Master Stonepolisher," Zalana said. "I'll take the offer. It will allow me to purchase a plot of land. Do you know of a lord or lady who might be inclined to sell a portion? Preferably away from a town or village. Over the last few months, I've found I prefer to be away from many people at once."

"Please, call me Moovy," he said.

He reached under his counter and pulled out a coin purse. He counted out thirty gold pieces of standard weight. Both sides were stamped as all the coins in the baronies. He started to slide them toward her and stopped.

"Would you like some of these in quarter gold pieces, silver coin, or maybe even coppers?" he asked. "Many places won't have change for a whole gold, if you plan on shopping in town."

"Yes, please," Zalana said. She hadn't considered it.

Moovy removed five of them from the stack and placed them back in the purse. It disappeared back under the counter, and another came out. He reached in, pulled a handful of mixed coins out, and started separating them.

As he was counting out coins, he said, "You know, my lady, it hasn't slipped past me that you haven't volunteered your name. Now, it's no concern of mine, mind you, nor is the child you carry. A little more than halfway there, I'd say."

He stacked the silver and copper coins and placed them beside the quarter golds next to the piled whole golds. He said, "Your accent places you from Gar-Noth, yet your style of clothes and the cut of the cloth tells me Minth."

He continued speaking, now looking at her, "Anyway, whatever reason you have is your reason. This barony is the farthest from Minth, and even farther from Gar-Noth, but if you're truly looking to live away from others, you might consider moving on to the Western Borderlands."

"The Western Borderlands?" asked Zalana, choosing to not answer the unasked question about the child's father. "Isn't that unclaimed land?"

"It was," agreed Moovy, "until about seven years ago. Lord Narvok is the lord of the Western Borderlands now. If you don't mind very few humans and traveling across the barony, the trip down and back out of the canyon, and the week or so to the village he started, that would be the place for you."

"Will I be able to grow a garden and pasture my horse?" Zalana asked.

"Garden?" laughed Moovy. "I'd say so. He'll give a farm to those looking to start a life there. His people will help start it."

"If he's willing to do that, why have so few moved there?" Zalana asked as she put her coins in her own leather coin purse.

"I said few humans," Moovy answered, "not Orcs. There are plenty of them there. He and the local tribal chief trade with Baron Arnwald. Fine wood, strong bows…and chickens. Do you know the black and white ones lay brown eggs? It's the strangest thing. Tastes the same, mind you, but the shell is as brown as my apron."

* * * * *

Chapter Fifteen

Marnell climbed down from the wagon and stretched, twisting back and forth. He looked over to see his brother Teel jump from the seat of the wagon to the ground. The boy was only twelve, but was nearly the size of a grown man. Marnell shook his head. There was a time he hadn't bothered to climb off a wagon, himself. Now, at twenty years old, it no longer appealed to him.

Since he'd learned to walk, Teel was always moving. Except, strangely enough, when he was hunting. The boy had learned to track and stalk like a Tarlok hunter from Zane and Penae and some of their neighbors in the collection of cabins across the grassland. Combined with the ability to stay still and blend into the forest taught to him by Orcs, the boy was as good a hunter as anyone Marnell knew, including other members of the Red Fist tribe.

Teel began unstacking the crates of chickens on his wagon, careful not to spill the wooden bowls of water any more than they already had. Several times a day they had to stop and refill them. It was a necessary chore when traveling for more than a week with the caged birds.

Marnell tossed his brother two small coins. "When you finish unstacking them, you can go get a sticky bun," he said. "Make sure you spend both copper pieces so you can bring me some. Don't eat them all this time."

Teel grinned and kept working. Honey covered sticky buns were worth the trip to Barony Arnwald, as far as he was concerned. Those and the chance to hunt one of the big cats as they came through the canyons, though he'd never seen one of the elusive beasts. He saw plenty of tracks, but never fresh ones. Marnell didn't doubt his brother would get one someday.

That evening, Marnell and Teel dined with Baron Arnwald. They were comfortable now around the baron, having stayed with him several times a year. The baron and his cousin enjoyed telling stories from their youth and of battle to Teel.

There was a time when Goblins would pour forth from the mountains like ants from a rotted log, or so they said. Marnell now knew it wasn't quite like they described it. It had taken several years to push them from the foothills at the edge of the barony years ago, but not in those numbers. Still, it made for exciting stories to a twelve-year-old boy.

In turn, Baron Arnwald and his cousin were enthralled with Teel's stories of stalking forest cats large enough to take down horses, or of wild boar weighing more than two men combined. As young as he was, Teel thought nothing of standing his ground and burying an arrow or two into the charging beasts.

Marnell let him tell his tales. Marnell could add to them, but it wouldn't be the same coming from a man. A boy, though, was a completely different story. He, like Teel, had learned from the Orcs that you must stand your ground. The cats, and even the boars, could sense your fear if you didn't. Occasionally, an errant shot didn't take the beast down. Teel carried two Orc-made axes, each a little larger than a hatchet, for those times.

After their meal, Marnell said, "We'll make our purchases, load the wagons, and leave by midday. Are there any looking to come west?"

Baron Arnwald glanced over at his cousin and said, "Narthon, how many have been waiting to make the trip?"

"This half year has seen the most, Arn," he answered. He looked at Marnell. "Is it only you and young Teel this time?"

"It is, sir." Marnell asked with a slight hesitation, "Why? How many will accompany us?"

"Twelve," Sir Narthon said. "Three are newly betrothed couples, all from farming families here in the barony. A family of five from the Kylin Barony bearing a writ from the baroness herself, vouching for them. It would seem she's with child again, and their small tenant farm was growing ever smaller. I've met the man; he spent some time as a foot soldier fighting back in the Minth skirmishes and started a family late in life."

"And the last?' Marnell asked.

"She's a late addition. Master Stonepolisher has vouched for her," he said with a shrug. "It would appear she comes from the coasts of Gar-Noth or some such. I've never met her. She's only been in town for two weeks."

* * *

The next day, near midmorning, Marnell and Teel finished loading the wagons. One was full of supplies requested by the families. The other was full of hobbled goats. Most were kids. There were enough to start a new flock. Marnell ensured they were loaded in the wagon Teel would drive. He didn't want their noise in his ears the whole trip. Strapped to the seat beside Teel was a crate with three young roosters, new blood for one of the farmers' flock. They crowed endlessly, each trying to outdo the other.

Each of the families traveling with them had their own wagons loaded with supplies. Several had animals tied to them and a crate or two of either chickens or ducks. The family of five had two dogs sitting in the back with their children. Marnell noticed the dogs kept their eyes on the four sheep tied to the wagon and ignored the birds and other animals.

The last to arrive was the lone woman. She rode up on her horse and stopped near Marnell's wagon. Marnell knew right away the horse was from the country he'd spent most of his life in. The Minth breeding was apparent. She wasn't as large as his father's warhorse, but she was larger than most he'd seen in the barony. The mare reminded him of those Coal had sired over the last few years belonging to Baron Arnwald and his cousin.

Marnell looked around and then back at the hooded woman. He could see part of her face and her long black hair. She settled her horse with a pat on her neck and turned toward him.

"Good morning, sir," she said. "Are you Lord Narvok's son?"

Marnell tried to see the rest of her face without being obvious about it. For years, his sister had chosen to hide hers, so he understood the desire. "I am," he said.

She reached up and slowly pushed the hood of her cloak back, letting it slide down her dark hair, and smiled. The whole journey, she'd been giving different names. She decided to use her real name on the last leg of her travels.

She said, "My name is Zalana. I'm pleased to meet you, my lord."

Marnell was speechless. He'd never seen beauty like hers. He eyes were a blue that reminded him of the seas he hadn't seen since he was Teel's age. They contrasted sharply with her hair, which was black and hung in loose curls, moving slightly in the breeze. Her smile took his breath away.

Teel spoke up, trying not to laugh as he said, "She called you a lord. Wait until I tell Katheen. You know she won't let you live it down."

Marnell glanced over at his brother and grinned. "You and the roosters mind your own business."

Zalana shook her head and grinned, too, when she realized the one in the next wagon in line was but a boy, despite his size. She looked back at Marnell and said, "Is the son of the lord of the Western Borderlands not a lord himself?"

"I suppose," Marnell agreed, "but I don't think about it. Papa tells everyone to call him Jynal. None of that 'lord' business, he says. I agree. It's only a title. Yes, someone must lead, especially when decisions must be made, but I don't feel I'm above any other."

Zalana tilted her head sideways and looked at Marnell in a new light. If she were being honest with herself, she would have already noticed he was a handsome, tall, strong man. Hearing this from a noble was eye-opening to her; it wasn't an opinion anyone shared in Gar-Noth. She found herself attracted to him—a revelation new to her, as well.

"Where's your wagon?" Marnell asked. "Your supplies? Livestock?"

"I have none," Zalana answered. "I have coin. I would purchase what I need when I get to Three Oaks. Is that not the name of the village? Three Oaks?"

"It is," Marnell answered, "but I don't think you understand. We don't have any shops. There are no craftsmen building wagons. No one has spare draft horses. It's a farming community. We barter and trade with each other and the Orcs. The Orcs have no use for coin. There are some who value precious stones, but I think it's for decorations and not for their value.

"You'd be better served buying a wagon, supplies, tools, and some livestock here. Unless you have something to trade, the coin won't do you much good unless you make the trip back here. It will be some time before Three Oaks is a town. Or a real village, for that matter."

Zalana didn't know what to say. She'd assumed she could purchase what she needed. She'd grown up a secluded noble's daughter. She'd followed it with nearly four years in the Halls of Magic. While she traveled west, she'd learned to be self-sufficient, but spending the coin she had was a large part of it.

Other than planting a small garden for herself, which she hoped she could accomplish, she'd thought she'd pay someone to build her home, barn, and fences. Perhaps continuing on to the Western Border wasn't a good idea. She could find somewhere in the Arnwald Barony instead.

Seeing the hesitation on her face, Marnell spoke quickly. He wanted to know more of her, and he wasn't about to let the opportunity slip past. "If you have the means to pay for them, I'll stay the afternoon and help you find what you need. Teel and the rest can start the journey. We'll catch up, as they won't be moving fast with the livestock they have with them. We can catch them before the canyons."

"What will I do about a home?" Zalana asked after considering his offer. "If everyone is a farmer, there will be no one with the time to build it for me. I don't know a lot about farming, but from my travels, I know it is a time-consuming endeavor."

"The home will be the least of your worries," Marnell said. "Everyone pitches in, and we'll have it built within a few days. What will take the longest is the fireplace. Stone must be gathered and stacked with mud. It has to dry."

"You can build a home?" Zalana asked, impressed.

"Well," Marnell said, running his hands through his hair, "yes, I can. I've helped Papa build them. I know my way around a hammer and saw. I'm nowhere near his skill on a forge, but I can make simple things. Nails, hooks, hinges. Simple hinges, not anything elaborate."

"Would it not seem unsavory, you building a home for me?" Zalana asked. "What will Katheen think?"

"What?" Marnell asked. He was confused by the question. "Why would my sister care? I helped build the home for her and Lur not half a year ago."

"Oh, my apologies," Zalana said. Her face flushed. "I heard him say wait until Katheen hears. I assumed she was your wife."

Marnell grinned. "No, I've not found a wife. Yet."

* * *

Teel and the others started the trip west, while Marnell took Zalana to purchase a wagon and a team to pull it. Marnell told her he knew draft horses and was certain he could find what they were looking for. The rest would be easy enough to buy, if Zalana had the coins she'd hinted.

Time passed quickly as they made their way around town and to nearby farms. Once Marnell realized she was truly starting with nothing, he wrote out a list on the back of the one his father had sent him with. When the list was compete, the wagon was nearly full.

They talked as they packed the last of the cups, pots, and pans. Marnell couldn't believe she'd crossed half of Kerr with only one small pot to cook in.

"It was all I needed," she reasoned. "It was enough to cook beans."

"Beans?" Marnell asked. "Just beans? What about cornbread, or soft rolls? What about fried eggs between two slices of fresh bread? Squash? Roast venison with onions, red root, and taters? What about stewed tomatoes with sweet peppers?"

He stopped and looked at her, his look serious. "No chicken and gravy over hard rolls?" He shook his head, looking down, then looked back at her and said, "You poor woman."

Zalana laughed out loud at him. She placed her hand on his arm and said, "Even if I had all these pots and pans and the food you mentioned, I couldn't cook it. I can only make beans."

The look of horror on his face made her laugh even harder. She'd never felt this comfortable with anyone. Well, anyone besides the woman who'd raised her and her friend Pelna. *A man, I have never felt this comfortable with a man,* she thought.

She shook her head to stop the thought. She was with child, and the child would be born without a father. Nothing could come from it. Once the truth was known, he would distance himself. His father was lord of the Wester Borderlands; even if he didn't act like it, he was nobility, and this type of scandal was always avoided at all costs.

They weren't a couple of commoners. It wasn't like her father's duchy, where a lord would order a widow to marry another peasant, giving them no choice in the matter. Landowners did this to the peasants living on their estates because the land *would* be farmed and taxes paid. The last thing a noble would do in Gar-Noth was come out of his own purse to support a widow and her offspring.

She dropped her hand and turned away, unaware Marnell slowly rubbed where her hand had been. She had no way of knowing Marnell felt the same about her. She tied her horse to the wagon and slowly climbed up to the seat. She told herself she would think no more of it.

Later in the evening, they stopped for the night. Marnell took care of the animals, staking them and watering them from the barrel. Zalana started a small fire. She didn't speak much to him, only answering necessary questions. She poured beans into her pot, adding more than normal for Marnell to eat with her.

He sat down on the other side of the fire. Zalana looked out of the corner of her eye and noticed him watching her. She found herself enjoying the attention, but unsure of what to say to him. She didn't want to mislead him.

Marnell asked, "What kind of beans are you cooking?"

"Dried beans," Zalana said. "I soaked them for a few minutes first."

"Alright," Marnell said, "but what kind are they?"

"I don't know," she answered as she stirred the pot with her knife. "They're beans."

"You do know there are many different kinds of beans, right?" Marnell asked.

"Well, yes," she answered. "The woman who raised me for my parents took me to the market many times. I know there are many. These are dried ones."

Zalana looked up to see Marnell laughing at her without making any noise. He covered his mouth to stop it, but the sound came anyway. Zavalla turned red and then couldn't help but laugh with him.

After they stopped laughing like youngsters, he looked at her with a thoughtful expression and said, "You say a woman raised you for your parents. You're nobility, too, then. Where are you from, and why would your parents have someone else raise you?"

Zalana was silent. She didn't know what to say. How much *could* she say? Should she even say it? She went to her wagon and retrieved two wooden bowls and spoons. Marnell divided the beans and set the pot aside. She pushed the beans around in her bowl, looked at Marnell, and decided to tell him of her youth, at least. She moved over beside him and sat against the wagon wheel with him.

She didn't look at him. She simply looked off at the starlit sky over the glowing embers of their fire and started talking. She found, once she started, she couldn't stop. It was as if everything she'd held inside as she traveled the last few months had to come out. Marnell let her talk. He asked questions when appropriate. He didn't judge her for how she was raised.

When she told him she had been sent to the Halls of Magic and of some of her training, he was interested, but he wasn't as curious about it as she'd have thought a farmer would be. After all, not many knew someone with the gift. Certainly not someone who carried themselves as he did, caring not about things of nobility and the opportunities they were given.

She asked him, "You act as if someone being able to do things others can't is something you see often. I mean, I'm glad you treat me no different, now that you know I have the gift, than you did earlier this evening. Thank you for that. But will you tell me? Why is it normal to you? Is there a mage in your family?"

It was Marnell's turn to talk. Zalana listened. She found herself crying as he told her in a quivering voice of the night his sister was burnt. She was amazed to hear of the miracle given to her, the spring, and of her becoming a shaman, a sister of faith. She asked questions when appropriate. She didn't judge him or his family for leaving without paying their taxes.

He stopped talking. They sat for a while, and he said, "I have to tell you something. I know we only met today, but I want you to know something about me."

"What is it?" Zalana asked.

"I...my family," Marnell said, "we are of the blood. That's why I'm a large man. Why Teel is the size of a grown man at the age of twelve. I'm part Orc."

There was silence between them as Zalana processed what she heard. She'd known of them, though she'd never seen one. All she had to go by was the stories she'd heard as a child, and what she'd learned from Master Stonepolisher over the last few weeks.

What he told her changed everything she'd thought she ever knew of Orcs. It was confirmed when she asked around the town, and she believed them. After all, this barony was the closest to Or-canth. They would know. No one had bad things to say of them, other than they'd never actually seen one. Only the elderly had.

Zalana asked, "Can I see your tusks?"

Shocked, Marnell looked at her in the dim light. She covered her mouth and started giggling. Finally she burst out laughing. He couldn't help himself. He laughed with her. On this night, it was the most either had laughed since they were children.

She smacked his arm with the back of her hand and said, "The Creator made us all. So, some are bigger than others. It's not like you're part Elf, you know."

"That's true," Marnell agreed as he settled back against the wagon wheel, aware of her closeness.

"Besides, if I had tusks, you would've seen them," Marnell said, "when I tried to chew those beans. Leather. I think they were leather beans."

When they stopped laughing again, she smacked his arm once more.

They sat there, each wondering where this might go, both more comfortable with each other than they had ever been with any other. Zalana wanted the night to last forever as she leaned against him slightly, feeling the warmth of him.

Softly, she whispered, "I have to tell you something about me."

* * * * *

Chapter Sixteen

Over the next few months, Zalana and Marnell grew closer. Her farm was a short ride from his family's, and he found himself there most evenings. The two of them learned to cook together, using his mother and sister's recipes. Zalana enjoyed his company. Neighbors came by often, sharing vegetables with her, and giving her pointers on her own growing garden. No one spoke ill of the woman, obviously pregnant with no husband.

One evening, in the quiet of the early night, they stood near the creek. The sound was soothing as she held his upper arm and leaned against him. He'd spent the afternoon and part of the evening finishing a three-sided shelter for her goats. Twice she'd cast a spell providing light so he could finish. It was nearing the time he left to ride back to his family's farm. She still had no idea where it was all going, but she was glad he was a part of her life.

"I want to ask you something," Marnell said.

He eased behind her and hugged her, his arms crossed above her stomach; she leaned her head back against his chest. They'd progressed to hugs in the evenings, and she didn't mind them at all. His hand strayed to her growing stomach. It was the first time he'd done this. She waited to hear what he would say.

"Will you be my wife?" he asked.

Zalana was at a loss for words. She knew she loved him, knew it the first night they traveled together. She'd thought he felt the same, but hadn't expect this question from him.

"I want nothing more," she answered, "but…" She placed her hand over his, mentioning it without saying it.

"I would marry you both," Marnell said. "Both."

Her tears fell. "Yes," she said. "Yes. I will be your wife."

Marnell turned her around slowly and looked into her eyes. He reached up and wiped away a tear with his thumb. "One thing, though. I won't lie to our son or daughter. I won't say who the father is, for that's not my place. But I think they should know the truth about why they aren't of the blood. I'll do everything in my power to let the child know I love him or her, and I chose them when I chose you to spend my life with."

"Love is all any child asks for," Zalana said as she held him tight.

* * *

Zalana went into labor before Katheen did, so Katheen was there with the shaman to help in the delivery. Marnell paced outside their home with his father, his sister's husband Lur, and his younger brother.

Teel had been the one to run the trails to the Red Fist village and retrieve the shaman. After four hours of running today, he didn't appear tired as he sat shaping an arrow shaft, not bothered in the least about what was happening.

The shaman had insisted someone let her know when the human sister of magic went into labor. As the mate of a member of the tribe, it was her duty to deliver the child, but even if Zalana hadn't been part of it, she would have come. Over the last few months, the shaman had visited for a few days at a time as Zalana taught her two more simple spells. All the shamans with the gift would benefit from them, eventually.

The only spells known by the few Orcs with the gift were simple ones. They were memorized, not written in a spell book. Zalana knew quite a few they didn't, and she didn't have to reference them, so she understood this technique of learning, but it limited how complex the spell could be.

She came to the realization after long talks with the shaman that even if she could memorize more complex spells and learn to push the right amount of energy in them, they might not be effective. It was as if Orcs only had the gift at the level of those with tan robes. In their talks, she learned how the few with the gift were kept from being burnt. She shivered at the thought.

* * *

10 years later

Garvant looked down at his ring and noticed it glowing softly red. He called out to the others. They dismounted their horses and walked over to him, all of them nervous.

"The ring glows," Garvant said. "You know what this means."

"Great," one of the men said, "he wants us back now. There goes the coin I spent on a horse again."

"Shut up about your horse," Garvant said. "I don't care about your horse. If he's angry about something, he could kill us, or worse. Worry about that, why don't you?"

"Maybe it's a real lead," one suggested. "Saints know we need one. We spent four years covering every estate, village, and rathole in Yaylok looking for her."

"And we're not having any luck here in Minth, except for an old man who sold a beautiful woman from Gar-Noth blankets years ago," Garvant said. "The last time we used the ring he gave us was when we got the lead here in Minth. Still, he half-killed the lot of us throwing us against the wall, so don't say anything. Let me do the talking."

Garvant took the ring off and put it on flat rock. He pulled a dagger out, turned it around, and smashed the stone with the hilt. The red glow grew to become a six-foot doorway. They could see into the room.

It was the lord mage's study. He stood there with his arms folded. He didn't look a day older than when Garvant was hired by him all those years ago.

"My lord," Garvant said.

"She's been found," the lord mage said. "Go to the Baronies West. Look for her in the Arnwald Barony."

"My lord," Garvant said, "the Baronies don't smile upon sellswords. We'd stand out."

The lord mage stepped closer to the doorway. "Clean yourselves up, you idiot. Do I have to tell you everything?"

"No, my lord," Garvant answered quickly.

Garvant stepped toward the doorway. The lord mage yelled, "Stop! I swear I'm surrounded by idiots. Don't come through. Stay there; you're closer to the Baronies.

"To be honest, I'd nearly forgotten about you until word of the necklace and swan pendant reached me. Her own father relayed the information of its sale by a traveling Gnome dealer. It seems a rival bought it to spite him. It astounds me what some people will do to try to gain favor and power. Anyway, that's irrelevant."

The lord mage threw something through the open doorway and said, "Find her and kill her. I don't need the distraction. Things are moving as planned. Slowly, but as planned."

The glowing red edges of the doorway slowly shrank until the opening blinked out of existence. Garvant bent down and picked up the broken ring. The stone was shattered, but the gold still held value. One of his men handed him the leather purse the lord mage had thrown.

He opened it. It was full of coins and another ring. Garvant slipped the ring on his finger and handed a few of the Minth coins to each of his men. It would tide them over nicely as they traveled. He saved the coins stamped with the symbol of the Baronies for later.

"I'm glad she wasn't in the Mountain Kingdom," one of them said. "I don't mind the Dwarves so much, but I hate tunnels."

The first man patted his horse on the neck and said, "At least this time we didn't have to go through and leave perfectly good horses behind like we did in Yaylok."

"True," another said as he mounted, "but did he actually say something about another man doing anything to gain power?"

"Shut up," Garvant said as he glanced at his ring to ensure it wasn't glowing. "You trying to get us killed?"

* * *

"My feet hurt," the man said.

"For the hundredth time, shut up," Garvant said.

They'd been walking for hours along the edge of the trees. This was the third farm they would check before they camped for the night. They would soon be close to the village. They had no idea whether they were in or out of Orcanth.

They'd taken a risk the day before, unsaddling their horses and turning them out near a herd they'd come across. The horses were descendants of those from the villages destroyed long ago, but the men had no way of knowing this. If anyone got close enough to the herd, perhaps the differences in their horses would have been noticed. As skittish as the horses were, Garvant doubted it would happen. The men buried their saddles and covered the dirt with leaves.

"All I am saying is, I lost another perfectly good horse," the man complained. "She'll probably get eaten by a big cat or wolves or something."

"Your horse is free, be happy for her," another of the men said.

"A saddle, too…" the man murmured.

"Shut up!" several said in unison.

They crawled to the edge of the trees and watched the house and barn. A big man came out of the barn and walked toward the cabin. Garvant put a hand on the hilt of his sword as he watched. He adjusted the crossbow strapped across his back. The man was too far away to be a threat, but he was a big man.

They continued to wait and watch. Their patience was rewarded when a woman came out of the cabin. She had long dark hair, but even at this distance, Garvant knew it was her. He had no doubt.

"It's her," Garvant hissed. "Finally this will be over. Ready yourselves."

"Until he sends us out on another wild swan chase," lamented the man with sore feet. "What's the plan?"

"We kill them both," Garvant said, as if the answer was plain as day. "We watch and see what they do, and we'll know if it's to be with sword or arrow."

"They're coming this way!" one said.

Zalana held on to Marnell's arm as they walked down to the creek. It was still their favorite spot. "Do you think it'll be two or three cows?" she asked.

"I don't know," Marnell answered. "Two for sure, maybe a third."

"I hope—" Zalana started to say.

She never finished the sentence. One of the two bolts in her chest pierced her heart, killing her. Marnell never knew what she might have been saying. One bolt hit him the throat. The other buried in his eye. The two of them…were no more.

The men dragged the bodies to the cabin. When Garvant was reaching for the latch of the door, it opened. He was startled to see a dark-haired young girl about ten years old. She looked at him, her blue eyes wide in shock. When she saw her parents laying there, she screamed.

She ran by Garvant as he tried to grab her. She didn't keep running; instead she threw herself down on her parents, screaming at them to get up, shaking her mother. Getting no reaction, she fell on her father, crying. Garvant looked at his men, stomped over, and grabbed her by the back of her clothes. They had a job to do, and he wasn't waiting to do it. He reached for his dagger with his other hand.

He snatched her up, dragging her backward toward the open door. She turned on him, and the dagger in her hand flashed silver as it caught the lantern light from inside the cabin. It sliced his face to the bone. Pain exploded, and one eye was blinded by the blood pouring from his brow. He struck out in a rage. His own dagger flashed, once, twice, three times.

Inside, one of the men grabbed a cloth from the table and held it tight against Garvant's face. He hissed in pain. "Put them in the beds. Get the bolts."

"You want these two in the same bed?" asked one of them. He indicated the bolt-filled bodies.

"Yeah," one of the others said, "the last thing we want is Narvok looking for us. If he sends those Tarlok hunters after us, they'll hit us like we did these two. We'll never see it coming."

He continued as he struggled to pull the bolt lodged in the skull, "She's a mage who left the Halls. Just ran off. Everybody who knows will suspect the lord mage. It's not like he hides that we took care of a few of the ones who did that in Gar-Noth."

"He's right," Garvant said. "You know what we found out about this place in the Arnwald Barony. Lord Narvok is a half-breed or whatever. A damned Orc. We don't need a tribe of savages hunting us down, either."

"Nobody is going to let Orcs pass," the first said. He looked around at the others for confirmation. "Will they?"

Garvant took his ring off. He put it on the wooden floor. Unable to see with one of his eyes, it took him two tries to smash the stone. The doorway appeared. The lord mage looked up from his desk, the top covered in pieces of parchment. He stood up and walked around his desk.

"Well?" the lord mage asked. "Is it done?"

Garvant stepped in front of the doorway. "It is, my lord," he answered.

"What happened to you?" demanded the lord mage.

Garvant moved the blood-soaked cloth and showed him. "You'll live," the lord mage said. "Show me her face." Two of the men carried her over in front of the doorway. "That's her." There was satisfaction in his tone.

"There was a child, my lord, of the right age," Garvant said, the cloth back on his face. "Do you wish to see her?"

"No," answered the lord mage. He waved a hand as if waving a bug away. "Pour what's left of the lantern oil around the room and step through."

The men dragged the body back to the bed. Garvant tossed the dagger on the table. They emptied two unlit lanterns over them, the girl, and on the floor and walls. After they finished, one of the men hung an empty lantern on a hook stuck high in a log. He reached up and jerked the lantern until it pulled the hook out. He dropped them against the wall.

They stepped through into the Halls of Magic. Before the doorway closed, the lord mage held up his hands, spoke words of power, and flames leapt from his hands into the cabin.

* * *

The next day around midmorning, two boys each led a large horned cow out of the forest on the trail to Three Oaks. They were surprised to see one of their mothers sitting on a rock near the creek waiting for them. What was even more surprising to them was when she grabbed the smaller of the two and held him tight. She whispered something in his ear.

He tried to push away, tried to deny it. He looked off in the distance and could see the smoke still rising in a thin stream. He buried his head in his aunt's shoulder and cried uncontrollably.

* * *

The scene faded into the swirling grey mists. Lan stood, her head down. This was the scene she'd dreaded showing the most. The truth of what had happened that night.

Kryder stood in shock, tears streaming. His body trembled as the rage built.

"Murdered," Kryder said through clenched teeth. "My parents. My sister Trenlis. They were murdered."

"I am sorry," Lan said, finally looking up. There was remorse in her eyes. "You had to know the truth. You had to see."

"Everyone thought they died from the fire and smoke that night," Kryder said. His voice was shaking. "I was told I couldn't see the bodies. They were burnt beyond recognition. All these years, I never knew. I never knew my sister had used this dagger to fight back." His hand slipped to his side and rested on the hilt of his smaller dagger. "She was only ten," he whispered.

He continued, his voice above a whisper now, "My mama had the ability to fight them, but never had a chance."

"No lad," Lucas said, "she never had a chance. And I'm to be betting your father would've gone through them as well if he could've reached them."

"I'll kill them," Kryder vowed, "and I'll find the lord mage and kill him, too. Take us back to the inn. Now."

Tog looked over at his cousin, his eyes glistening. He clinched a massive fist, its knuckles whitening. "We had them. We had them in our hands."

"Who?" Kryder demanded. "Those men?"

Then it dawned on him. The scar. Four men. It had been the same four, only they were older now. Those men were part of one of the mercenary companies looking to earn coin in the upcoming war, a company with a bad reputation. Kryder planned on ensuring they never earned a copper.

Kryder and Tog were in Yaylok because the kingdom was on the verge of war with Gar-Noth. For the last year they'd been part of Baron Arnwald's troops. The Baronies were prepping to defend themselves, should King Westell and his ally the lord mage succeed in their attempt to take this kingdom. The two had volunteered to travel to Yaylok so they could come back with first-hand reports.

If they were successful, the invaders would move their armies north through the forests of Tarlok to attack the Baronies, or they would pull back and go above to the kingdom of Minth to defeat it. King Westell had his eyes on all of Kerr. It was only a matter of time.

"I can't," Lan said. "There is more I must show you."

Once again they found themselves in another time and place.

* * * * *

Chapter Seventeen

Kryder was exhausted. He'd been running all morning. He sat against a tree trunk, his knees up with his arms around them. His head down, he stared through to the ground. Looking over, he glanced at the wooden bowl beside him. He didn't want to think about eating the mixture of dried fruit, nuts, and dried meat. He wasn't sure what the meat was. It could be deer, or it could be goat. It didn't matter. He was too tired to eat.

For the last three days, he'd run four hours in the morning and four in the evening. It wasn't the pace causing it. He doubted they'd covered half the distance Orc warriors could over open terrain as they ran through the trails in the forests of Orcanth. It was the relentless movement. Nonstop, one foot after another, following the shaman as she ran ahead of him.

He looked over at the warriors of the Red Fist tribe making the journey with him. They laughed and joked with one another as if it was a normal day. Kryder went back to staring at the ground. *What am I doing?* he asked himself for the hundredth time. There were hot spots on his feet. He thought about what had led him to this point.

Two weeks ago, he lay in bed with a fever, his Aunt Katheen hovering over him with a cold cloth, wiping his face and forehead. When it happened again a week later, she sent his Uncle Teel the next morning to let the tribe's shaman know her suspicions.

Teel returned after noontime with the shaman. She stayed in Three Oaks, waiting. When his fever happened again, she felt his head, asked him some questions, and nodded, her mind made up.

197

The next morning, they started running. The closest patrol peeled off from their duty and escorted them.

Since they'd started, warriors had led them down the trails, their long strides eating up the distance. Kryder didn't ask where they went. He concentrated on keeping up with the shaman. At fourteen years old, Kryder was in exceptional shape…for a human. He ran often with Tog through the forest. He suspected the old shaman had slowed even her normal pace for him, which made him push himself harder.

The fourth day, they were met by two more shamans at the base of a mountain rising up out of the forest, with its top in the clouds. One of them, from the Fang tribe, he had met before. The other he didn't know. She looked him over and told him to remove his boots. He understood most of it. Like all shamans, she spoke the human language, but she also knew Kryder was learning Orcish.

She checked his feet over, took note of the blisters forming, and reached for the small leather bag she carried. She rubbed a reddish-colored powder on them and prayed in Orcish. Whatever deity she asked, answered. Kryder saw a soft blue glow; the powder faded, and so did his blisters.

Later in the evening as they waited for others, Kryder saw his shaman cast a spell other than a prayer spell for the first time. She used magic. Once the mix of leaves and small sticks were stacked, she didn't take out the stone and steel Kryder was used to seeing start the fire. She didn't loosen a bow string or wrap a stick and use it to spin on a piece of wood. She didn't use any of the different methods he knew to start a fire.

She held her hands close and spoke in a language he first remembered hearing his mother use years ago. Sparks flew from her fingers, and several started the tinder burning. As he watched the fire build when additional wood was added, his mind wandered five years back.

He and his sister used to delight in convincing Mama to blow out the lanterns and cast a light spell. The three spheres would light their entire home. Every now and then they could talk her into making one of the goats or a chicken slow down.

It was mage-speak. He knew the language. He spoke it. He could write it. From a very young age, his mother had them practicing the letters and words in the ancient language. "Just in case," she'd tell them. "Just in case." It was expensive, but she made sure to purchase parchment and ink whenever someone made the trip to the barony. Kryder never asked where the bag of coins she used came from.

Seemingly on its own, his hand reached to his belt and the bag tied to it, holding a small book wrapped in a piece of sheepskin. As he shifted it to make himself more comfortable, he thought of its contents.

It was his mama's book of spells. He could read it. He could say the words, pronouncing them as his mama had taught him. Nothing happened when he did it, though. After she and the rest of his family were gone, he continued to practice, for her sake. Just in case. He couldn't make the lights appear, or cause the ring he now wore to slow the goat or chickens, but he tried it anyway.

Tog walked over and sat down beside him. "Are you alright?" he asked.

"Yeah," Kryder said, "I'll live, I think. It doesn't help when I get a fever every night now. How do you do this?"

"What?" Tog asked. "Run? I just do it. I've always done it. All warriors run. Going back and forth between Three Oaks and Red Fist Village, I ran. My Uncle Tro made me run as soon as I could walk. I run with my papa, though he doesn't run like the warriors. You know he couldn't run at all when he was young."

"Yeah," Kryder said. "His leg was healed. It's a nasty scar."

"They let me go on patrols now," Tog said. "If I couldn't keep up, they'd leave me. It's bad enough they wallop me with blunt axes all the time. Can you imagine being left a half day away? No thanks, I run."

"They wallop you because you're too slow," Kryder teased. "You don't get the handle up in time to block the blow."

"Whatever!" Tog laughed. "You can't lecture me on being slow. We've been running at an old woman's pace, just for you. Besides, I'm getting faster. I hit Uncle Tro with a solid blow the other day."

"You did?" Kryder asked leaning forward. "You got past his guard! I wish I was there to see it. That's great!"

"The chief saw it." Tog grinned. "You're right, it was great."

"How's he doing?" Kryder asked. "I mean, you know."

"He says he's ready," Tog said. "He says my father's father is ready to be chief, and he's ready to meet the gods."

"The shamans can't do anything?" Kryder asked, his voice lower so the shamans wouldn't hear him.

Tog shrugged. "They asked. He still grows sicker. The gods heal as they see fit. Changes come."

One of the shamans looked over and said, "He has lived a long life; the gods save their healing for others."

"She heard me," Kryder whispered. "Goat droppings!"

Tog laughed. "When Sar becomes chief, that means I can proclaim members of the tribe or allies. If you weren't already accepted, I'd claim you."

"Thanks," Kryder said, "but Uncle Lur did that long ago. Did you realize, I'm the only member of the entire Orc nation with no trace of Orc blood? I mean, besides our Nana, but she's a tribe member's mate, so it doesn't count."

"Yeah," Tog said. "I remember them talking about it. The council of tribes debated it for days. The chief of the Running Boars was against it. It took trade deals to make it unanimous."

"So what are we waiting for, anyway?" Tog asked. He looked over at the three shamans.

"From what they told me, it takes at least five of them," Kryder said. "I think that's where the warriors went. To other tribes to get their shamans."

"What will they do when they get here?"

"I have no idea," Kryder answered. "They didn't say. Keep me from being burnt somehow. I don't know."

"You're going to be alright, aren't you?" Tog asked. He was serious now.

"I hope so," Kryder said. "No, that's not right. I will be. Aunt Katheen says there are no burnt Orcs. She said very few ever show signs of the gift, but every one who does becomes a shaman. That couldn't happen unless they were successful. Either way, I'm glad you came with me."

"I'd like to see someone try and stop me." Tog grinned. "Besides, there was no way I could wait back at Three Oaks to see what happened to you. I mean…I've seen the baron's stable boy. He's a nice man, and the horses love him, but he's not all there. I'd be so nervous I couldn't eat."

"The day you can't eat is the day the Creator ends all of Kerr," Kryder said.

Tog shrugged. He couldn't deny it. "Speaking of that, I hope we eat more than the patrol's food. I'm tired of nuts and berries."

The next morning, three more shamans arrived. The group began the trip up the mountain. They followed a worn trail, sometimes descending in order to get around a rock cliff or deep chasm. Kryder was glad they were no longer running. Two hours into the climb, they came across a mountain stream. They followed it.

After a half-day's climb, they came to its source. A cave loomed before them, the stream running from it now narrow enough to jump, though that wasn't necessary because it was less than knee deep.

Inside the cave, a pile of furs rested on a rock ledge. Each of the shamans draped one over their shoulders, the ends dragging. All of them came from great bears. One was handed to Kryder.

"Carry this," he said. "You will not need it until after."

Tog reached over and clasped his cousin's forearm. "I can't go any farther," he said. "I have to stay outside with the warriors. Only shamans or those who'll become shamans can enter."

"Yeah," Kryder said, "that's what they told me. Did you notice all the shamans are brothers and sisters of magic? Some are both of magic and of faith, but none are only faith."

"I didn't notice," Tog admitted, "maybe that's why Mama didn't come. Well, that and she'd never be able to keep up. She wouldn't have had a prayer."

Kryder looked down and shook his head. Leave it to Tog to joke when things were getting serious. He turned to follow the shamans, stepping into the stream. He turned back to look at Tog.

"This water is cold," he said, "freezing cold. You don't think…?"

Tog raised his eyebrows and said, "Better you than me. I'll be out here in the sunshine. I might even take a nap."

"Thanks a lot," Kryder said.

Kryder followed the shamans into the cave. The light shining from behind them grew dimmer. One of them cast a light spell. A single globe of light lit the inside of the cave. Kryder could see the cave continued on beyond the circle of light.

Another rock shelf held two metal boxes. A shaman opened one and handed candles to the others. The other box held five stones. Each of them took one.

A shaman Kryder didn't know cast a spell and touched his finger to the candle he held. He used it to light the others. They continued deeper into the cave. The stream followed one wall, allowing them to walk alongside it. Kryder was relieved they were no longer walking in the stream. His boots were soaked, and he was getting cold. He debated throwing the fur around his shoulders like the others.

The sound of a waterfall came from up ahead, and when they rounded a bend, the source of the sound came into sight. A small waterfall fell from the darkness above. It wasn't very big, but it sounded as if it were, as the noise echoed in the dark. The water landed in a small pool and flowed from there.

The shamans sat down on one side of it. Four of the candles were blown out. Kryder sat with them and waited. It didn't take long before the fever came on again. He lay down, using the fur for a pillow.

They checked on him every few minutes. Time passed slowly, as outside, the sun set. Finally the Red Fist shaman said, "It is time. Take off your shirt."

Kryder sat up, his face sweating despite the chill in the cave. "What? My shirt? I'll freeze."

"Yes," she answered, "everything but your britches. Remove your ring. And yes, you will very nearly freeze."

Reluctantly Kryder did as she asked. They lit the other candles and placed them around the pool while he did so. He was starting to realize what was expected of him. *This is going to hurt*, he thought. He felt himself getting hotter even with only his britches on.

She made him lie in the pool of water. The cold caused shooting pain as he lay in it. It was deep enough that it covered his entire body. He shifted, trying to get comfortable. He had to hold his head up to keep his face above water. One of them handed him his shirt. He balled it up and put it under his head.

Kryder's hands and feet went numb, and his teeth chattered uncontrollably. He struggled to sit up but was pushed back down. The last thing he heard was the beginning of another spell.

The shamans knelt beside the pool on each side of Kryder's head. Each reached a hand out, placing it on his head or face. They held a stone in the other hand away from them. One after another, the shamans spoke words of power. The stones glowed red and began emitting sparks.

The five of them stayed in that position for nearly an hour. One by one the stones stopped throwing sparks. When the last was finished, they removed their hands, and the glowing stones faded. Moving quickly, they pulled Kryder from the water. They wrapped him in his fur, and four of them carried him away from the pool, guided by the other shaman holding a candle high. In his other hand were Kryder's belongings.

Once the group was out of the cave, they put two of the robes down between the cliff face and the large fire they'd instructed the warriors to build when they entered the cave. They placed Kryder on them and covered him with the remaining furs. More wood was placed on the fire, and the warriors moved away into the dark.

An hour later, Kryder was gently shaken awake. The shaman sat him up and handed him warm stew. He sipped from the bowl. The feeling was back in his hands and feet. As he sat there, he started to feel normal, except for the pressure.

The Red Fist shaman sat beside him. The others gathered around. "What do you feel?" she asked.

Kryder said, "I feel...I feel a pressure inside."

"It is the gift," the shaman said. She touched her chest. "We all feel it. It is greatest in the beginning. In time, you will not notice it."

Kryder said, "I don't feel it only in my chest or my head. It's like my whole body is trying to release it."

She glanced at the other shamans gathered around and continued, "It is tradition to train a young shaman. Teach them the spells so they may use the gift fully. Our sister of faith in Three Oaks says you know spells."

"I do," Kryder said. "At least, I think I do. I can read magespeak. I can write it. I hope I pronounce the words right; it's been years since I was taught. From listening to you cast your spells, I think I do, but they've never worked for me before."

She nodded. "You have your mother's written spells, do you not?"

"I do," Kryder answered. "When…when my home burned, it was wrapped and deep in a chest below winter furs. The wall it was against didn't burn completely."

"Do you remember any of them?" she asked. "Or do you need to read them?"

"I remember the light spell," Kryder said. "It was my sister's favorite. She loved it when Mama cast it for us."

"Yes," she said, "that one will do. Speak the words."

Kryder set the bowl to the side and pushed the furs off his shoulders. He held his hand up and spoke the words he'd memorized years ago. They rolled off his tongue as if he'd been speaking them for years. In reality, he had. He'd been trying to cast the spell for more than four years. Above them, eight spheres of light lit the night sky.

The shamans all looked up at the lights. In silence, they gave each other a knowing look. The Red Fist shaman said, "Kryder Narvok, brother of magic, I would tell you my name."

The others did the same.

* * * * *

Chapter Eighteen

They were back in the Inn. Kryder blinked several times and looked around. Nothing had changed, except the room was a little cooler. Lucas stood up, walked over, and added two logs to the coals. Tog picked up one of the cold taters in front of him and took a bite.

"I know you told me they put you in the water," Tog said around his mouthful, "but the way your teeth were chattering, you didn't do the story justice. That looked painful."

"Yeah, it was. I had no idea what they did after the sleep spell," Kryder said. "I wonder how those stones were enchanted. From what we learned, it takes a binding spell from a scroll to make an item."

"They've been on Kerr since time began," Lan said. "As have others. There was a time when transfer stones were in every kingdom."

The deity looked at each of them and said, "The lord mage and others have managed to consolidate the other stones on this world. They have perverted the gift given by our Creator. In the beginning, the gift was given to those designated as protectors. The bloodlines have dispersed over time. Now the attempt is being made to consolidate them again. Now that you know, what you do with this knowledge is up to you."

"Whoa," Tog said, "what do you mean up to us? You're the goddess of time. You just did the impossible. Can't you smite them?" He slammed the side of his fist in his palm and twisted it. "Make them two hundred years old instantly or something?"

"I cannot," Lan said. "It is forbidden, lest the balance shift. All thinking mortals have been given free will. We cannot interfere. I showed you what happened. I did not alter the events tonight, nor when they happened."

"But we saw Tog's mama saved," Kryder countered. "Mine managed to cross all of Kerr by herself. I'd say you or another god was involved."

"All the decisions were made by mortals," said Lan. "The decision to send Marnell for brother Pynon was made by your grandfather. The very spells Pynon prayed for were answered when he asked for help. Not before. We did not interfere. We must not. The only one who may do so is our Creator."

"Well," Kryder said, "the first thing I'm doing is finding the four who murdered my family. Then we can decide what to do."

"Aye, lad," Lucas said. "I'd say they need a dose o' what they have coming to them, and I'm to be lending a hand."

"Then I say we make the journey to the Halls of Magic," Tog suggested.

"It will take planning," Kryder said. "We can't just come through the front gate demanding he face us. He's the most powerful mage in the world."

"Is he?" Lan asked. She tilted her head slightly, looking at Kryder in question.

"Yeah," Tog answered, "he's the lord mage. We..."

"Wait," Kryder said. He looked down at his ring. "My ring. I've never had real training. I have my mother's spell book, and I can cast the simple spells. The more difficult ones I've been hesitant to try.

But this ring, my mother's ring. The enchantment is the slowing spell."

He continued, "I never thought about it. But earlier tonight, I really pushed into it when I used it."

"You didn't only slow him, lad," Lucas said, realizing what he was saying, "you stopped him completely. And you *held* him."

"Eight," Tog said. "You always have eight of them."

"Eight what?" Kryder asked, confused at the change of subject.

"Eight balls of light," Tog said. "Aunt Zalana cast three. The shamans have one. Even Pelna could only cast three."

Kryder thought about it for a moment and realized something else Tog had said was important. "Pelna. We need to go to Minth. She can teach me to use the other spells. Maybe teach me new ones."

"It's been twenty years," Tog said. "Do you think she'll remember your mother?"

"We'll have to find out," Kryder said, "but first, we have to find those four. Something tells me they still work for the lord mage. If they do, the mercenary company isn't here to fight for Yaylok. They're here to infiltrate. Maybe murder the knight commander, or even the king."

Kryder turned to ask Lan a question. She was nowhere to be seen. The goddess of time was gone.

"That was rude," Tug said. He reached for another tater.

"Aye, lad," Lucas agreed, "but I'll not be the one to tell her."

* * *

Lan answered the summons as soon as she heard it. She looked around. She found herself in a hall she'd never seen before, never in all of time. One by one, all the deities appeared. Even ones forgotten centuries ago by mortals.

She looked over toward Minokath and started to ask him if he knew why they'd been summoned. It had never happened in the history of Kerr. His eyes widened, and she turned to see what had startled him.

On the other side of the hall, one by one, the demons of Kerr started appearing. It was obvious they'd been surprised by the same summons. From the way they were acting, they'd been taken from whatever pit of darkness they resided in. The lesser of them immediately began jeering at their counterparts. The larger ones stood silent, contemplating what might be transpiring.

Lan realized there was only one reason all the immortals had been called together. As soon as the thought came to her, she was proven right. The Creator was coming.

Every immortal in the great hall felt the presence solidify. The demons fell silent. Some cowered behind others. The deities on the other side of the hall all dropped to their knees, or the equivalent.

Some demons claim to the misguided mortals who follow them that there are none greater then they. They delight in leading them astray. As with all things, those demons lie. Here, now, they feared for their very existence.

A voice rang out in a language understood by all. *"Since the time of this creation, you have been entrusted with it. Each assigned a place. One among you has chosen to do other. One of you has tilted the balance so those who worship you will dominate this world. I watched, and I waited to see if you would chose to remember your place. Free will is a gift given to you and to the mortals of this world. Your place is according to my plan. The free will of thinking mortals are of my plan.*

"The balance between good and evil shifts slightly, according to the decisions by the mortals, as was foreseen. There will come a time when their decisions will determine their fate. Only I know the time. The balance has been offset.

"One of you has enacted your own plan for this world. You have enabled some mortals to live well beyond their design. This is not your place. In denying your place, you deny your Creator."

Across the hall, Lan saw a large demon suddenly stand and arch in pain. Its body immobile, it was lifted into the air and brought to the center of the great hall. All eyes were now on the Creator and the demon floating in the center of the vast room.

"Lethrall. In you, I am displeased. You are no more."

The huge demon folded in on itself several times, growing smaller and smaller. Wadded like waste parchment, it continued shrinking, until the demon Lethrall was gone.

"The rest of you, see to my creation. Answer the prayers and requests of mortals as you will. Seek to influence as you will. Here, there will be good and evil, so the mortals may choose between the two."

The Creator's physical presence began to fade. Before it was gone, the voice rang out. *"I have put in place what is necessary to right the balance. It is now up to the mortals to do so. Even in this, I would have free will. Know your place."*

* * *

L an found herself back in the inn. She stumbled, startling the three men. They scrambled, caught her, and eased her into a chair, each man afraid to ask what would cause a deity to do this. They sat quietly until she was ready to speak.

"I have shown you all I am to show you," she said. She looked at each of them in turn. "Our Creator has deemed all is in place to right the balance. What happens from here is left to mortals."

"Wait. You mean us? By ourselves?" Tog asked.

"I think so," Kryder said. "She can't directly interfere. We have to get our hands on those stones. That has to be what this is all about."

"But you said we can't bust the gate down on the Halls of Magic, take on all the guards, and chop through every closed door to get to the lord mage." Tog said.

"I didn't quite say that," Kryder reminded him. "But no, we can't go through the front gate."

"I'm just planning ahead a little." Tog grinned at Lucas.

"If I were a few years younger, I'd go with ye," Lucas said. "That's to be the kind o' plan I like. Me boys now, the two o' them would be all for it."

"Yes!" Tog said. "How are they with an axe? Can they swing one?"

"An axe is not their first choice, to be sure," Lucas admitted, "but they both swing hammers down at the quarry most days before working the inn for me. I'm to be thinking they'll break a shield and the arm holding it."

"That could work," Tog said. He rubbed his chin. "I could show them a few blocking moves with the handle. It's similar to an axe in some ways. For defense, anyway. I wonder if we can get our hands on some with hardened handles. Maybe we can find war hammers with steel hafts."

"'Tis a good question," Lucas said. "The problem is, all the Dwarves here in town are to be merchants, not warriors or even blacksmiths. To get our hands on quality war hammers, we'd need to go to the Mountain Kingdom."

"Yeah," Tog agreed, "that's true. Unless the merchant's guards are Dwarves. They may sell us some."

"Well now," Lucas said, "there's a thought."

"Whoa," Kryder said. "Slow down, you two. First things first. There's the matter of the four men who murdered my family."

"We're only planning ahead, lad," Lucas said. "You can be sure your cousin and I haven't forgotten what we saw tonight. I'm to be thinking those four get theirs on the morrow."

Tog slammed his fist into his palm. "Yes," he said, "tomorrow."

Kryder turned toward Lan. He wasn't quite sure what the deity would think about their plans to kill the four men, even if it was justified. She was staring of into the distance, her eyes focused somewhere else.

She turned to him and said, "Those who commit foul deeds do so knowing full well they may pay for them one day. What you decide is not for me to judge, Kryder Narvok. I must go. There are prayers I must attend to."

She stood and paused, once again staring off. She looked down at the three of them seated around the table. Finally, her mind made up, she said, "The stones may be the least of your worries. I wish the three of you well. May your choices be wise. The balance of Kerr may very well depend on them."

The goddess of time slowly raised her hood and disappeared.

"What did she mean by that?" Kryder asked.

"I don't know," Tog answered, "but I don't like it." He reached for the last tater. Kryder beat him to it.

* * *

The next morning, Lucas introduced his sons, Sethon and Marn. Both were large men. Not the size of Tog, but they towered over most. Marn was near their age, while Sethon was a year younger. He also introduced his daughter Julia. She shyly waived and hid behind her father.

Sethon said, "Papa says there's a handful of men what needs done for. Are we to beat them senseless, or...?" He let the sentence drag out.

"If they're to meet their maker early," Marn added, "I'm afraid you're to be telling me why first. We'll have no part o' murder."

Lucas explained to Kryder and Tog, "I didn't tell them why, lads. I thought it best to leave that to you."

Tog looked at Kryder and nodded. Kryder described the four men, reminding them it was the ones they'd thrown out into the street. He explained they hadn't know it was them, or it would already have been taken care of. Slowly at first, the pain still fresh, he told them of the night his family was taken from him.

"Aye," Marn said, "that'll do."

"We're to be on our way right now, then," Sethon agreed. He started for the door as he punched his fist into his palm, over and over.

"Wait," Kryder said, stopping them. "We need a plan. They're part of the Razors. We're going to have to figure out how to separate them, or risk fighting the whole company of mercenaries."

"And the king's forces too, if they're to be contracted already," Lucas added.

"Yeah," Tog said, "we need a plan. The only way to get near them is to catch them out one night like they came here."

"I don't think they'll be going out any time soon. Not here, any-way." Kryder said. "It seems like forever, but it was only last night they were thrown out."

"It was, wasn't it," Tog agreed. "That means they know our fac-es, so we won't ease up on them like a couple of Tarlok hunters. There has to be a way to get someone near them. Someone in the company with them."

Lucas laughed. "Good luck finding anyone honest enough to help you out in their company. A group of outlaws, oathbreakers, and sell-swords they are. They aren't professional fighters like most companies."

"Maybe we can contact a local sneak-thief to join them and lure them away," Tog suggested. "Every town has a few."

"We don't have that kind of coin," Kryder reminded him. "We need someone to join the Razor's and lure them away."

Lucas, Kryder, and Tog looked at the brothers. Tog grinned and nodded. Kryder raised an eyebrow. Lucas crossed his arms, waiting.

"Fine," Marn said, throwing up his hands in disgust. "We're to be joining the worst mercenary company o' the lot o' them. Come on, Sethon. We're off to make a few coppers."

* * * * *

Chapter Nineteen

On the edge of town, several mercenary companies were camped between it and the king's castle. Marn and Sethon could see the different flags waving over the commanders' tents. The solders contracted to each had various shelters, ranging from small tents to lean-to type protection. One of the companies looked to be calvary only, judging by the amount of horses tied near their tents.

Closer to the castle was a small unit. Flying in the cold breeze was a black flag with a silver shaving blade on it. The blade dripped blood. It was the Razors' camp. There weren't as many tents around the commander's tent in this unit as there were around the others. They made their way to it, passing the rest on each side of the road.

Outside of the commander's tent was a small folding desk where a man sat, busy writing on a piece of parchment. He was dressed in hardened leather armor with strips of steel linked to it. He glanced up at them, then back down to his writing. He dipped the quill in ink again and wrote several more lines. He finished, picked up the parchment, and blew on it.

He put it on the desk, looked up and asked, "Are you looking to join the Razors?"

"We are," Marn said, "if the wages are right. We're not to be fighting for free, mind you."

"Ah," the man said, "a couple of locals. Why are you trying to join a mercenary company and not the king's forces, or even your local unit? With your size, it would be an easy decision for them."

Sethon answered, "Let's say, for conversation's sake mind ye, that we're from a town on the coast a half day's walk from here. We may or may not have cleared a tavern o' men one night after a wee bit o' drinking. Let's also say the locals are not too fond o' us, being as how the local sergeant o' the guard was included in the eight we left sleeping on the tavern floor."

Marn added, "Lost a tooth or three, that one. The local forces won't have us, and there's to be no recommendation to the king's own."

The man grinned. "As the captain of the Razors, if two men with that sort of problem were to come around, looking to join, I'd say they're the type of men for me. I'd offer a fair wage and throw in some leather and a weapon of choice from my armory. On loan, of course."

"Where do we make our mark, then?" Sethon asked as he stepped up to the table.

* * *

K ryder and Tog waited in the Hobbled Goat with Lucas for his sons to report on their attempt to join the mercenary company. It was getting late. They'd spent the evening at the bar counter itself, telling him more of their youth and of how their village of Three Oaks had grown from what he'd seen on the trip through time with Lan.

"Another village has started on the site of one of the ruins," Kryder said. "It has a good water source and plenty of farmland around it."

"A lot of good fruit comes from Waypoint," Tog added. "You'd be amazed how far the orchards spread after a hundred years of no upkeep. It was like a forest of apple and pear trees. Over the last few years, they've been able to keep them trimmed for the most part."

"More trips are made to the barony these days, I take it," Lucas said as he wiped the counter.

"Yes," Kryder answered. "It's coming up on thirty years since Jynal Narvok became the lord of the Western Boundaries. Some years a dozen families came, looking for a new life."

"Then there are the hunters," Tog reminded him. "They don't have their cabins close to each other like a village, but in their stretch of forests, there're at least thirty families. Probably more, now. Many with children. Zane and Penae's daughters aren't much older than we are."

"Those two!" Kryder laughed. "They make a game out of deer touching."

Lucas rubbed his chin. "It may be I've spent me time in a town most o' me life, but what would be deer touching?" he asked.

Tog tipped his mug, wiped his mouth with his sleeve, and put it down. He leaned closer to Lucas as if he was about to tell him something not to be believed. Which made no sense after the hours they'd spent with the goddess of time.

He said, "They trail a deer near midday, when most deer are on the ground sleeping, you see. They ease up on the deer and touch it without it knowing they're there until they do it."

"They do not," Lucas said in disbelief. "A deer would smell them if it didn't hear them, to be sure."

"It's true," Kryder said. "They circle around to keep the wind from blowing their scent toward the deer."

Tog slid his mug toward the innkeeper and said, "The stories you hear about Tarlok hunters, they're all true. Not only can they shoot a bow as accurately as an Orc, they shoot faster. I mean, they can't shoot an arrow as *far*, but's that's only because they can't draw a bow as stout as we can."

"You learn something every day," Lucas said as he slid the mug back over. "Tell me, lads, what o' the tribes? Do they all accept that humans border them again?"

"They do," Kryder answered. "All the tribes either trade with the Western Borderlands or through it to the Baronies. The ten tribes who make up the council and all the sub-tribes have come to accept it and realize humans respect the boundary. Only those of the blood or who are invited can cross it."

"Are there others besides your family o' the blood living in Three Oaks now?" Lucas asked.

"There are," Kryder said. "Several have come. One knew his tribe was the Fang. His great grandfather made the trip years ago and learned of it. The man was able to name the place where the tribe had raided. The names of members he'd met were passed down in their family. The shaman verified it from the etchings. The chief of Fang acknowledged him and his family."

"That's interesting, to be sure," Lucas said.

"Kryder may have stretched the truth about humans respecting the border," Tog said with a grin. "Boys will be boys. Some girls, too. They learn their lesson, though. When a young one sneaks across, the switch across the backside as they run back is a good teacher. They can't outrun it when a warrior is chasing them. "

Lucas threw his head back and laughed, causing several patrons to look over, wondering what might be so funny. He wiped his eyes. Kryder nodded in confirmation.

Lucas put his rag down, leaned on the bar, and looked at Tog. "Tog, when ye acknowledged me and said I was o' the Red Fist tribe…"

"Yes," Tog interrupted him, "I have the right to do so. Lucas Trant, you're a member of our tribe, and by that, so are your children."

"It has been spoken," Kryder said. "It is so. I'll inform the tribal council of new members of Red Fist."

Tog grinned. "I'm the son of the son of the chief." He nodded his head sideways. "He's one of our shamans. There can be no denial." He took a long drink from his mug, wiped his mouth, and looked satisfied. It was the first time he'd had a chance to do it.

Lucas reached across and clasped forearms with Tog. He did the same with Kryder. He wasn't sure what to say. He only wished his mother was there to hear it.

"Oh," Tog said, "I forgot to tell you one thing. We have a feud with the Running Boar tribe. Well, not a feud, really. Nobody's killing anybody, but we don't like each other. That's been going on since they were made to leave the border and Red Fist became one of the border tribes."

"Good to know," Lucas said as he raised his mug. "I'd hate to be drinking with the wrong sort one day. Never liked those Running Boars, anyway."

Tog spit out his sip of beer, laughing, causing Lucas to say, "Right. Now that I know yer in line to be me chief, I suppose I have to clean up after ye?" He wiped the counter, grinning.

Kryder said, "Tell him about the time we went with Uncle Teel into the canyons to hunt the great cat."

Tog leaned on the bar and said, "Four years ago, Uncle Teel decided we all needed to die."

Lucas looked at him in obvious disbelief. Tog continued, "No, I'm serious. He wanted to finally track and hunt one of the cats roaming the canyons. It wasn't smart, because one could have pounced on us at any time. Their fur is the color of the sand and cliffs, so if they lie in wait; you can't see them. It was dangerous."

"He told Tog he was going without him because he didn't want him hurt," Kryder explained, "so you *know* Tog demanded he be allowed. I was foolish enough to go with them."

"You know you were glad you went," Tog argued. "Anyway, so there we are, in a boxed-in gully south of the mining site. We learned from the miners which direction the cat was dragging the goats it killed."

Kryder added, "It had been causing problems for the mining camp. It was only a matter of time before it attacked a miner or someone traveling through, so Uncle Teel decided to do something about it."

"Yeah," agreed Tog, "you don't hunt what you can't eat unless there's no other choice. So after stalking it for hours, we cornered it, and Uncle Teel put it down. We were skinning the cat when we heard a sound I'll never forget."

"I'm with you," Kryder agreed. "At least twenty goblins came growling and screaming around the bend behind us. The sound was like something out of a nightmare. Now *we* were the ones boxed in."

"They were less than a bow shot away," Tog said. "Teel dropped his skinning blade and starting firing arrows. I shot two, then readied my axe. Kryder slipped to the side and threw fire into the first one charging. I can still smell it. Goblins smell bad enough because they don't bathe, but one burning is enough to make you lose your last meal.

"It caused them to back up and let Teel empty his quiver. Then he pulled four from mine, but there were still six left."

Kryder said, "Teel was killing most of them, and Tog wasn't having any of it. He charged into the group of them, slinging his axe. Limbs flew, heads flew, it was bad. He was cut in three places. They have these blades with serrated edges they never clean.

"Aunt Katheen had to treat the cuts for infection. It's a good thing she was able to do it with poultice and not prayer. I don't know if the gods would answer a prayer for someone so foolish."

"Goblins?" Lucas asked. "They came from their mountain lairs? I haven't heard o' that in years."

"They've been moving lately," Kryder answered. "We heard the Tarlok stopped some raiding down into the northern end of their kingdom's forests."

"If one were to believe the legends," Lucas said, "there's only one thing that would stir the lairs up enough for them to move down into human lands."

"Elves," Kryder answered, "but why would Elves hunt more goblins? They breed them as slaves already, or so they say."

"Who knows?" Tog said. "Nobody's actually seen an Elf in over a hundred years, probably longer."

"I saw a Half-Elf once, I think," Kryder said. "She was in town, in Arnwald's barony. She adjusted her cloak and was around the corner before I could get a good look."

"If ye saw one, she didn't want to be seen, to be sure," Lucas said. "If you think humans treat those o' the blood bad, ye don't know what Elves do to those who dare to be born Half-Elf."

"Do you really think they send out a team to hunt them down?' Tog asked. "Slipping around at night and all that. It seems like a story claiming that some escaped from Zar is just something to keep the young ones in their bed at night."

Lucas looked at Kryder and said, "Speaking of the Arnwald Barony," he said, "why are ye and Tog here on a mission for the Baronies? How did that come about?"

Kryder said, "Three years ago, Tog and I went to visit the baron's cousin, Lady Shynae. I wanted to see if she could help me with my mama's spellbook. I could read the more difficult ones, but wasn't sure if I was pronouncing some of the words right. She helped me a little with it. Some she didn't have enough of the gift to cast, but I learned to use a few more. While I was doing that, Tog spent some time with the Lord Narthon and the baron's archers, teaching them the best way to volley arrows with the bows they'd traded for. They weren't comfortable with the distance and angles."

"They now have our bows," Tog explained, "but the ones they get from us are for young Orcs and aren't as strong as mine. They can't draw one like mine. Only a few of the strongest can, but not for shot after shot. The bows are of better wood and stronger than any they make, so it was simple for me to show them the ranges they can now use."

Kryder continued, "We joined the baron's forces. Lord Narthon commanded a unit made of those from all the Baronies. As you know, the Baronies West are allied with Minth. We camped on the border of Minth and Gar-Noth, fighting a probing war. Mostly skirmishes, until they pulled back and turned their attention south, here in Yaylok."

"The Baronies were looking for someone to make the journey to learn firsthand what's happening. Things like whether there will be war, or will your king submit to the king of Gar-Noth, and either way, what're the intentions of the Gar-Noth forces. Will they go back through to finally take Minth, or will they come toward the Baronies, because everyone knows King Westell intends to rule all of Kerr."

Tog said, "Except for Zar. Even if you could get through the swamps, nobody's ruling over the…"

Right then the door flew open, and the breeze blew through the tavern. Sethon quickly pulled the door shut behind Marn before anyone could throw mugs. They hurried over to the bar. Both were wearing patched hardened leather and had hammers with four-foot handles strapped behind a shoulder.

"Elves," Sethon said in a whisper only they could hear. "Elves."

"How did you know what I was going to say?" Tog asked. He squinted his eyes at the brothers, looking a little sideways at them.

"What?" Sethon asked. "I'm to be having no idea as to what ye were saying before we came in."

"It's the Elves," Marn said. "We were across town at the Spitted Rabbit with some o' the ones in our company. They were celebrating our joining, only tradition held we were to be buying the drinks."

"A few cups o' spiced wine, and they were talking like they've known us for years," Sethon added. "The Razors aren't here to infiltrate. 'Tis a done deal between our king and the king of Gar-Noth. He's to become an archduke."

"Gar-Noth will rule us," Marn said. "The Razors escorted no less than fourteen mages from the Halls of Magic here."

"Was the lord mage with them?" Kryder asked, quickly getting off his stool.

"No," Sethon said. "Garvant, the man with the scar, said he's still back in the Halls preparing for something. The others are named Gelton, Rarvid, and Narve."

"What about the Elves?" Tog asked. "You said Elves."

Marn looked around the tavern to make sure no one was listening. He leaned in and said, "One of the men with Garvant was saying King Westell and the lord mage are allied with the Elves, so there'll be no stopping them. They'll rule all of Kerr, giving the Elves some of Yaylok in return. Garvant made him shut up before others heard. He told us to hold our tongue about it as well."

"This may be far more than Baron Arnwald and the others are concerned about," Kryder said.

Elves were the stuff of nightmares. The last time they'd come through the swamps separating them from the rest of Kerr was well over a hundred and fifty years ago. They were pushed back into their homeland by the combined armies of several kingdoms. Two of those kingdoms had been swallowed up by Gar-Noth since then. It would seem Yaylok was to follow them.

The stories passed down about the Elves were too consistent to be dismissed. Elves were slightly shorter than humans, slender, with dark hair. The most striking features were their pale skin and dark eyes. It was said their eyes were of such a dark brown color, it unnerved you.

In battle, they wielded a sword and a small shield with a knife attached to the top edge. It let them fight with two weapons and still provide protection for themselves. Most murals showed them in a type of chainmail over leather armor, the rings larger than those used by other kingdoms. Those same murals took care to show the Elves for the evil monsters they were, the expressions on their faces nearly demonic in delight at the bloodshed around them.

Their armies drove before them hordes of Goblins. The Goblins themselves were a force to be reckoned with. The creatures were a little over four feet in height, brandishing all different types of short blades. Some were hooked, some were serrated, while still others were made up of odd angles.

None were forged of the best of metals, but it didn't matter when facing one. If the blade of the one you were fighting broke, it didn't stop. It attacked with the broken pieces, claws, and teeth. Nor would it stop the others around it, for they attacked as a group.

They had a habit of looting the dead as they went, donning helmets that were too big, or upper pieces of armor that covered most of them. They took blades and other weapons from enemies and their own dead to use as they went, dropping weak or broken ones as the battle continued. They, like their masters, not only killed the enemy forces, they razed entire villages, killing the elderly, women, and children.

If the scenes on murals weren't enough to frighten those looking at them, others showed the Elves holding back huge wingless dragons in chains, keeping them from getting too far ahead of their forward lines. The beasts were depicted ripping men and horses apart. It was said their scales turned blades away.

The most famous dragon story told how three of them were finally killed by a company of Dwarves. Their picks—used in mining and battle—were able to penetrate, and their hammers dealt crushing blows to the flesh beneath the scales.

If one offered a round of drinks and sat with any of the local or traveling Dwarves, they were happy to tell the version their clans repeated. They all had a story. It seemed as if all of them claimed some kin to that particular company.

Kryder looked at Tog as realization came over him. Tog reached up and rubbed his chin. Kryder knew he was thinking the same thing. He had to be sure the brothers had heard what they thought they had.

"Did the man say anything else?" Kryder asked. "Are you absolutely sure he said Elves?"

"Oh, I'm to be sure," Marn said. "He was on about losing another horse if they had to step through. Then he said Elves probably ate horses, and even if they didn't, Goblins did."

Sethon added, "I've no idea why the man is obsessed about losing a horse. 'Another horse,' he said to me. At first I was sure he'd already been drinking. I asked what he meant, and that's when he told us o' the Elves."

Marn turned to his brother and said, "That he did. And what was all the 'stepping through' business?"

Kryder knew it had to be true. Sethon and Marn had no idea of the spell they'd seen used with the breaking of the stones on the enchanted rings. For them to mention the very ones who'd stepped through and hear one complain about losing another horse proved it beyond doubt.

Lan was right, the enchanted stones were the least of their concerns. The thing of nightmares, the stories told to bad children in an attempt to frighten them into behaving, was going to become real. Elves were coming.

* * * * *

Chapter Twenty

"What do we do?" Tog asked.

Kryder looked off, thinking. He turned and said, "We have to let Baron Arnwald know. If there isn't going to be war here in Yaylok, then Gar-Noth will go north into Minth. Once the king of Yaylok swears fealty to King Westell, Gar-Noth grows even bigger. Their armies combined will be bad enough, but if the Elves are coming out of Zar to join them, I don't know if they can be stopped by the combined armies of the Baronies and Minth, even if the Mountain Kingdom gets involved because of the Elves."

"One big pile of wild boar droppings is what this is turning out to be," Tog said, "and we're down here right in the middle of it." He shook his head, pursing his lips. The big man sighed. "I'm beginning to think seeing more of Kerr wasn't the best of ideas."

"Yeah," Kryder agreed, "staying in the Western Borderlands or deep in Orcanth sounds a lot better, now that we've left it."

"Aye, lad," Lucas said, "but there's a reason you're to be here now. Saint Lanaeth wouldna taken us where and when she did without reason, I'm to be thinking."

"Saint Lanaeth?" Sethon asked. "Just how much beer have you had tonight, Papa?"

"Not enough," Lucas said. "Not near enough."

"We'll have to explain later," Kryder said. "What we need to know now is the timing. When will it happen? When will the Elves come through the swamps?"

"You don't think they'll try and come traveling through days of swamps this time of year do you?" Tog asked. "It grows colder every day here. I mean, it's bad enough now."

"I hope not," Kryder said. "The last time they did, it was well into spring." He thought for a moment and said, "Unless they plan on coming without the Goblins. It's too cold for them, for sure."

"Aye, " Lucas agreed, "the goblin lairs are in those mountains full o' volcanos. Most o' them are quiet these days, but the fissures still run through them. They say a man starts sweating the deeper into those caves they go."

"Who would go into their lairs?" Tog asked. "Someone with a death wish?"

"There's always the ones, lad," Lucas said. "Them that looks to find looted treasure from centuries past. There's no telling what those creatures have hoarded up in those mountains. It's not as if they haven't sacked castles and whole towns before."

"You won't catch me going into those caves," Tog said. "I don't mind the heat, I've never even seen snow, but I don't need old coin and whatever else they have tucked away. Not if it means never coming back out into the sunlight again."

"I'm with you," Kryder agreed, "only don't tell Uncle Teel. He'd get a few of his Tarlok friends and Nok, and he'd try it."

"I could see Nok going with him," Tog said. Nok was his Orc cousin, the son of Tro. "He gets bored on patrols and always wants to trail any great bear tracks we come across. He goes into the den after them."

"Sounds like someone we'd like to drink a beer with," Marn said. His brother nodded in agreement.

"You two get back to the camp before they suspect something," Kryder said. "Take a few bottles of wine with you, if that's alright with you, Lucas."

"If I have it and ye need it, it's yours," Lucas said. "That's what kin does for one another."

"Kin?" Sethon asked. "How are we kin? Nobody ever tells us anything. After we take care o' the four what has it coming to them, somebody needs to explain some things, I'm to be thinking."

"What will we be needing the wine for?" Marn asked.

"You tell them you know the owner of this inn," Kryder suggested. "Let them know you drink for free here. If they say anything about the fight last night, tell them you'll come back and take care of the big one, and they can get revenge. See if you can talk them into it, and if they come, we'll get them to draw steel first."

"That we can do," Marn said. "They already think we're to be fond o' a good tavern brawl. We're to be wary o' their crossbows, though. We watched them hitting targets the size o' yer fist from twenty paces."

* * *

Sethon and Marn stood near their tent, each with a hard roll and bowl of mush. The Razors fed their men, but they were quickly learning it was nothing like the meals from their father's inn. They didn't complain; they took their wooden bowls and moved away from the cook fire and the wagons used by the camp followers.

234 | STEVERSON & ACKERMAN

It wasn't long before Garvant and the other three men made their way over. Three of them had a bowl and a roll. The other had managed to talk his way into getting three rolls. Marn raised an eyebrow in question.

"I can't eat another bowl of the swill," Narve explained. "I fill up on the bread. Maybe it'll help soak up some of the wine."

Garvant said, "Wine? You don't have any wine in you. If I recall, you emptied your gut several times last night."

"Maybe," Narve said, "but it can't hurt."

"It was good wine," Garvant said, "it's a pity you wasted so much. Where did you two get four bottles of good wine, anyway?"

"We're to be knowing the owner of The Hobbled Goat," Marn said.

"That place?" Garvant said. His eyes narrowed. "Wait, that is where I saw you two before?"

"We pick up a few coins there," Sethon said, "or get paid in drink. We break up fights, keep an eye on the server's sticky fingers, and the like."

Marn grinned and asked, "Was it ye four we dumped in the street the other night? Four men were taken down by only two." He shook his head. "Shameful, that was. Wouldna happened to us, I tell ye."

Garvant was offended. "What are you saying? We could have taken them if one hadn't used magic."

At hearing this, the brothers looked at each other. Sethon said, "Are ye sure o' that? It could have been the beer in ye. Now if yer to be looking for a little payback, well, we don't need the coin from there anymore. We can take care o' the big one while you four work the other over."

"We can call them out o' the place," Marn added. "Give ye room to work, so to speak."

Garvant scooped the last of his oatmeal mush onto his roll. He ate the piece, thinking as he chewed. He reached up and touched the ugly bruise on the side of his face. They could see by the look in his eyes, he wanted revenge.

"My memory of that night is a bit hazy," admitted Garvant. "It's hard to believe only two men did that to us. One of them a half-breed, at that."

"Don't look at me," Narve said, "look at my nose. It'll never be straight again. You three let him tackle me and didn't even lend a fist."

Gelton, wearing his half helmet as always, threw his roll at Narve. He said, "That would be because the one as big as your stupid horse came at all of us. He knocked me cross-eyed, and probably would have crushed my skull if I hadn't had my helmet on."

"Hey!" Narve said as he stepped over and pointed a finger in his face. "My horse is not stupid. You take that back, or we can go at it right here."

"Shut up, you two," Garvant said. His tone indicated he was constantly keeping them from fighting. "Let me think."

After a moment, he said, "Alright. Here's what we'll do. You remember the arrogant lord we had to take care of? The one with his manor on the cliffs by the sea?"

"Yeah," Gelton said. "We took out his guards at thirty paces. Left him and his son to you to take care of. Easy coin, it was."

"Right," Garvant said, warming up to his idea. "These two," he nodded to the brothers, "get them to come outside, and you and crook-nose there, you take the shots. Both of you kill the smaller one. If he can cast a spell, I don't want him to have the chance."

He paused and said almost to himself, "I still say we should kill every mage without gift enough to join the lord mage anyway. It's not wise letting any go at all."

The offended man reached up and touched his nose. "As long we don't let him get close enough to tackle me again, I'm good with it. I prefer the crossbow anyway…and the distance."

Garvant nodded. "I'll carve the half-breed up." He reached a hand down to the grip of a sword. He wore two of them.

He continued, "If anyone tries to interfere, the rest of you keep them away. If the local guard shows up, threaten them with the fact their king is about to swear fealty to Gar-Noth. Tell them who we are. Kill them if you have to. Nothing will be said for it; even the captain knows we work for the lord mage himself."

Marn asked, "When do you want us to do it?"

"We need to do it tonight," Garvant said, "because tomorrow or the next day, King Westell and his forces arrive to make sure the people don't rise up. They aren't going to take kindly to becoming part of Gar-Noth."

"Politics," Rarvid said with a disgusted tone. He spat. He was the quietest of the four. "I hate politics. I suppose sticking around here and dealing with troublemakers is better than going with the unit being sent to Zar. I don't envy them, traveling through the swamps with winter coming on."

"It was bad enough when we rode with King Westell's men into the swamp this last summer," Garvant agreed. "At least our job was easy, escorting the two mages."

"The Elves seemed to respect those two mages more than the knight commander leading the whole thing," observed Gelton. "I wonder why? Do you think they have mages?"

"I couldn't tell you," Sethon said. "Me 'n me brother, we're to be the muscle. All that mage business, and lords and knights and such, isn't fer us. Ye point the way and tell us who to fight, and we're to be happy."

Garvant grinned and pointed at him. "And that's why I'll put in the good word for you two. Maybe it's time there are six of us taking care of the lord mage's business."

"What about our contract with the Razors?" Marn asked. "We wrote our mark, ye know."

"You let me worry about that," Garvant said. "You notice the captain doesn't have us out there swinging blades in training." He nodded toward an open area where the other members of the Razors we sparring.

He continued, "We do our own training. It helps to know the right people."

"Ye can have the blades," Marn said, as he reached over a shoulder and tapped the head of his war hammer. "We've only used hammers for busting rock, but it feels right in the hands as a weapon, too. We'll figure out the rest."

"I don't doubt it," agreed Garvant. "We'll go over to the inn this evening. This morning, Rarvid here will show you some blocking moves. He uses an axe and not a hammer, but it's close. He used to use a hammer."

The six of them sparred at half speed all morning. The brothers learned to do more than simply swing the hammer. They were far from the skills the other four had, especially Garvant, but they made up for it in sheer size and strength.

In the afternoon the four sell-swords practiced using their crossbows. Each of the brothers stood near the two who would shoot bolts into Kryder. They intended for the men to become used to their bulk near them and think nothing of it. They feigned interest in the shooting technique.

Come evening, the six of them made their way across town to the Hobbled Goat. The sun was setting as they made final plans outside the inn. The dim light wouldn't be a problem for the shooters as long as it happened soon.

"I'll go in, see if they're still staying here, and make an excuse to send them out," Sethon said. "I'll tell them the guard wants a word with them. Don't fill me full of crossbow bolts. I'll come out first and move to this side with Narve."

"Right," Garvant agreed. "No quick fingers. Once he gets beside you, Narve, take the man out. Both of you loose at the same time. Leave the half-breed to me."

Garvant drew both his short swords, the movement fluid. A brawl was one thing. With both swords in his hands, it was another matter entirely. He looked at each man in turn and then nodded to Sethon.

* * *

Kryder looked up when the door opened. He was relieved to see Sethon enter. After the big man closed the door, he came straight to him. The look on his face meant it was happening tonight.

"Are they here?" Kryder asked as he stood.

"They are," Sethon said. "They plan to ambush ye, too. Two o' them brought crossbows. They plan to take ye out before ye can cast a spell. Then Garvant aims to take on Tog."

"Does he?" Tog asked. He popped his knuckles and made fists.

"How are they set up?" Kryder asked. "I can cast a shield, but if they're on both sides of me, it won't protect all of me. It's a simple spell; I don't know others."

"I was going to ask ye about that," Sethon said. "You casting spells. They were talking about the lord mage and all kinds of things. Just what are ye and Tog about?"

"We'll have to tell you later," Kryder said. "After we take care of this business."

"Nobody tells us anything," Sethon complained. "They're to be on both sides of the door, about ten paces away."

"Can ye keep them from using the crossbows?" Lucas asked his son.

"Aye," Sethon said. "I'll go out first to get out of the way. As I pass him, I'll give his crossbow a wee tap o' the hammer. Marn will be watching and do the same. After that, it's up to the two o' you. If ye need us to help, all ye have to do is ask."

"No," Kryder said, "if they don't have the crossbows, we can take them."

"You going to spell them?" Tog asked.

"No," Kryder said. "After what they did, they deserve the blade."

"I like it," Tog agreed. "Lead the way, Sethon."

"I'll keep anybody from leaving the inn," Lucas said. "We don't want anyone getting caught up in it, do we now?" He threw his rag down and came out from behind the bar. He had a studded steel club in his hand.

Sethon walked out the door of the inn. He turned to his left. Kryder waited a few moments, and then he walked out, followed by Tog. Lucas pulled the door shut. He wanted to go out with them, but he had his part to play in this.

Kryder glanced to his left in time to see Sethon swing his hammer up where he had it casually in one hand. The head, the size of two fists, caught the crossbow. Not only did it break one of its arms, it sent it flying out of Narve's hands.

Kryder quickly turned the other way, drawing both daggers as he did so. He watched Marn kick a broken crossbow away from the man he'd knocked down. The man was unhurt, and he scrambled to his feet, drawing his sword. It was a longsword and could be held with one or two hands. Right now he had two on the hilt.

"You bastards," hissed Garvant. He stood with both swords in his hands. He pointed one at Sethon. "After we take care of them, you won't walk away from here."

"Maybe," Sethon said as he held his hammer in both hands, spread about a foot apart on the handle. "But if ye do, it'll be a fair fight, to be sure."

"Do you really think you can handle your own?" Garvant asked. "Against us? You're only now learning how to use those hammers as weapons."

Rarvid, quiet as usual, stepped forward, his axe in hand. He'd been teaching the brothers all morning how to block and attack. He knew their limitations and would make short work of them. Garvant crossed his arms, still holding his swords.

"Teach him a lesson, Rarvid," Garvant said.

"I don't think so," Kryder said.

He strode forward, both daggers blade downward. "They're here to keep you from attacking as one. This is between me and the four of you. You interfere, I'll hold you where you stand and burn the lot of you."

Garvant wasn't sure if Kryder could do what he said, so he stepped back out of the way. The other two men watched, both wary of the huge hammers ready to strike them before they could do much. Neither dared to attack the brothers, because the Half-Orc was there, ready to join either in a two-on-one fight.

Kryder shifted slightly to one side. The man he was facing countered effortlessly. Kryder realized the man knew his business with an axe. The weapon was balanced in a two-handed grip, chest high. Kryder feinted with the dagger in his right, following with a swipe at the man. The first was blocked with the handle, the other with the flat of the blade.

The man kicked his left leg forward, aimed at Kryder's stomach—the move designed to gain room—followed by a sweeping blow with the axe. Kryder anticipated the move when the man kicked. He'd seen similar versions when sparring with members of the Red Fist.

He didn't step forward thinking the man was off balance and vulnerable after the kick. To have done so would have put him in the path of the oncoming blade. He allowed the momentum from the light kick to move him back, out of the strike area. That clearly surprised the man.

Before the man recovered from the swing, Kryder bounced back and struck with the same attack he'd used before. This time he aimed for the man's hands, and not the body. When the handle came up to block the first dagger, the blade cut his fingers to the bone. The smaller dagger followed almost instantly, cutting even deeper on the other hand, severing two fingers.

It was a move Kryder had perfected in sparring with his tribe. The Orc warriors used blunted axes when training. Kryder used dull wooden blades in much the same way. The axes, though blunt, hurt when they hit and left a nasty bruise. His wooden blades rapped knuckles, causing intense pain to those holding the handles of their axes. In the beginning, he'd suffered many bruises. In the latter years, his opponents were leery of his blades, especially Tog.

"Ohhh," Tog said, "the fingers." He sucked air in through his teeth and shook a hand. "That hurts, believe me, I know."

Furious, the man brought the axe down in a mighty overhead swing, his hands bloody as they struggled to grip the handle. Kryder slipped to the side, spun his body, and buried both daggers in the man. The larger dagger didn't penetrate deep with a killing blow because of the leather armor. The smaller dagger, his father's, was a different story. It sank to the hilt, its blade piercing the man's heart.

"That's for Mama," Kryder said as the man sank to the ground, trying to hold himself up with the handle of his axe, the head stuck in the ground. He died staring up at Kryder.

Kryder turned toward Marn and the man beside him. Marn pushed Gelton forward, and he circled, his sword held in two hands. Its blade was much longer than a short sword. Like the others, he knew how to use it. He watched Kryder move, looking for an opening.

Kryder used the oldest trick in the book. He moved awkwardly as he tried to follow the man moving around him. He didn't step over, each foot balanced, he kind of shuffled. He held the dagger in his right hand with the blade up, the other down. Thinking his victim was not only uncomfortable moving in that direction, but that he was off balance, too, the man struck.

Kryder flipped his smaller dagger over and met the blade with his own two crossed in front of him. It was a battle of strength as they each pushed, until Kryder kneed the man low. Surprised, Gelton stepped back in pain. Kryder watched his eyes and saw the confusion in them. The man realized Kryder wasn't an easy opponent to fight.

This time Kryder initiated the circling, stepping over each foot, balanced and on his toes, ready to move, changing his tactics completely. Both blades were held down, his fist gripping tight, his forefinger over the end of the hilt. He slid his blades over one another, slowly, knowing the movement and sound would put the man on edge. Several times the man attacked, and each time it was turned away. The dance continued.

Kryder initiated the next move and rushed in. Gelton swept his sword downward at an angle, a move design to only allow one dagger to block, giving him a chance to strike Kryder's body. He spun around the man's arm as it extended across his body, still holding the sword in a two-handed grip. Kryder's hand came across the front and side of his neck with the smaller blade. It sliced deep. Gelton dropped his sword and grabbed his throat.

"That's for Papa," Kryder said as the man dropped to his knees and fell sideways, his hands and arms soaked. The helmet fell off and wobbled, the circles becoming smaller, until it settled beside his head.

Garvant stepped forward a pace. "You bastard! You'll die for that."

"Don't do it," Tog warned.

His bow was in his hand and an arrow was nocked. He and Marn both moved toward the leader of the men. Garvant stopped, furious at being unable to do anything. Sethon moved to the side and motioned Narve toward Kryder.

Kryder breathed heavily as he watched the man move toward him. Narve held his sword out; it was slightly longer than a short sword, with a thinner blade. Narve reached to his belt and drew a dirk. The weapon was longer than a dagger, with no edge. Its guard extended up the blade a hand's length, and the tip of the weapon ended in a well-defined point. It was designed to block, disarm, and puncture. Kryder had no doubt it would puncture his hardened leather.

Their blades clashed. Kryder moved away, his arm nicked. The man was fast. The next strike was a feint, followed by a thrust of his dirk. Kryder spun away from the extended arm—it, like his, now cut.

The next time they came together, Narve caught Kryder's long dagger between his dirk blade and its angled guard. He flipped the blade out of his hand. Kryder didn't hesitate. He came in, the small dagger flashing. His opponent was overconfident, since Kryder only had one blade left, knowing it was the smaller of the two.

Too close to use his sword, the man easily blocked the blade coming at him with his dirk, again and again. Suddenly his movement stopped, surprise showing on his face. He fell to one knee and dropped his sword, the arm holding it useless. Underneath his arm the shafts of two bolts angled out oddly. Kryder had grabbed them from the quiver on the man's back and rammed them through the opening of the armor into the man. He jerked his hand forward, holding them, before he moved away from the man, dislocating the shoulder.

Kryder kicked him in the side of the head, dazing him, and came down with his dagger, burying it. Pulling his blade free, he kicked the dirk away and stood over the man, looking down.

"That was for my sister," he said.

The sun had nearly set, and the light was dimming noticeably as Kryder looked up at Garvant. He stepped forward. Garvant swept his swords back and forth, ready.

"Who are you?" Garvant asked. "Who sent you here? Are you from Gar-Noth? You keep saying this is for your family. Who? Which one? I want to know before I kill you."

He shifted slightly, his blades moving in an easy, yet intricate pattern. "You won't take me with daggers. The rest may get to me eventually, but *you* will die for what you did here."

Kryder stopped and asked him, "Do you know this dagger?" He held it up. It didn't catch the dying light from the setting sun. It couldn't, even if the sun was higher. The blade was covered in blood.

"That?" Garvant said with an attitude. "No, I don't know that dagger. How would I know a dagger?"

Kryder held up his hand and spoke words of power. The area lit up brightly around them. Above him, eight spheres of light floated. Garvant's eyes widened at the display of magic. He'd been around it enough to know that multiple lights meant a gift rivaling the lord mage's own power.

"It knows you," Kryder said. He ran a finger down his face, imitating the scar on Garvant's own.

Garvant's eyes narrowed, his mind racing. Kryder could almost read his thoughts as it dawned on the man. He realized who Kryder was. The blade, his scar, the girl...the girl was his sister.

"Twins," Garvant said. "She had twins."

Kryder stared, refusing to answer the man.

"Go ahead, then," Garvant said, letting his hands drop. "You can't take me man to man in a fair fight. Cast your spell, mage. I'll die knowing you couldn't avenge your family by blade."

Kryder stepped forward, only to be stopped by a large hand on his shoulder. "No," Tog said. "You only have the dagger. Let me have him."

Kryder glanced sideways at his cousin—more like a brother—and back at Garvant. He turned to Tog, his decision made. It was Tog's family, too. He nodded and stepped aside.

Tog handed his bow to Kryder. He reached over his shoulder and pulled his axe free from its loops. He took his quiver off, held it by the leather strap, and laid it at Kryder's feet. The huge man rolled his neck and stepped forward with his dual-headed axe held loosely, midshaft, in one hand.

Garvant smiled. Despite the size, he was confident he could easily take down the half-breed. When they sparred, Rarvid never stood a chance against him with his axe. This would be no different. He rolled his wrists, looping the swords, and brought them up, ready for the fight.

Tog gripped his axe with both hands, and with a speed Garvant would never have believed if he wasn't facing it, he twisted slightly, brought the axe up over his shoulder, and swung down. Garvant was faster than the giant man, and he brought his hands up and crossed his swords to block it below the blade.

What he hadn't counted on was the raging strength of an Orc. The force of the blow slammed through the man's crossed blades, knocking his hands away, and the axe blade buried in Garvant's head. The swords clattered to the ground as he fell to his knees.

"That's for Kryder," Tog said through clenched teeth. He kicked the body away, dislodging his axe.

* * * * *

Chapter Twenty-One

The sergeant of the guard and four men stepped into the light. Johan walked over to Tog and looked down. "Came back for more, did they?"

Tog shrugged a shoulder and waited to see what the man said next. It would be their word only in the explanation of the bodies. Honest self-defense wouldn't land them in prison if it was proven. Now, anyway. Who knew what the laws would become under King Westell.

Johan looked over at Kryder. "I'll be honest with ye, we were coming fast when we saw the fighting. None of ye noticed us, so caught up in it were ye. I slowed the lads and stood in the dark and heard this one say ye were looking to avenge yer family."

He pointed to Garvant's body. "I'm not so old I don't remember me own family, and it's been years since the saints took them. This lot got what they had coming, I figure. Get what ye claim from them, and I'll have the lads haul the bodies away. I'm still in charge o' the watch, for now. I said it, and it's a done deal. To the pits with their captain and his lieutenant. Now, which o' ye is to be buying an old sergeant a beer?"

Kryder walked over to Garvant's body, bent down, and got what he wanted. He and Tog cleaned their blades and went inside with Johan. Marn and Sethon collected the slain men's weapons. They wrapped them in a cloak, brought them into the inn, and put them in a back room behind the bar.

Lucas pushed a couple of tables together in the back corner, farthest from the fireplace. No one was seated anywhere around them. The six of them sat down with pitchers of beer and enough mugs to go around.

"We need to figure out what we do next," Tog said. He poured himself a beer.

"Agreed," Kryder said. He leaned back in his chair and crossed his arms, deep in thought.

Tog looked down at his bench and behind him to the wall. Satisfied he wouldn't fall, he leaned back himself, beer in hand. He waited to hear what Kryder had to say.

"There's a few choices to be sure, lads," Lucas said. He filled the other mugs. "Ye have to let the baron know what's happening, and ye need to be making yer way to the Halls o' Magic to take care o' that business."

"Yeah," Kryder agreed, "before he finds out what happened to his sell-swords."

Johan looked back and forth at them. He looked at Marn and Sethon, men he'd known their whole lives. They both shrugged. They didn't know what the three were talking about, either.

"Somebody needs to let me know what's going on, to be sure." Johan said.

They told him, in bits and pieces at first. He interrupted with questions of disbelief until he realized they were serious. When Marn and Sethon told him what they'd learned of the Elves and the expected arrival of King Westell, that verified it for him. He knew of King Westell's upcoming arrival. It wasn't common knowledge in the town, and those on the watch were to remain silent about it on orders from their current king.

"It seems like ye need to be in two places at once," Johan said. "Even if ye have the gift, I doubt ye can do that."

"No," Kryder agreed. "That's not a spell I've even heard of. I'll admit, there are many I don't know, nor will I ever, but it can't be done."

"Well," Johan said, "whatever ye decide, I'm to be with ye. I'll not stay with the local forces and fall under King Westell. If they do give some o' the kingdom to the Elves, I'd just as soon not be a part o' it."

Lucas said, "With yer experience, they're sure to send you with the force to invade Minth, old friend."

"I'll not have any part o' that, either," the old sergeant said. "I'll make for the Western Baronies or look for a job as a traveling merchant's guard or something."

"I'm with ye, old friend," Lucas said. "I've a few coins saved over the years. We'll get a wagon or two and leave Yaylok." He looked at his sons. "If the two o' ye are to be fighting, it'll not be for King Westell, if I have to box yer ears and make ye leave with me and yer sister. With Elves around, there's no telling what they may decide to do with them that's burnt."

"That's it!" Kryder said as he sat forward. "*You* can take a message to Baron Arnwald. Tog and I can go to the Halls of Magic. Most of the mages are here now. We'll only have the guards to worry about, and some apprentices, maybe. We might have a chance to get to the lord mage."

"How are we going to do that?" Tog asked. "By the time we get there, he may be gone. We could cross paths with him and never know it."

"That's true," Sethon said. "King Westell and his forces are traveling a different route than the Razors used escorting the mages here."

"Not if we step through," Kryder said. He placed the ring he'd taken from Garvant on the table in front of him.

Tog reached over and picked up the ring. It looked like a child's ring in his hands. He turned it over, looking at the red jewel. "This is the same ring," he confirmed.

"I think so, too," Kryder said. "From what I saw, breaking the stone creates the doorway. I didn't know someone without the gift could use an enchanted item until we saw him do it. Both times it led to the lord mage's study. Maybe the enchanted item is there and the ring is an extension."

The lord mage had a ring like this one, but with a bigger jewel," Lucas said. "I remember seeing it."

"It may be the one," Kryder said. "If it's the case, we may not step through into his study. It'll be wherever he is."

"He could be in a room full of guards," Tog observed. "That could be a problem."

Johan said, "I don't believe a few guards will stop the likes of one such as you. Ye handle an axe like it's a part of ye."

"I think it may the only way to get to him while we know where he is," Kryder said. He paused a moment, looking at Tog. "If we use the ring, we may not survive it. He's the most powerful mage on all of Kerr. But…I have to do this. I have to face him."

"No," Tog said. "*We* have to face him. We do this like we've done since before we could walk. Together."

There was silence at the table, each lost in their own thoughts. Kryder and Tog thinking both of what was ahead, and their past, facing everything as family should, together. Lucas, after knowing the two of them for a few days—though in reality it had been far longer while they traveled with the goddess of time—felt he'd found a part of him, a part of his family he'd been missing for decades. His sons, Sethon and Marn, knew what it meant to their father. They felt the kinship themselves and would face a demon without hesitation to protect their little sister.

Johan knew he was past his prime as a fighter and a leader of men. It would be one last mission, and a way out of a kingdom that would as soon forget him as it transitioned into something he'd never thought he'd see.

Johan leaned forward, ran his hand down over his grey mustache, straightening it, and said, "First thing in the morning, we get our hands on two wagons. We need three teams to pull them. Two fer each wagon, and two to spell them if one goes lame or throws a shoe."

He warmed up, the leader in him showing through. "You two get back over to the Razor's camp. Find the horses what belong to those four, pack their bags, and bring them to my place right below town. If anyone asks, tell them yer only doing what the scarred one ordered ye to do. It might buy us a few days before anyone even thinks to ask where they went. If we can't use their gear, we can use the horses fer certain, though I don't know if they can carry you two and Lucas. I think it's the wagons fer ye."

Marn and Sethon stood; Johan had asked, and they didn't hesitate. "We'll get the other two crossbows and all the bolts, too."

Lucas watched them go. He turned to Johan and said, "Maybe we should've had them under you on the watch years ago. They always did listen to you without complaint."

"They're good lads, Lucas," Johan said. "Ye raised 'em right. I never did have me own family. Them and their sister are like the nephews and niece I never had. Now, speaking o' the lass. After ye shut down tonight, ye need to pack her things, and yers, so when we pull up in the morning with the wagons, we load them, go to me place, and prepare to leave. We'll buy supplies, food, anything we need tomorrow evening, a few towns away."

"What'll you do with the inn?" Tog asked. He reached for the pitcher.

"I'll leave a note in the kitchen with enough coin to keep it going a while, saying I decided to go to Minth, where me family's from. I'll leave it to the cook. She's been working for me for nigh on six years now. It's the best I can do for her."

Kryder said, "When King Westell gets here, there'll be many who pack up and leave. They'll eventually put a stop to it, I imagine, but the first week or so, no one will question anyone missing from here."

Johan nodded, stood, and said, "I need to be going. I'll catch up with the lads who took the bodies away. I'm to be making sure they're good and buried tonight. Come to think of it, not a one o' them was keen on the whole King Westell thing. Don't be surprised if I show up with the whole squad, bags packed. None o' the four have a wife, nor planning on it yet, young as they are."

After he left, Lucas said, "He's a good man, to be sure. He was me own sergeant back in the day. I haven't seen him act so young in years. We'll light out by noon tomorrow. When will the two of ye leave?"

Kryder picked the ring up from the middle of the table. "We'll go in the morning, if this works. After a good night's sleep. We don't know our way around the Halls of Magic. Night is not when we want to try and learn it."

"Good," Tog said. "I was afraid you wanted to go now. I mean, I'll step through whenever you're ready, but some of that hog and taters sounds good right about now."

* * *

I t was quiet in the Halls of Magic. The majority of mage instructors were in Yaylok by now, or close to it. The apprentices had been sent home for the winter—an unusual move, but necessary. Besides the lord mage himself, only two other mages were still there.

The servants were still in attendance, as those with the signs of the gift filtered in every now and then. Mage Jonthia walked briskly down the hall. It always surprised the guards when he went past. At his age, to have so much energy was amusing. He waved with one hand as he went by, a stone in the other.

It was his night to transfer the heat if one of the soon-to-be apprentices showed signs of their fever rising to dangerous levels. More than likely he would simply spend the night in the small room with a bunk next to the transfer room.

On the other side of the Halls, the lord mage looked down at a sheet of parchment bearing the names and places the newest apprentices came from. He checked another sheet, which let him know which mage would be with those with the gift maturing.

"At least it's Mage Jonthia tonight, and not Mage Kaynald," he said out loud.

No one was there to hear him. She was from the Baronies West and was the only full mage to stay from there. Others had left when they'd finished training. Not many from there earned the black robes. In his opinion, she wasn't exceptional, but she had accepted the offer to stay, so she'd earned the red robes of an instructor.

Keeping her here instead of with the others moving to meet with the armies of King Westell wasn't a hard decision to make. She didn't show any enthusiasm over the looming battles. As a matter of fact, she always seemed bored, unless she was on her own time studying in the library.

Mage Jonthia, on the other hand, was a favorite of his. It was too bad the old mage couldn't handle the strain of travel; he'd relish using magic to fight. The man was well beyond his prime, and his sanity was slightly suspect from a riding accident years ago. Instructing was about all he could do these days.

The lord mage looked at the large ring on his hand, then spun it around his finger, thinking. His mind made up, he reached down and opened a drawer on his desk. He pulled out a small gold box and shook it. It was nearly empty, and only one item could be heard rattling inside. He put it down and opened it.

He reached inside and took out the small ruby. He put it on his desk and reached for the smooth stone holding a stack or parchment in place. He smashed the jewel and waited a moment. A red glow formed on the desk in front of him.

It grew to a half-foot square window. When the connection between the two places was complete, he found himself looking at a pale face with dark hair. The brown eyes nearly blended with the pupil. It was one he spoke to often.

"Chauncy," the Elf said, speaking in human. "I wasn't expecting you to connect tonight. You have used the last distance stone, by my calculations."

"Mraynith," the lord mage said, "it's the last, but we won't need any more of them. All is in place. I plan on leaving from here tomorrow evening. I'll step through in Yaylok to ensure everything goes as planned, and I'll winter there."

"Good," the Elf said. "I will arrive with the emperor and the horde in late spring. Once the new border of Zar is in place, the horde and your King Westell's armies will be ready to move north and take the kingdom you call Minth."

"Agreed," the lord mage confirmed. "Then you and I will decide if we want to kill your emperor and our king, or wait until they capture the rest of Kerr for us."

"Indeed," Mraynith said, "then we rid ourselves of the two over us with no gift. They do not deserve to rule. After we eliminate any who would say otherwise, we will rule all, and split the world between us."

"According to plan," the lord mage agreed. "It's been a long time coming."

"The years have been worth it," the Elf said. "Speaking of years, do not bother attempting to extend yours. It will be a waste of blood. Save your next...donor until I resolve what may be happening. I performed the ceremony twice this last week, and nothing happened. It would seem Lethrall will not grant the years. I will endeavor to determine what has angered the demon prince."

"Perhaps he was not pleased with the sacrifice?" the lord mage suggested.

"They were both untouched human girls," Mraynith argued. "I did nothing different. It is the same ceremony we Elves have used for the last hundred years."

258 | STEVERSON & ACKERMAN

He continued, "It was the last two I had available. The breeding does not go well lately."

Chauncy Ashdale, lord mage of the Halls of Magic, waved a hand in dismissal and said, "Come late spring, there'll be plenty available for you. Perhaps Lethrall wishes more than one at a time. We'll figure it out. He hasn't abandoned us."

The window slowly closed until the red glow blinked out. The lord mage leaned back, satisfied with the future.

* * * * *

Chapter Twenty-Two

Kryder reached out and clasped Lucas' forearm. "Be safe," he said.

Lucas grinned. "It's not us who needs to be worried, lad," he said. "The two of ye are stepping into far more danger this morning."

Tog clasped the innkeeper's forearm and said, "Maybe, but think of the tale if we survive it."

"Just be sure ye do survive to tell about it," Lucas said. "Here, take this bit o' coin. You're to be needing it to make yer way to Minth after."

Kryder took the small leather purse from Lucas. He bounced it in his hand. There were more than coppers in it. He raised an eyebrow at the innkeeper.

Lucas waved it off. "I been saving fer years. It's not like I needed to spend any on good food and beer, ye know."

"He's right," Tog agreed. He looked around the empty tavern. "Maybe when I grow up one day, I'll own one so I can eat and drink for free."

"Aunt Katheen says you'll never grow up," Kryder reminded him.

"She's probably right," Tog agreed. "I'm good with it."

Kryder held his small dagger in one hand and the ring in the other. He was wearing his traveling cloak. The plan was to travel light. The rest of his gear and his horse were at Johan's place already. The

260 | STEVERSON & ACKERMAN

old sergeant was delighted to ride the Minth-bred horse, taking care of it for Kryder until they met in Arnwald's Barony. The horse was descended from a warhorse his grandfather had owned years ago and those bred by his mother.

Tog had his traveling gear on. He didn't own a horse. For someone his size, only the largest of draft horses could carry him for long. It didn't matter to him. Like all Orcs, he could run for hours. When they traveled, he remained on foot. His axe on his back, he held his bow, an arrow already nocked.

"You ready?" Kryder asked. He placed the ring on the wooden floor.

Tog rolled his head around on his huge neck. He paused and said, "Wait." He turned to Lucas, reached up, and pulled the piece of leather sewn to his hardened leather top. It ripped free easily for him. He handed it to Lucas.

Lucas turned it over in his hand and saw what it was. The imprint of a fist in a deep red dye. He looked up at the two, unable to speak.

"If you ever go beyond the Baronies into the Western Borderlands," Tog said, "you'll need that token to go a little farther. Make sure you tell them we gave it to you, and they're to let the council know."

He turned to Kryder and said, "After you. Stay low. I may need to loose one right away."

Kryder knelt down and smashed the jewel with the hilt of his dagger. A red glow formed in front of him. It grew to the size of a doorway. Through it he saw a desk. No one sat there. Staying low beneath Tog's line of sight, he stepped through, Tog on his heels.

* * *

Kryder looked around as he stepped forward. The study was empty. Behind them, the doorway remained open for the same length of time as the ones they'd seen when they'd traveled with Lan. The red glow faded behind them as the door shrank and disappeared. Kryder glance back when it did.

"Where do we go?" Tog whispered.

"Well," Kryder said, "there's only one door. I say we start there."

"Is there anything on the desk worth taking?" Tog asked. "What about the parchments?"

Kryder looked through them. "There's nothing here, supply requests, inventories, nothing of…wait. This is interesting. I found a map. It looks like the one the baron has. Gar-Noth is drawn much bigger, though. It has arrows and dates with question marks by them."

"Bigger," Tog said. "Of course it is. Snatch it up. That sounds like part of the plans for their armies. Does it have anything about Elves?"

Kryder rolled it up and slipped into an inner pocket of his cloak. "Yeah, it had yellow flags beside the symbols for King Westell. I got it. Let's go."

Unsure of what might be on the other side, Kryder opened it quietly and looked down a hall. It was empty in the direction he could see. He pushed it open and stepped out quickly, followed by Tog. He heard the sound of Tog's bow as he released the arrow. There was a shout immediately following it.

Kryder spun in the other direction to see one guard pinned to a wooden door ten feet away, and another running toward them, sword out. He didn't hesitate; he threw up a hand and spoke. The

262 | STEVERSON & ACKERMAN

man slowed before he could reach them. Tog released another arrow and ended the threat.

Tog pulled the arrow free, wiped what he could off on the man's tunic, and put it back in his quiver. When they got to the door, he pulled the other out, nocking it as the body fell. He looked down at the man's armor.

"They're wearing chainmail," he observed. "We get too much distance between us, and we run the risk of the arrow not penetrating deeply enough or breaking a tip. The bow is strong, but an arrow can only take so much. These don't have the type of head we need for puncturing chain or steel armor, for sure. If I'd known we might need it, I would've brought some. Larn Narthon had an armory full."

"We were supposed to be scouting in Yaylok, not sneaking through the Halls of Magic," Kryder said. "Not your fault."

Kryder cracked the door. He didn't see anyone. This time when he opened it, he was ready for an attack from the other direction. None came. He looked around and realized he was in a library. The walls contained shelves of rolled parchment. He didn't see any books here.

A woman walked around a corner, looking down and reading as she walked. She sat at a table where several other sheets were unrolled, held by smooth rocks as paper weights. Tog shrugged at Kryder. Kryder raised a hand, ready to cast. The woman was wearing red robes. He cleared his throat.

She looked up, startled. "Oh, what are you doing in here? How did you…" The question trailed off.

In a glance she took in the arrow pointed at her and the dagger in Kryder's hand. Looking closer she noted the cut of Kryder's thin leather cloak. Taking in the sight of Tog as well, she tilted her head slightly and asked, "Are you from the Baronies?"

Recognizing her accent, Kryder said, "A little west of there, actually. But yes, in a sense, we are. Why?"

"The cut of your cloak," she said. "He's at least Half-Orc. Maybe more. The dagger you carry, did you know it came from deep in the great northern desert above the Baronies? There's a clan of Gnomes, known for their technique of forging blades, roaming there. I can see the design is very old. Is it true it needs no sharpening? From what I've read, the technique is so complicated, they never make more than dagger-sized weapons. For them, of course. That may be why it appears smaller than a normal dagger in your hand. Do you..."

"Not to be rude," Tog interrupted, "but you talk more than a Gnome. Are you from the Baronies?"

"I'm sorry," she said. "I tend to do that if the subject is interesting. Yes, I'm from the Baronies. As a matter of fact, I'd be there right now instead of facing an arrow if I wasn't needed here. Would you mind terribly not pointing that at me?"

"What do you mean needed?" Kryder asked. "I though all the mages went back to the Baronies. It's not like there are many there."

"That's why I stayed," she said, standing slowly. "My baroness asked me to. I'm memorizing spells beyond what I'm allowed to copy in my books." She paused for a moment, considering whether she should say more. "I'm also doing research. I must find a way to create something. Something desperately needed."

Kryder glanced at Tog. "You can ease off. She won't sound the alarm. You're trying to find the spell to bind to a transfer stone."

Her hand flew to her mouth. "How do you know of them? No one but mage instructors know of the stones. Mages who earn the black robes but leave aren't told of them. They've been kept here for decades."

"There's no time to explain everything," Kryder said. "There is no spell. The stones came with the enchantment when mortals were given the gift. They can't be created with a binding spell."

"How do you know?" she asked. "I mean, that would explain why there's nothing in the archives about it. Unless the lord mage has locked the knowledge away in his personal library."

By her tone when she said his title, Kryder knew she didn't care for the man. "Where is his library? Isn't this it?" He waved his hand around.

"No," she said. "He travels to his library through a spell. None of us know where it is. I suspect it to be somewhere in the same desert your dagger comes from. Sometimes when he takes the books back to his study, he returns with parchments of the area."

She indicated the library. "All this is knowledge copied from other places. Other than books in mage-speak designed to learn the language itself, none of it contains words of power. Daily someone retrieves the spell books he selects to learn from and returns them to his study."

She continued, "Over the last few years, I've filled my books with spells, but there are some he'll never share. There was a time when many mages could travel to other places. Other than he, there are none I know of with the spell now."

"Yeah, well," Tog said, "the spell will die with him today."

"I see," she said. "My name is Kaynald. If you wish to end his life, I'll tell you where to find him. He's at breakfast in the main dining hall. It's in the next building, to the left. There will be many guards. Eight that I can think of."

428

"That was easy," Tog remarked to Kryder. "Why?"

"The man is a monster," Kaynald said. "We had an apprentice take her life; she told me why before she bled out in my arms. I would do it myself, but he's too powerful. My own gift isn't strong enough to face him. I plan on leaving tomorrow when he's gone."

"You were going to leave?" Kryder asked. "Without learning of transfer stones?"

"I planned on taking one of them," she explained, "to use in the Baronies. Never again would we have to send a child here." She stood defiant, as if she dared them to stop her.

"I can see that," Tog said.

"Are you the only mage here," Kryder asked, "besides the lord mage?"

"No there is one other," she admitted. "He's strong, but he grows old, and his mind isn't what it used to be. I think I could prevail against him."

"Jonthia," Kryder said. "How many stones are there?"

"There are three," Kaynald answered. Again she was surprised he knew more then he should. "They are located in a hidden closet in a small room where the gift is matured."

Kryder thought for a moment. "Where is Jonthia now?" he asked.

"He's eating with the lord mage," she said. "They'll be there for the next hour. He's giving final instructions before he leaves."

"How many are here and need the stones now?" Kryder asked.

"None," she said. "The last matured last night on Jonthia's watch. We've been taking in very few with the gift lately. Minth and the Baronies are being denied. It's very rare to receive anyone from Tarlok. They cannot pay what the lord mage demands."

"The Tarlok live off the land and what they hunt," Kryder agreed. "You're right, they can't pay the fee. If you help us get to the lord mage, we'll end him, and the other if he chooses to fight. You can take a stone and go to the Baronies. Leave us the others. Don't wait for us; get a horse and ride. Go to the nearest port and book passage on the next ship to Minth, if you can find one."

She said, "I'll have to get to the coins in the administrator's office on my way out. It should be no issue. I'm a mage instructor."

She looked around the room. "I hate to leave all this, but it's all copies. Somewhere in the desert is the real library of mages. If Minth stops King Westell and the threat to the Baronies ends, I'll find it."

"If we survive," Tog said, "we may go with you. A desert sounds good. I'm tired of the cold down here."

Kaynald looked at him with a strange look on her own face and said, "It's not yet winter."

"Don't remind me," Tog said. He curled his lip in disgust.

* * * * *

Chapter Twenty-Three

Kryder said, "Lead the way."

They followed her back out into the hall. She glanced at the bodies and looked away. She led them down a flight of stairs to another set of large doors.

She stopped and said, "There will be four guards between the buildings. In the next building is the hall leading to the dining area. Follow it. There will be two guards outside the hall, and two inside. There are another ten not on duty now. Once the fighting starts, you can be sure they'll come. Their barracks are upstairs in the same building."

"Four outside," Kryder said. "Got it. Where do you need to go?"

"The stones are in the other building on the left side of the courtyard," she answered. "I can help you with the guards."

Tog nocked his arrow. "I'm ready."

Kaynald opened the door and stepped outside. The guards glanced her way and went back to their conversation. She put a hand up and spoke words of power. A gust of wind flew from her hand against the four. Two were knocked down. One was pinned against the building, his shield catching the wind and holding him there with it against his chest. The other man turned his back and ducked his head, trying to avoid the sand and leaves.

Tog and Kryder stepped to each side of her, and when her hand dropped, they rushed across the courtyard. Tog let his arrow fly on the run. It struck the man in the shoulder right above his shield. The arm dropped, unable to hold the weight of the shield with the arrow lodged in the shoulder.

They were able to close the distance and attack. Kryder blocked the short sword of the man in front of him and caught him with a dagger. It sliced the length of his forearm. He kicked sideways, pushing the next man away.

Tog dropped his bow and drew his long dagger. His axe would have to wait. He swung hard several times, backing his opponent up into the man behind him. As he stumbled, Tog found his opening. He left his dagger there, reached over his shoulder, and drew his axe.

Kryder ended his fight when he slipped inside the man's reach. He turned to help Tog but saw the last man fall. Without his shield, he didn't stand a chance against the axe. Tog retrieved his arrow and his dagger.

"So far, so good," Kryder said. "None of the other guards came out of the building. Help me drag these under those trees in case someone looks out a window."

They entered the building, turned, and eased down the hallway. When they rounded the corner, Tog let fly another arrow. The guard dropped. His partner shouted and rushed forward. Kryder tossed Tog his axe when he dropped his bow. Tog met him halfway across the open area.

His axe sliced deep into the man's shield and stuck. Tog jerked it with all his strength, pulling the man to him. Tog grabbed the arm holding the sword and pushed it back. Kryder heard the shoulder snap, and the man screamed. Tog finished it.

Knowing they'd been heard, Tog kicked the door. It flew in and slammed against the wall. Inside, the lord mage and the older instructor were on their feet already. One of the guards was near them, the

other rushing to the door. Kryder raised his hand and spoke. A ball
of flame flew from him and hit the man in his chest. The force of it
knocked him back, and he fell, his tunic burning. The man rolled,
trying to put the flames out. The other guard circled a long table,
coming around to Tog's side. Tog was ready.

Kryder turned and saw the lord mage with his hand up. He dove
to the floor and rolled. A ball of fire hit the wall behind him and
blossomed. Kryder came up and cast the only protection spell he
knew besides the simple shield. He'd never cast it before, and he had
no time to wonder if he'd pronounced the words correctly.

The lord mage held a hand in the air, and one of the rings glowed
red. Nothing came from him. Kryder held his had in the air and felt
the push against it. He gritted his teeth and put more into the spell.
The pressure against him eased.

The lord mage dropped his hand as the glow faded from his ring.
His mouth was open in surprise. Kryder had no idea what spell the
ring held, but it hadn't worked. He had no idea he should be unconscious.

Kryder dropped his hand and threw his other up as he spoke
again. This time he was sure of the spell. From his four fingers darts
of light flew across the room like arrows. The lord mage rejected
them with one word as another ring glowed softly. The darts flew in
different directions. Two hit walls, one struck a tapestry on the wall
between windows, burning through it to splatter against the blocks
behind it, catching the tapestry on fire, and another burned through a
table, causing it to smolder.

Kryder cast the rejection spell again. The moment he spoke the
last syllable, the flames coming from both of the lord mage's hands
blossomed five feet from him as if they'd hit a giant invisible shield.

Kryder raised his other hand and pushed with all he had. Slowly, inch by inch, the fire blossom backed toward the lord mage. Kryder took a step, moving it closer. He felt his arms tremble. He took another step. The flames moved closer to him.

Kryder's back foot slipped. He slid an inch, then two. He gritted his teeth. Running through his mind was the sound of his mother's voice, encouraging him and his sister Trenlis to try again. They almost had it right. "Say it again slowly," she said. "When you're sure you have it right, say it with conviction. One day, if you have the gift, you must be sure of yourself, of the spell. *Know* it will work and say it like you mean it."

Kryder meant it. Right now, there was nothing else. He pushed harder. This spell, this one, would hold. He would not falter. *I will hold*, he screamed in his mind. He stopped sliding. The flames moved away from him slowly. He took a step. The lord mage stepped back.

Kryder kept pushing. His eyes darted to the lord mage's face across the room. The man was straining, a look of disbelief on his face. Kryder took another step. The flames moved back another foot with the force of his rejection. Anther table started smoldering as the flames blossomed over it.

Across the room, Tog was engaged with the guard. Unlike the others, the man wielded an axe, and he knew how to use it. There was a reason he was the commander of the guards in the Halls. Tog continued to move the man back, though. His opponent was good, but he couldn't compete with the strength behind each of Tog's blows. Tog's blade cut through the hardened wooden handle, and the blade embedded in his chest. Tog turned to see several places in the room start to burn and felt the heat from the battle of fire and will between the two mages.

He stepped toward the lord mage and felt an agony he'd never felt before. His muscles spasmed as he dropped to one knee, his hands on the floor. The knuckles of the hand holding the axe ground into the stone as the grip tightened. After a moment, the pain eased. He turned his head to see the old mage grinning, his hand out, a knife in the other.

The mage lowered his hand and walked toward him without a care in the world, until he realized the huge man before him had never hit the floor, and the mage was completely immobilized with shock. The old man's eyes widened as Tog stood on shaking legs. Just as the mage started to raise his hand and speak, the axe hit him square in the chest, having spun once in flight. Tog dropped to his knee again then stumbled to his feet, walked over, and jerked his axe free.

The flame and rejection shield were now closer to the lord mage. It was moving slower away from Kryder now. The lord mage dropped his hands, and the flames dissipated between them. Kryder stood defiant, breathing heavily.

"Who are you?" demanded the lord mage. It was nearly a shout. "You never came through here. You can't be a mage! You should be burnt!" The man was shouting now.

Kryder reached into a pocket of his cloak, took something out, and threw it at the lord mage's feet. The ring with the shattered stone rolled against his boot. The lord mage's eyes widened when he recognized it. He looked at Kryder with the obvious question in his eyes.

"My mother put him to sleep once," Kryder said. "My cousin put him to sleep permanently."

As the lord mage's expression changed to disbelief, several guards came into the room, shouting, and rushed Tog. The lord mage used the distraction. Instead of casting another spell, he pulled the large ring from his finger, spun, and threw it at the wall, shattering the large stone.

A red glow formed in front of him, growing to the size of a doorway. Kryder could see beyond him into a large room. The walls were stone, but of a shade of reddish brown he'd never seen. Books lined several waist-high bookshelves.

Kryder threw his dagger as the lord mage stepped toward the doorway. Silver flashed as it spun. Like Tog and his axe, Kryder hit where he aimed. Hours had been spent between them since they were young throwing at a tree. It never grew old. The only thing they changed was the size of the target as Tog's axes grew heavier.

The blade embedded into the lord mage's back, severing his spine. He fell, his legs useless. Reaching toward the doorway, he tried to drag himself. In his panic, he couldn't find the strength to cast a spell. Kryder looked back at Tog, his axe swinging, fighting several men at once. He didn't give the bleeding mage another look.

Kryder raised his hand as he moved toward his cousin and spoke the words written on the inside of his ring. Two of the men slowed, nearly stopping their movement. Tog's axe cut the man down in front of him, and he swung a swiping blow the other way and killed both men.

Kryder reached Tog's side, grabbed the hilt of his cousin's dagger, and pulled it free. He turned with Tog, a dagger in one hand and nearly a short sword in the other. His hands shook slightly. Inside he knew it would be dangerous to cast another spell without rest, even the simple ones he knew made stronger by sheer will.

Together, they fought off the next wave of guards until there were no more. Kryder bled from a cut on his arm, and Tog bled in several places, none serious. Breathing heavily, they turned back toward the lord mage. The doorway still stood, its edges glowing in the smoke-filled room. Two more tables and a paneled wall burned.

The lord mage was almost halfway through the door as he strained to pull his lifeless legs behind him. The trail of blood was heavy. Tog started to speak when the door started shrinking. He never got a sound out as they watched the mage claw the smooth floor in the room through the doorway. There was nothing for him to grab, no crack in a stone floor to aid him. He panicked and screamed, tearing his nails as the door continued to grow smaller.

The door shrank to nothing, its glow no longer visible to Kryder once it cut into the lord mage's body. It cut clean through, leaving half of the man in the hall with them. The other was wherever the connection was. Kryder reached down and pulled his dagger free. He wiped it on what remained of the man's robes.

Looking down he said, "I'm not a mage. I'm a shaman."

* * * * *

Chapter Twenty-Four

Tog ripped the leg off one of the tables and held it in the flames. Once it caught, he nodded to Kryder, and they left the room. In the hall, they ran into several of the servants. Tog casually walked over to a set of floor-length curtains and set them on fire.

"I'd leave if I was you," he warned.

The servants ran. Tog and Kryder continued to set the building on fire as they left. Occasionally, Tog would cut into a paneled wall and hold the flame to it until it caught. The number of servants they encountered grew fewer and fewer as the word spread through the halls. The servants were gathering their belongings and anything else they could and leaving.

"I wonder why we haven't seen any of the apprentices?" Tog asked as he held the flame to the wooden rail of a stairwell.

"I think Kaynald told them to leave," Kryder said. "Speaking of her, we need to see if she left the other two stones."

"Sounds good to me," Tog said. "We need to go to another building, anyway. This one is too smokey, and I don't intend to leave a single one standing, anyway."

After a moment, he turned to Kryder and asked, "Can you burn stone?"

Kryder laughed. "No, it doesn't work that way. Besides, I'm exhausted. Use your torch. Make me one, and I'll help."

Tog reached down, snapped a rail from the stairwell, and handed it to his cousin. Kryder put it to the flame. They left the building and went to the one holding the stones. Right where Kaynald had said they'd be, in a hidden cupboard with its door open, were two stones on a shelf. Kryder slipped one into each of his front pockets.

The last building they walked into was the one with the Library. Knowing everything was a copy of a work somewhere in the desert, Kryder decided to put it to the flame, too. As they came back downstairs, they met one last person. He was probably the only person in the entire Halls of Magic left, the others long gone.

The administrator froze in his tracks. He stared wide-eyed at them. In his hands he struggled to carry three sacks bulging with coins, jewelry, and loose stones. Tog looked at the man and raised an eyebrow. The administrator put two bags down. He handed one to Tog, reached down, and picked the other two up. He backed up slowly, his eyes never leaving theirs until he turned and ran.

Tog looked at Kryder and shrugged. He dug in the sack and pulled out a handful. He put it in one of his pockets. He put one more in another pocket and offered one to his cousin. Kryder took half of the huge handful and divided it between several inner pockets. They left the rest on the floor.

* * *

Kryder and Tog walked down the road away from the Halls of Magic. Tog asked, "Do you think we have enough coin to book passage on a ship?"

"I think so," Kryder said.

"Will they feed us? Wait, what do they eat on a ship, anyway?" Tog asked.

"Fish," Kryder suggested, "and flat bread."

"I saw," Tog said, "but I think that's if you get sick. I don't get sick. I can eat anything."

"I hope they have taters," Tog said wishfully.

Kryder shook his head and grinned. "You want to run?"

"No," Tog answered. "My legs hurt."

# # # # #

About Kevin Steverson

Kevin Steverson is a retired veteran of the U.S. Army. He is a published songwriter as well as an author. He lives in the northeast Georgia foothills where he continues to refuse to shave ever again. Trim…maybe. Shave…never! When he is not on the road as a Tour Manager he can be found at home writing in one fashion or another.

Website: www.kevinsteverson.com

Instagram: kevin.steverson

Facebook: https://www.facebook.com/kevin.steverson.9

Twitter: @CallMeCatHead

* * * * *

About Tyler Akerman

Tyler Ackerman is a singer/songwriter and an international touring artist. He is one half of the duo Cypress Spring. He lives in Ohio, where he and Melissa are raising their two boys. A fan of the fantasy genre, his first foray into writing stories as opposed to songs is a collaboration with the novel Burnt.

* * * * *

Get the **free** Four Horsemen prelude story "**Shattered Crucible**"

and discover other New Mythology titles at:

http://chriskennedypublishing.com/

* * * * *

The following is an
Excerpt from Book One of The Milesian Accords:

A Reluctant Druid

Jon R. Osborne

Available Now from New Mythology Press

eBook, Paperback, and Audio Book

Excerpt from "A Reluctant Druid:"

"Don't crank on it; you'll strip it."

Liam paused from trying to loosen the stubborn bolt holding the oil filter housing on his Yamaha motorcycle, looking for the source of the unsolicited advice. The voice was gruff, with an accent and cadence that made Liam think of the Swedish Chef from the Muppets. The garage door was open for air circulation, and two figures were standing in the driveway, illuminated by the setting sun. As they approached and stepped into the shadows of the house, Liam could see they were Pixel and a short, stout man with a greying beard that would do ZZ Top proud. The breeze blowing into the garage carried a hint of flowers.

Liam experienced a moment of double vision as he looked at the pair. Pixel's eyes took on the violet glow he thought he had seen before, while her companion lost six inches in height, until he was only as tall as Pixel. What the short man lacked in height, he made up for in physique; he was built like a fireplug. He was packed into blue jeans and a biker's leather jacket, and goggles were perched over the bandana covering his salt and pepper hair. Leather biker boots crunched the gravel as he walked toward the garage. Pixel followed him, having traded her workout clothes for black jeans and a pink t-shirt that left her midriff exposed. A pair of sunglasses dangled from the neckline of her t-shirt.

"He's seeing through the glamour," the short, bearded man grumbled to Pixel, his bushy eyebrows furrowing.

"Well duh. We're on his home turf, and this is his place of power" Pixel replied nonchalantly. "He was pushing back against my glamour yesterday, and I'm not adding two hands to my height."

Liam set down the socket wrench and ran through the mental inventory of items in the garage that were weapons or could be used as them. The back half of the garage was a workshop, which included the results of his dabbling with blacksmithing and sword-crafting, so the list was considerable. But the most suitable were also the farthest away.

"Can I help you?" Liam stood and brushed off his jeans; a crowbar was three steps away. Where had they come from? Liam hadn't heard a car or motorcycle outside, and the house was a mile and a half outside of town.

"Ja, you can." The stout man stopped at the threshold of the garage. His steel-grey eyes flicked from Liam to the workbench and back. He held his hands out, palms down. The hands were larger than his and weren't strangers to hard work and possibly violence. "And there's no need to be unhospitable; we come as friends. My name is Einar, and you've already met Pixel."

"Hi, Liam." Pixel was as bubbly as yesterday. While she didn't seem to be making the same connection as Einar regarding the workbench, her eyes darted about the cluttered garage and the dim workshop behind it. "Wow, you have a lot of junk."

"What's this about?" Liam sidled a half step toward the workbench, regretting he hadn't kept up on his martial arts. He had three brown belts, a year of kendo, and some miscellaneous weapons training scattered over two decades but not much experience in the way of real fighting. He could probably hold his own in a brawl as long as his opponent didn't have serious skills. He suspected Einar was more than a Friday night brawler in the local watering hole. "Is she your daughter?"

Einar turned to the purple-haired girl, his caterpillar-like eyebrows gathering. "What did you do?"

"What? I only asked him a few questions and checked him out," Pixel protested, her hands going to her hips as she squared off with Einar. "It's not as if I tried to jump his bones right there in the store or something."

"Look mister, if you think something untoward happened between me and your daughter—" Liam began.

"She's not my pocking daughter, and I don't give a troll's ass if you diddled her," Einar interrupted, his accent thickening with his agitation. He took a deep breath, his barrel chest heaving. "Now, will you hear me out without you trying to brain me with that tire iron you've been eyeing?"

"You said diddle." Pixel giggled.

"Can you be serious for five minutes, you pocking faerie?" Einar glowered, his leather jacket creaking as he crossed his arms.

"Remember 'dwarf,' you're here as an 'advisor.'" Pixel included air quotes with the last word, her eyes turning magenta. "The Nine Realms are only involved out of politeness."

"Politeness! If you pocking Tuatha and Tylwyth Teg hadn't folded up when the Milesians came at you, maybe we wouldn't be here to begin with!" Spittle accompanied Einar's protest. "Tylwyth? More like Toothless!"

"Like your jarls didn't roll over and show their bellies when the Avramites showed up with their One God and their gold!" Pixel rose up on her toes. "Your people took their god and took their gold and then attacked our ancestral lands!"

"Guys!" Liam had stepped over to the workbench but hadn't picked up the crowbar. "Are you playing one of those live-action role playing games or something? Because if you are, I'm calling my garage out of bounds. Take your LARP somewhere else."

"We've come a long way to speak to you," Einar replied, looking away from Pixel. "I'm from Asgard."

"Asgard? You mean like Thor and Odin? What kind of game are you playing?" Liam hadn't moved from the workbench, but he had mapped in his mind the steps he would need to take to reach a stout pole which would serve as a staff while he back-pedaled to his workshop, where a half-dozen half-finished sword prototypes rested. From where he stood, though, he didn't feel as threatened. He knew a bit about gamers because there were a fair number of them among the pagan community, and he had absorbed bits and pieces of it. Maybe someone had pointed Liam out to Pixel as research about druids for one of these games—an over-enthusiastic player who wanted to more convincingly roleplay one.

"Gods I hate those pocking things," Einar grumbled, rubbing his forehead while Pixel stifled another giggle. "Look, can we sit down and talk to you? This is much more serious than some pocking games you folk play with your costumes and your toy weapons."

"This isn't a game, and we aren't hippies with New Age books and a need for self-validation." Pixel added. Her eyes had faded to a lavender color. "Liam, we need your help."

* * * * *

Get "A Reluctant Druid" now at:
https://www.amazon.com/dp/B07716V2RN

Find out more about Jon R. Osborne at:
https://chriskennedypublishing.com/

* * * * *

The following is an
Excerpt from Book One of The Shadow Lands:

Shadow Lands

Lloyd Behm, II

Available Now from Blood Moon Press

eBook and Paperback

Excerpt from "Shadow Lands:"

The combatants, for lack of a better term, were both resting at the edges of the dance floor. To the left was a very butch-looking blonde in what looked to be purple leather, along with her entourage, while to the right, a petite, dark-skinned Hispanic in a princess outfit stood, surrounded by meat popsicles wrapped in leather. Vampire fashions make no damn sense to me, for what it's worth. There were a few 'normals' huddled against the far wall, which showed signs of someone's face being run along it, repeatedly. Sure enough, the London 'Special' was in the DJ booth. He killed the sound as soon as he realized we were standing there.

"Ladies and gentlemen, may I introduce the final players in our little drama, the Reinhumation Specialists of the Quinton Morris Group!" the Special said into the mike.

"Fuck me running," I said.

"With a rusty chainsaw," Jed finished.

The two groups of vampires turned to face us.

"Remind me to kick Michael in his balls when we get back to the office," I said.

"You're going to have to get in line behind me to do it," Jed replied.

"You can leave now, mortals," the blonde said with a slight German accent. She had occult patterns tattooed around her eyes, which had to be a bitch, because she would have had to have them redone every six months or so. Vampires heal.

"Like, fershure, this totally doesn't involve you," the Hispanic said, her accent pure San Fernando Valley.

"Jed, did I ever tell you how I feel about Valley Girls?" I asked, raising my voice.

"No…"

"Can't live with 'em, can't kill 'em," I replied, swinging my UMP up and cratering the Valley vampire's chest with three rounds into the fragile set of blood vessels above the heart. Sure, the pump still works, but there's nothing connected to it for what passes as blood in a vampire to spread. On top of that, company-issue bullets are frangible silver, to which vampires have an adverse reaction.

With that, the dance was on. The damn Special in the DJ booth at least had the good sense to put on Rammstein. *Mien Teil* came thundering out of the speakers as we started killing vampires. Gunny ran his M1897 Trench Gun dry in five shots, dropped it to hang by a patrol sling, and switched to his ancient, family 1911. I ran my UMP dry on Valley Vamp's minions, then dropped the magazine and reloaded in time to dump the second full magazine into the Butch Vampire as she leaped toward the ceiling to clear the tables between us and the dance floor. As soon as Butch Vamp went down, the remaining vampires froze.

"Glamour," the Special called, stepping out of the booth. "I can control a lot of lesser vampires, but not until you got those two randy cunts thinking about how much they hurt."

"You. Fucking. Asshole," I panted.

Combat is cardio, I don't care what anyone else says.

"Yes?" he replied.

I looked him over. He was wearing a red zoot suit—red-pegged trousers and a long red jacket with wide shoulders over the ubiquitous white peasant shirt, topped with a red, wide-brimmed hat. He even had on red-tinted glacier glasses.

I felt his mind try to probe mine, then beamed as he bounced off.

"My that hurt," he replied.

"You know, we don't work with Michelangelo for nothing," Jed replied. Apparently the mind probe had been general, not specific.

I went through the messy side of the business—staking and be-heading—assisted by Capdepon. Crash helped Jed sort out the normal survivors, followed by prepping the live lesser vampires for transport. The Special leaned against a wall, maintaining control of the lesser vampires until we could move them out. Once all the work was done so the cleaners could move in, and the lesser vampires were moved out of Eyelash, I stepped wearily to the Special.

"What's your name?" I asked.

"You can call me," he paused dramatically, "Tim."

I kicked him in the nuts with a steel-toed boot. Even in the undead, it's a sensitive spot.

* * * * *

Get "Shadow Lands" now at:
https://www.amazon.com/dp/B07KX8GHYX/.

Find out more about Lloyd Behm, II and "Shadow Lands" at:
https://chriskennedypublishing.com/imprints-authors/lloyd-behm-ii/.

* * * * *

Made in the USA
Monee, IL
02 March 2020

22553034R00164